KEEPER
OF THE
ARCHIVES

LYNNE STRINGER

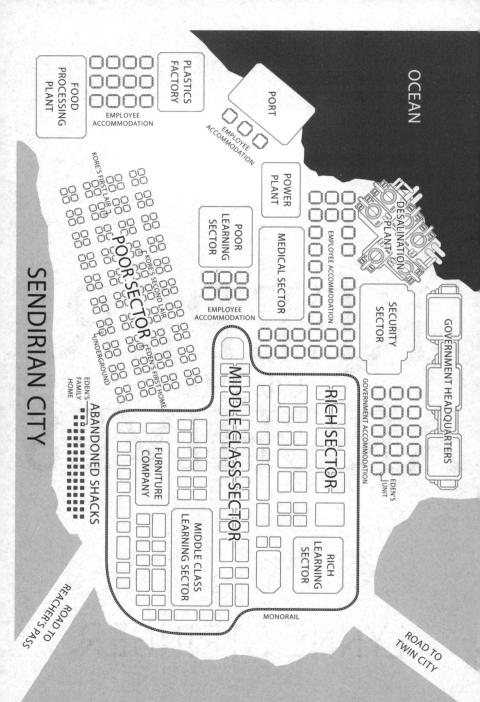

To Jeanette and Adele,
my fellow authors, supporters
and friends.

CHAPTER ONE

I stretched out my hand, grasping for anything in the thick smoke that wrapped me in its choking tentacles. It felt like a living being, winding its way down my throat, coating it in filth. I struggled for clean air, but there was none to be found.

Lenny quivered where he hung strapped to my back. Usually, he was unfazed by anything. In his two-year-old eyes, life was a perpetual game. He could always find something to amuse him, even amongst our scant belongings and dysfunctional family. He hacked up a cough in my ear. At least it told me he was alive.

I could feel Jed's hands clinging to my shirt, felt it when he bumped against Lenny, desperate not to lose me in the darkness. He'd only turned thirteen a few weeks earlier. We'd made as much of a fuss of him as we could, even managing to keep Dad away. It couldn't end like this for him.

Was Mother still behind him? *Please, please, let her still be there!* She had insisted on bringing up the rear, five-year-old Kathleen strapped to her back. Mother had always said I was as small as a bird and she wasn't much bigger than me. I hoped the weight wouldn't be too much for her.

I stretched out, my hands disappearing as I felt my way around.

The smoke stung my eyes, so I closed them. It made no difference if they were open or shut. I longed to feel the scratch of peeling plaster under my palms, a sign that we had reached our goal—the emergency exit on our floor. Surely we should have got there by now.

I continued to grope, looking for anything solid. What if I'd been turned around somehow? No, that wasn't possible—I would have bumped into Jed and Mother. I had to be going the right way. Where were the stairs? Why weren't they there?

My shin connected with something and my heart leapt with hope, but then I realised that the bundle I'd walked into was soft, not scratchy with flakes of paint coming off in strips. Dread ran fingers down my back as I realised what it was.

A body.

Who was it? One of our neighbours? I found an arm, then a shoulder. Should I check for a pulse? I didn't know how to do that. They had taught us only a little about pulses and heartbeats at the learning sector, nothing that would help in a life-or-death moment.

I stepped around whoever it was. I felt it when Jed connected with the bundle and tried to steer him around it. But then he stopped.

Oh no. Mother wouldn't try to help, would she? She couldn't! My head was spinning and I gave another wracking cough. We wouldn't get out at all if we didn't keep moving. But I couldn't draw breath to speak, couldn't tell her she was being ridiculous, couldn't order her to put her family first. How could we help our neighbour if we died as well? This corridor could be our tomb.

I dragged Jed with me, only to collide with something else. It was harder than the bundle on the floor, but hands reached out to hold me upright. I felt a padded suit and the smog parted for a moment and I saw the visor of a man from the emergency sector. He towered above me, his face hidden in his helmet, where I knew he was probably breathing fresh, clean air.

'How many of you?' he said, his voice distorted by the mask.

I couldn't speak, so tapped him five times on the arm. I felt guilty for not including the body on the floor in my tally, but my family was still alive. At least, I hoped they were.

The fire officer grabbed my arm, moved me in front of him, and pushed me against the wall. I clutched at it, feeling the first hint of relief. A moment later, Jed was next to me, and I could feel Mother's presence on the other side.

The officer pulled me to the left and forward, and I was in the stairway. 'This way,' he said.

'A man ...' My mother's voice ended in a fit of coughing.

'I'll come back for him. Let's get you out first.'

He led us through the swirling smoke, keeping us moving despite our stumbling steps. The air felt like it was on fire. The rail was so hot it seared my hand. It was five floors down and the man stayed with us the whole way, encouraging us, holding us up, until finally, we staggered out into the night.

More emergency officers were milling around, none with their visors on, presumably saving the air for a journey into the building behind us. As I fell onto the pavement across the road from our unit block, I looked back up. All fifteen floors were alight, the flames stretching up into the sky, as if to make a mockery of the tiny sprays of water some of the officers were directing at it.

Mother coughed, unstrapping Kathleen from her back. My sister wailed and retched, turning to the pavement and vomiting. Mother patted her back before grabbing the arm of the officer who'd saved us. 'A man ... on our floor. You must get him out.'

The officer turned to head back into the fire, only to be stopped by a colleague. 'We're supposed to wait for instructions.'

The officer shook him off and headed back inside.

I noticed that a lot of the fire officers were doing nothing. 'Why

3

are you standing there?' I demanded, trying to get the words out despite the fire burning in my throat. 'People are dying!'

Some of my other neighbours, also writhing on the concrete, turned their ire on them, as did others I recognised. I knew they had family in the building. Finally, a group of officers donned their helmets and raced in.

The first officer had returned by then, a body slung over his shoulder. He dumped it next to us and my mother immediately turned from her children, who were coughing and retching, tears making tracks in the soot on their faces, to the stricken form beside her.

'Mr Ivanov!' she said, turning the man's face up toward hers. 'Can you hear me? Quick, Eden, see if you can find some water for him.'

I hurried as quickly as I could over to one of the emergency officers, gasping for breath all the way. 'Do you have any water? I think a man is dying over here.' Probably more than one.

A woman from the medical sector raced over, wheeling a canister behind her. 'Where is he? I have oxygen and water.'

By the time we'd returned, Mother had cleaned some of the grime off Mr Ivanov's face. His eyes were unfocused, the breaths rattling out of his body. He grasped at the mask the medic put on him as if it was his last hope.

Other medics appeared and finally, my brothers and sister were able to get some water and oxygen themselves. I waved it away, making sure that the three of them were okay, while Mother hovered over Mr Ivanov, getting in the way more than anything, I thought.

Mr Ivanov's skin had a sickly pallor. His lungs heaved, hands shaking as they clawed at the mask. He seemed to calm, his body relaxing. I was about to shriek that he was dying when his eyes flashed open wide, his hands pulled the mask away and he pointed at a nearby alley.

'Izrod!' His yell was barely loud enough for us to hear. 'Look out! Izrod!'

The medics looked around in confusion, but the people from our building understood instantly. 'Izrod is here!' someone yelled.

'He's come to snatch the dying from the street!' another local shrieked.

Panic erupted around us, adult survivors throwing their bodies protectively over their children, bystanders running toward the alleyway, others running away from it. The medics looked fearfully over their shoulders. The security sector people, who had been directing traffic, hurried over.

'What's going on?' one said.

'Izrod!' Mr Ivanov said again, his hand shaking as he tried to keep pointing.

The security officer looked at me. 'Izrod?'

'It's what he calls the Freak.'

Her face dawned with understanding. Everyone knew who the Freak was—the huge monster of a being who stole people off the street for Kore Luddan to experiment on. Rumour said that Kore, a local crime boss, had genetically altered Izrod and others, turning them into deformed creatures that only vaguely resembled their human selves.

Mr Ivanov spat the name out every time the Freak was mentioned. 'It means ugly, hideous, deformed,' he'd told me. 'At least, so my grandmother said. What word is better to describe such a disgusting monster?'

The security officers followed Mr Ivanov's gesture, running for the alley, past the fire trucks where I could see more officers donning their protective gear before they headed into the still-burning unit block. Soon more people were brought out and laid next to us, some gasping for breath and calling hoarsely for oxygen, some too far gone to save.

I doubted they'd catch Izrod. He'd been terrorising everyone here in Sendirian City for months, but despite the media sector constantly lauding the heroic efforts of our security sector, no one had even come close to catching him. Sure enough, it wasn't long before the security officers returned, shaking their heads.

***

I shivered in my jacket as I hugged Lenny and Kathleen close, trying to ignore the stench of smoke that still clung to them. Jed leant into Mother's side. Mr Ivanov had been taken away long ago, but the medic tending to him had been grim-faced and wouldn't look at us. I was sure we wouldn't see our neighbour again.

I turned my gaze to the other residents of the smoking wreck that used to be our home. Coughs had lessened, looks of despair taking their place. Mrs Murphy came over and sat by Mother. The contrast between them was immense—Mrs Murphy was broad and red-headed, my mother slight, wispy blond hair covering her haunted eyes.

Mrs Murphy rubbed her hands together and blew on them. 'Where do we go now? What do we do?' She looked around. 'There should be someone from government here. There has to be!'

There were at least eighty of us standing on the footpath—men, women and children—all with no home. Would a government worker come and tell us where we could go?

Mother's energy seemed to have slipped away with Mr Ivanov, so I dragged myself to my feet and headed off to where I could see a bunch of our neighbours. I thought there were likely to be answers there, even if they weren't good ones, if the yelling and gesticulating were anything to go by.

They were snarling at a man who stood in their midst—a man with a suit holding a computer pad; something that made him stand out like a beacon in this neighbourhood. It marked him as a government worker as clear as day. Government sector workers were among the few in this city who could afford fancy suits. If he'd

6

had any brains, he would have come dressed like a doctor from the medical sector or stolen one of the padded suits and pretended he was with the fire sector.

He wouldn't find much congeniality here in the poor sector, or the 'lower socioeconomic sector', as they called it. It was a polite way of saying that everyone who lived here had nothing and nobody cared enough to do anything about it. Definitely not the people who lived in the government sector or the stuck-up snobs who lived in pristine units right next door to it. The stinking rich, in other words.

The man tucked the computer pad under his arm and held up his hand, trying to quell the questions and accusations that rang out like a clarion around him. 'I understand how concerned you must feel. We will make it our business to find new homes for you as soon as possible, but it can't be done tonight. Please, try and find a place with friends or other family members for now, and we'll work things out in the days to come.'

'But where will we go?'

'I don't have any family. What am I supposed to do?'

The man didn't answer, just turned and fled. Some of our neighbours raced after him, still jabbing him with questions and pleas, but he jumped into a government vehicle and drove away.

The emergency officers were still trying to get the fire under control but I didn't think it was likely anyone else would come out alive. They brought out a few shrouded shapes. I didn't look too closely.

'What do we do now, Eden?' Jed asked.

I could see some of our neighbours wandering off, probably those who had friends and family they could impose on. Unlike us. About ten different family groups remained, all looking lost.

A large woman walked up to us. She had the feel of government in the way she held herself, but her clothes lacked the formal cut of the man who'd disappeared so quickly. There was grey on her temples, the long thick mess of hair drawn back into a bun. Her face was all angles. She raised her voice, letting it ring out among those of us left. 'I can take you to somewhere you can sleep,' she said. 'It's not much, but you'll be safe there, at least for tonight.'

Some other people—men and women, folks I wouldn't normally trust if I passed them on the street—started shepherding us away. I wasn't keen on going with them, but what choice did we have?

The big woman encouraged us as we moved off, and I saw her meet my mother's eyes. 'Is it just you and the children?'

Mother's eyes darted to us, then away. 'Yes,' she said, turning back to the woman. 'Just the five of us.'

'This way.'

She led us past the alley, and even though I wasn't sure I still trusted her, whatever hell she was leading us to wouldn't be as bad as the one we'd known for years. I checked the alley carefully. Not for Izrod, like a normal person in this city might have done, but for the man who had made my life a misery ever since I'd been old enough to walk.

And there he was—huddled in the corner, passed out and reeking of urine. My father. What would he do, in the morning, when he woke up and found the home of his punching bag had burned to the ground and he couldn't find my mother to beat her senseless until she gave him more money for drink?

I hoped with everything I had that he would never find out where we were. But we'd never stayed hidden from him for long.

***

The large woman, who'd never bothered to tell us her name, had been right. It wasn't much. It was less than that.

We'd been living in our new 'home' for a few days. It was an old shack, one of several in an uneven row. They couldn't have been used for years. They were made of some kind of wooden slats, not something you saw in our city all that often, and any glass in the windows was long gone. Doors hung creaking on rusty hinges. They looked so old they could have been erected before the Unbidden Conflict. That could account for all the damage.

We hadn't seen the woman since, and definitely nothing of the man from government. I knew several of our neighbours trudged in to the government sector day after day, trying to find someone to help us.

I watched Mrs Murphy return as I added another board to the place where a window used to be. She'd taken up residence in the shack next to ours.

She peered in. 'No luck again.' I could feel her rage heating the boards I was installing. 'Government don't care. We're too poor to be of concern to them. We're just an inconvenience.'

I didn't see a reason to respond, so she wandered on, sharing her ire with some other neighbours, where she probably received the outrage she was looking for. But I had to give Mrs Murphy credit for trying. And maybe government would help us just to shut her up.

After the next board had been fixed in place, Jed handed me another.

'Where did you get these boards?' I asked.

He shrugged. He'd probably stolen them, most likely from another abandoned shack since they were actual wood. I had to hope no one lived there and decided to come searching. Even if they did, I'd fight tooth and nail to keep them.

Mother looked up from her laptop. We were lucky … in one way. She organised the budgets for a few local companies and one of them had given her an old laptop to replace the one the fire had destroyed. It was a small mercy, but since our only income came from the meagre hours my mother eked out fixing budgets, we were grateful.

'Don't block all the windows, Eden,' Mother said. 'We need some light coming in.'

Was she crazy? 'Mother, you know Dad will climb in the window if the door's locked.' Hell, he'd probably break down the wall if he had to.

'I'll turn the lights on.' Jed yanked on the cord hanging from the ceiling. It fell off in his hand. Not to be beaten, he grabbed a chair, climbed up and stretched up on his toes to take hold of the tiny bit of cord that still hung from the light fitting. A dim light came on, then it flickered off again.

'We may have to get someone to look at that,' said Mother.

'I'm not sure anyone could fix a problem out here. And you know the electricity is never reliable anyway.' Of all Sendirian City's utilities, power was the worst. The lights were always failing, even in places like the learning sector. Fortunately, the power in wall sockets usually stayed on, but maybe that was why they hadn't fixed the power to the lights. Everyone could work in the dark.

I picked up another board, turned back to the window and froze. My father's bleary eyes leered at me through the small gap remaining.

I didn't bother to stop him as he tore the boards off. Kathleen, who had been playing on the floor with Lenny, grabbed her brother and fled into the room they shared.

My father came in the window, his thin, wiry frame pushing the boards out of the way. His skin was parched and sallow, but although he wasn't hugely fit, working as a labourer had built up some strength in his arms, as we knew from bitter experience.

He jumped onto the floor, gazing around at us. But we weren't all that interesting to him. We were only his family.

'I need money. I know you got paid today.' He grabbed my mother's wrist, holding her link to his. 'I'll leave the computer … this time.' But he eyed it with calculated desperation. He would be back for it sooner or later.

'No, we need that money to buy—'

He slapped her across the mouth. Jed and I were about to race to her rescue, but she held out her hand. She would let him take it. She always did.

I ended up being the one to hold Jed back. He held up his fists, his face turning red, but I knew there was no point in that, especially since Dad wasn't drunk enough to pass out this time. Of course, now he had what he wanted, he wouldn't hang around either.

He climbed back out the window and was gone.

I managed to catch Mother before she hit the floor. 'Jed, fetch the cloth from the kitchen.' I helped her back over to the battered lounge and dabbed the cloth on the cut on her face.

'Eden,' she said, looking at me with desolate eyes. 'You need to get out of here.'

'It's all right. Let me fix you up.'

She took my hands. 'No, I mean really. You're just about to finish your studies. The learning sector has said you did really well. You can go and get a job. Earn some money. Maybe you'll be lucky enough to get an employer with accommodation.'

I doubted that. Companies in each sector usually employed people who lived nearby. All other city-dwellers worked remotely unless they were required in some official capacity in the government sector or the medical, learning or security sectors, and you had to have high-level training to be employed by them and get a spot in their supplied accommodation.

But even though my results had been better than average, I wasn't going to be a doctor, accountant or office manager. There was nothing that made me stand out.

'I guess I can try.' I would say anything to get the look of hopelessness off her face.

Jed leant down and scooped up a newspaper from the floor. Our city gave them away for free, although you could also watch broadcasts from the media sector on special screens in your home if you had the money to buy one. We'd had one once. It was probably a smoking shell on a dump somewhere. Mother must have been given the newspaper when she'd gone to the market earlier.

'Look at this, Eden.'

My eyes ran over the headline.

IZROD STRIKES AGAIN!

Someone from the media sector must have been there the night of the fire and heard Mr Ivanov's nickname for the Freak. I guess it looked more impressive in a headline.

My eyes scanned over the article.

> *Last night, yet another citizen disappeared, thought to be the latest victim of the creature who has become known as 'Izrod', and has been linked to the dangerous crime boss, Kore Luddan.*
>
> *Andrew Redmond, a junior keeper in government's Archives, disappeared after an evening out with friends. Senior officials in the security sector have confirmed that he checked in to his accommodation in the government sector later that night, but he failed to respond to a security check the following morning, when it was discovered that his unit was empty.*
>
> *'The security sector is investigating the matter to see what can be done,' said Governor Jerrill. 'We ask all citizens of the city to stay calm and please come forward if they have any information that would lead to Mr Redmond's safe return.'*

The article continued, but I didn't bother to read anymore. So what if Izrod had taken someone else? He should come to our neighbourhood and try. No one from government would care if we disappeared. They'd probably thank Izrod if it meant people like Mrs Murphy stopped going in there to make a fuss day after day.

'There, see that?' said Jed when I didn't respond.

'What?'

'A government worker has gone missing. Someone working in the Archives. Maybe you can get a job there. They'll need a replacement now.'

It seemed a bit gruesome to take the job of Izrod's latest victim, but Jed had a point. However, I didn't know if I had what it took to be a junior keeper. I would need to ask at the learning sector when I did my exit interview next week. Perhaps they could arrange something.

Mother's eyes started shining. 'That's a brilliant idea, Jed. Not only would you get paid, they have their own accommodation. It would be perfect.'

I hated to stomp on her enthusiasm, but ... 'I don't think they'd let us all stay there.' If it was a job that someone as unqualified as me could apply for, I doubted the unit would be bigger than a broom closet.

Mother wrapped her arms around me. 'That doesn't matter, Eden. Someday you're going to start off on your own. It may as well be now. And it's not like you won't be able to help us. With the extra money you bring in, especially if we can keep it from your ...'

Yes, what if Dad didn't know we had an extra source of income? He knew what Mother earned and how to squeeze that out of her, but if I was giving her more on the side, maybe she could move out of this hole and find somewhere else, somewhere Dad couldn't follow. Although that seemed like too much to hope for.

'Get a new account,' I said, 'just in case. The money needs to be somewhere Dad can't find.' While every account we had could be accessed on our links, if he didn't know it was there, he wouldn't think to look. Although he was the kind of guy who could smell credit through concrete, so maybe I was being a bit too confident.

But it was worth a shot. My family couldn't stay here, not when my father knew where to find them. Not to mention that there was the ever-present danger of one of them being snatched by Izrod, although he seemed to favour skilled workers over dregs like us.

Maybe the Archives was exactly what we needed.

CHAPTER TWO

It was like I was being lowered into the bowels of the earth. But maybe that was just an effect of the light … or lack of it.

Considering the Archives was part of the government sector, I'd been expecting a little better. The lobby I'd walked through minutes ago had been pristine, with large grey tiles covering the floor, faux wood fittings and doors with shiny metal doorknobs, not to mention suited people rushing to and fro on their way to who knew where.

The administrator had smirked when I'd told her which job I'd come to apply for. 'The newly vacated position?' she'd said, polishing her long red nails as her sceptical dark eyes looked me up and down.

'Yes, the one in the Archives.' I'd made sure I showed no response to her disdain. And it wasn't like I didn't feel sympathy for this Andrew Redmond. In a way, he was one of the lucky ones. The junior keeper had been found babbling like a madman a few days ago and tried to kill three people before guards from the security sector had hauled him away. He'd been gone for more than a week before he'd turned up, knife in hand, slashing at anyone who wandered too close. Most of Izrod's victims were never seen again. If I were Andrew's family, I would be glad to at least know he'd escaped Kore.

But this woman's reaction made me realise why I'd scored an

interview in the government sector. It seemed no one was lining up around the block to replace Izrod's victims and there had been quite a few from the government sector lately. People seemed to prefer staying alive, even with the offer of good pay and supplied accommodation.

I looked at my guide. He'd met me at the elevator and had said nothing since we'd gotten in. He'd punched the button marked 'A' with a grimy hand, wiped his nose, and that was all. He wasn't much older than me, but his darting eyes reminded me of my father and that was to be avoided at all costs.

He squinted at me as he chewed a fingernail. 'What did you say your name was?'

'Eden Fittell.'

'Ah, one of the famous Fittells.'

There were no famous Fittells, certainly none I was related to. It must be his attempt at a joke. A gruff noise that could have been a chuckle sounded in his throat.

'Don't say much, do you?' he said, giving me the once over. What did he see when he looked at me? Someone young and impressionable, entering the workforce with wide, innocent eyes? Probably he saw exactly what they'd seen in the learning sector. I'd managed to pass under the radar for most of my years there. I kept everyone at a distance and made sure they only saw what my warped mirror showed me— brown hair with bangs. Thin. Short. Expressionless. Uninteresting. My hair and my height weren't my doing, but everything else was deliberate. Blend in. Be smaller. Go unnoticed. Give nothing away.

We jolted to a halt and the doors groaned open.

I stepped into a cavernous room. White lights shone at regular intervals above my head, growing distant and dimmer the further they stretched, then they were blocked by shelves. Lots of shelves, mostly made of faux wood. Rows and rows and rows, stacked high with books. Not all of them were in straight lines, either—some crisscrossed through corridors further down. I craned my neck, looking for a path.

There were people too, drifting in and out of the aisles between the shelves, pushing carts stacked with more books and boxes filled with tiny digital files. Every so often one of them stopped at a shelf, ran a finger along the top of their cart, selected a book and put it in its place.

It was riveting stuff. This was my future.

They were all wearing uniforms. Nothing fancy, just a blue outfit with ARCHIVES—JUNIOR KEEPER scrawled across the back and on the front left just under the collar. The guy who'd brought me down in the elevator wore one too, although his was devoid of writing. If I got this job, I wouldn't even have to worry about buying new clothes. That was a relief. I'd had to hunt in dustbins for the shirt and skirt I was wearing, doing my best to make them look passingly decent.

In front of the shelves was a series of desks. All of them were stacked with papers and each had a small computer, but only one desk was occupied. A woman sat there, her spindly hands folded under her chin, her grey hair falling in waves down her back. Unlike the other employees, she wore a suit, still blue to match theirs, but closer in cut to the suits I'd seen in the lobby. I expected her face to be as distant as the faces of the officials I'd seen, but there was an expression of mysticism in her faded grey eyes and a benign smile on her face. I wished I knew if it was genuine.

'Ah, thank you, Derek,' she said to my guide. So he had a name. Had he told me? Possibly.

Derek bobbed his head. 'Certainly, Head Keeper.' He looked at me. 'This here is …' His face froze. 'This here is …'

It looked like I wasn't the only one who hadn't been paying attention. 'Eden Fittell,' I said.

His nose spread wider as he smiled. 'Yes, Eden Fittell, of the famous Fittells.' I guess he thought the joke was good enough to repeat.

The old woman seemed neither annoyed nor amused by her employee. Her eyes turned to me. I kept my expression neutral as she held out her hand. It took a moment to realise what she wanted. 'Oh, I'm sorry.' Of course she wanted my forms. I uncurled my fingers and gave her the file.

She fed it into her computer and examined the screen. 'Thank you, Derek.'

'Yes, Head Keeper.' Derek bobbed his head again and headed back to the elevator, the grinding sounding again after the doors had closed behind him.

The head keeper took her time looking over the forms. 'Do you mind if I call you Eden?'

'No, ma'am.' She could call me whatever she liked as long as she employed me.

'Then you may call me Susan. Or Head Keeper, if you feel like being formal. When any officials grace us with their presence, it would be best to use my title.' She pointed to a badge pinned to her chest with her name and position on it.

I hid the relief that flowed through me. It *sounded* like she was going to accept me. But I kept my voice neutral. 'Do they come here often, ma'am?'

Her eyes admonished me. 'Susan.'

'Susan.' I couldn't remember ever calling anyone my senior by their first name.

'They do. We also take files up to various offices. It depends on the requirement. Admittedly, they have been coming down here a lot of late.'

'So am I to start work here then, ma'am?' I asked.

Her faded eyes regarded me with a puzzled expression. 'Aren't you curious about why our government officials have been coming here so frequently?'

18

That thought hadn't even occurred to me. 'No, ma'am ... Susan.'

She stood. Her shoulders were hunched and her hands seemed paper-thin, but there was no sign of weakness as she came around the desk and regarded me. 'Eden, you're a puzzling creature. Usually people who want to work in the Archives have some interest in the records we have here.'

Did I need to show enthusiasm? 'Yes, ma'am ... Susan. I mean, sure, I'm curious, but I just didn't think that you'd be allowed to discuss things our officials wanted. You know, confidentiality and all that. Especially given what's been happening with Kore and Izrod.'

That seemed to please her. 'I'm glad you're up to date with current events. Yes, it was a great shame that Andrew was taken. A terrible thing for his family.'

She waved her hands at the looming shelves behind her. 'Come, let me show you what we have here.'

Am I employed or not? I wanted to scream it, to shake her, to demand a response. But she was showing me around. That had to be a good sign, didn't it? Surely she wouldn't do that if she was just going to turn around and kick me out?

She led me in between the shelves. In the first few rows, the lights on the ceiling lined up with the walkways between each shelf, creating a cold shaft of light on our path. There was barely room for the two of us side by side, so I followed most of the time, especially when we had to squeeze past a worker with a cart. I was met by curious looks from one. Maybe he thought I was brave for taking Andrew's place. Another gave me a resentful glare. Maybe she thought I'd try and advance myself over her. The kids in the learning sector had talked about things like that.

Susan indicated some metal drawers. 'This is where we store the digital records. They're the most recent and the most likely to be required.'

'They aren't stored on the computer system?' All the digital files in the learning sector had only been available online.

'Yes, they are, but these are master copies in case of a system failure.' She gestured to the left. 'This way holds information on the city, its inhabitants, local problems, crime waves. This is the side the officials are usually interested in.'

She turned to her right. 'Here we have the digital records for infrastructure, then flora and fauna, ecology, then the history of Sendirian City. It covers its regeneration fifty years ago when it was re-established after the Unbidden Conflict. Further down there'—she pointed down a crossway at shelves I couldn't see clearly—'we have paper records. They basically follow the same pattern—the most recent first, with infrastructure, ecology and other related information, then the history of our city. Right at the back, we have pre-conflict history and some ancient records, and although they look like books, they are, in fact, newspapers.'

She pulled a book off a nearby shelf and opened it. 'See? There's a catch here.' The pages of a number of the papers were fastened under the catch, which was operated by a lever. She unlatched it and the cover loosened. 'We can remove individual papers if we need to, but we bind them together, each book folder holding a certain section of papers, sometimes a few months' worth, sometimes the papers printed for a full year. The cover helps to protect them.'

She put the book on the shelf and strolled back towards her desk. I slowed my steps, pretending to look around me, assessing the different categories. Truth be told, I saw virtually nothing.

She resumed her seat at her desk and once more clasped her hands before her. 'Eden, you're a quiet girl. That's a good thing here. We prefer silence as we look over our records and care for them. I had worried at first that because of your age, you might not be suited to this kind of work, but I think you will be. Your teachers in the learning sector gave you a glowing review and your results show a dedication to learning and a seriousness of mind. You're seventeen, are you not?'

'Yes … Susan. Just finished my last year in the learning sector.'

'Congratulations, you're our new junior keeper. When can you start?'

Although I felt myself relax, I held rigidly still. If she noticed anything, she didn't say so. 'I'm happy to start tomorrow.'

'You'll need a uniform or two. Unfortunately, I don't have any here right now. When you come tomorrow, Derek will show you where to get some. You'll also need one of our living units. All government employees, even lowly ones like us, live in the government sector. Is that satisfactory?'

'Yes. I'm looking forward to starting out on my own.' Wasn't that what Mother had said to me?

It must have been the right thing to say because she beamed as she turned to her computer console. 'Yes, I think there's one free in the sixth segment. I'll send the details to your link.'

I felt the link on my wrist buzz as the information was processed. I knew it would tell me which unit was mine and would allow me access immediately.

A cacophony of grinding sounded from the elevator shaft before a loud groan pulled the doors apart. There was Derek again. Behind him were two men and two women, all suited up, hair neatly coiffed, faces full of their own importance. No stuffy uniforms for them, just the most prestigious officewear money could buy.

Susan rose from her desk and headed over to them. 'Ladies and gentlemen, so good to see you. You need more from our Archives?'

One of the women raised an eyebrow at me. A man smiled before turning his attention to Susan. 'Yes,' he leant closer, but I still heard what he said. 'After what happened to Andrew …'

'They're still out after last time. Please, walk this way.'

They *did* have files on Kore's gang. Of course they did. Fear of him

21

had sometimes even made me hurry home. Mother was always frantic when I wasn't back on time. 'He'll get you, that terrifying Izrod! You mustn't stay out too late.' But there were plenty of times when Izrod seemed less dangerous than the monster we usually had to face.

I looked up to see if Derek was waiting for me to follow him to the elevator, but his gaze was fixed on the men and women walking amongst the looming shelves. With a quick look around, he followed, and unable to stop myself, I joined him.

I kept further back—I had no business being there until I started work the following day—but soon I heard the shush and squeak of small wheels as other carts found it necessary to head to where the group of officials set themselves up.

There was a large table in an opening I hadn't seen during my brief tour of the Archives. It was littered with digital files and papers, some in orderly sections, others strewn about. A screen stood at one end of the table and Susan turned it on. As a grainy image appeared on it, the other keepers shuffled over, their eyes fixed on it. I wondered if they always did this or if it was their terror of Kore and Izrod that transfixed them.

A moment later, the screen revealed the image of a large man falling off the side of a building.

'You see,' the younger of the two men said, pointing. He had black hair and hazel eyes that scanned the image before him. 'It's him. I told you!'

The two women regarded the screen. 'Izrod himself,' one of them pondered, her spectacled eyes blinking rapidly.

'I don't know where that ludicrous nickname came from,' the other one sniffed.

And it looked like it was Izrod. If the huge well-muscled shoulders, meaty hands and stumpy, strong legs weren't enough to tell us that, even I could see the halo of sand-coloured hair flailing around him as he fell.

'So that's it?' said the second woman. She was a little older and heavier than the first. 'He's dead?'

The first man struck the table with his fist. 'No one could survive that fall.'

The second man leant forward. His face was more open than the first, his eyes serious. 'I wish that were true, Gary. But unfortunately ...'

Susan handed him a remote control and with the press of a button, a new image filled the screen. A different angle showed a body lying on the ground at the base of the building. As it started playing, Izrod picked himself up, shook his head, and lumbered away.

The other three gasped, a sound that was echoed by the keepers. I clamped my lips shut. It was better they didn't realise I was there.

'That's not possible!' Gary declared. 'No one could survive a fall like that.'

'We think this footage was taken just before he snatched Andrew. We're working on ...' The other man turned, frowning, noticing the crowding keepers for the first time.

Susan turned to her employees. 'Now, now, ladies and gentlemen, it's time for us to return to work.'

I ducked into the shadows, hoping no one had noticed me snooping. But I heard the group of suits as they continued to talk.

'Look, I know that Izrod is an issue,' said the older woman, 'but he's not the only problem we have. There was another unit block fire last night. We need to do something about them. I've received reports that the construction of units isn't meeting basic city safety guidelines.'

The younger man groaned. 'Give it a rest, Cynthia. There'll be plenty of time to look at that later. You know the media sector is way more interested in Izrod than a few little fires, especially in the poor sector. He's the bigger problem we need to deal with.'

I could feel the heat rise in me at his casual dismissal of the poor. Just meaningless, faceless problems that weren't worth a moment's thought. Not real people with needs greater than these stuffed shirts with their government-supplied meals and safe, secure accommodation. But then, Andrew Redmond would have been snatched from one of those very units. Maybe he'd lived next to this suit. Had he been a step away from abduction himself?

I kept my footsteps soft as I made my way back to the elevator. By the time I arrived, Derek was already there, his head bowed amongst the other keepers, their voices too low for me to catch anything, but the fear on their faces spoke volumes. They were rattled by the sight of Izrod apparently uninjured after that fall.

'I heard he was using genetic engineering,' one said as I came nearer.

Derek turned as I approached. 'Oh. You,' he said.

As he led me to the elevator, I thought he might discuss Izrod with me, but although he glanced my way several times, he said nothing. Maybe he'd realised I shouldn't have seen all that, at least, not until I'd officially started work.

But I wasn't thinking so much about Izrod as I was about the fires. Another unit block fire? How many had there been? I wondered where the survivors of this one would go. Or had there only been shrouded, smoking bodies left on the roadside?

It had occurred to me that working for government might mean I could get some help for my family and our neighbours, but that hope deserted me as the elevator doors slammed shut. I would have to make sure I didn't mention it when I went home. I couldn't have Mother all starry-eyed, telling Mrs Murphy I'd fix everything. But then, the more people Mother told, the more likely it was Dad would hear about it. That should ensure her silence.

And now I could leave that old shack and strike out on my own. It would be hard to leave my family behind, but I couldn't deny that the thought of getting out of there filled me with relief.

CHAPTER THREE

I walked down the concrete steps of the building that housed the Archives. It had an impressive façade, that was for sure. Six pillars graced the entrance but if you squinted, you could see the pit marks and the dirt. Even the doors with their glass panes were stunning until you came near and saw the edges lifting and the latch that didn't work anymore.

It said a lot about Sendirian City, about the entire government sector. I kept my head down as I moved through it, dodging the people on the street going about their business—suits, most of them.

I had no grandiose plans of becoming someone big in government. They'd demonstrated pretty clearly that people as lowly as me were worth little more than the dirt on their shoes, but all government employees had special accommodation in their own sanctioned areas. You couldn't just walk in off the street; security made sure of that. No one entered unless they lived there.

But even though I knew my new address was on my link, I had to go home first. I needed to get my things and make sure my mother had that new account ready to go.

I left the government sector and moved out into the middle-class sector, tall towers crowding on every side, their looming shadows like concrete monsters. Monorails hummed past me. It would have been nice to score a ride, but I had no money for such luxuries.

I travelled through several more crossways, each building growing gloomier and more careworn the further I went. Even the sky seemed darker here. Was that rain? Unlikely. It had been a year since any rain had fallen and we wouldn't see any for months. Even then, there was a good chance it would still carry pollutants from the bombs they'd told us about in the learning sector.

When this planet had run low on water, countries everywhere had fought for it, sometimes dropping bombs that decimated entire cities. Of course, that meant that they polluted the water in the ravaged cities as well, so it seemed a really stupid thing to do, but I guess people didn't think straight when they were desperate. I'd seen enough of that in the poor sector to cement it in my mind.

Even though our city had been spared the bombs, it didn't mean we'd gotten off scot-free in the Unbidden Conflict. We'd still been invaded, what with our desalination plant blinking like a beacon of hope right next to the wharf. The plant had been destroyed, apparently by our own people. I guess they'd done it to teach the bad guys a lesson. Pity it had left all the locals without a water supply.

But that was ancient history. In the last fifty years, things had been rebuilt. We generated our own water, power and some other services, with some fresh food coming from Reacher's Pass and other goods from Twin City. These days ships even brought additional items from other countries, although sometimes there weren't enough luxuries to go around.

My pace slowed as I reached the edge of the poor sector. I passed by the burnt-out unit block that used to be our home. Where we lived now was so lowly it wasn't even classed as poor accommodation. The smell of smoke filled my nostrils. Was that from the fire the suit had talked about?

I passed by several food vendors. Their tiny carts were a common sight around here. There were a few in other sectors as well, where they had larger carts, some even with storefronts, although it was impossible to score work in them. Usually, they were family-owned and operated by people in the same sector.

Michael the food vendor was closing up and wheeling his cart away as I passed. Alfred the drink merchant was still making offers on the corner. He tipped his cap at me and I stopped myself from sneering at him.

'Hello, Eden. I've done good business today.' His satisfied chuckle hung in the air like a warning. I passed by the familiar alleyway but couldn't see any comatose drunks there. That was a bad sign.

It had taken me a long time to realise that there was a reason my old home had been so close to the drink merchant's corner. Further away from the shoe repairers, the barbers and the street vendors who sold more upmarket products like clothes, confectionery, maybe even jewellery. No, we'd ended up within walking distance of alcohol.

I continued past all the old unit blocks, past the crumbling and burnt-out buildings that nobody used anymore, until I got to our dilapidated shack on a ramshackle street. I checked all the windows to make sure the boards were still in place. I even punched one that seemed a little loose. It stood its ground.

I went up to the door. I didn't need my link to get inside here. These doors were too old for electronic locks. Even if they'd had them, we would have replaced them with something more secure.

I knocked softly. I heard rustling inside, then I heard Jed's voice. It sounded a little lower than usual. Did he really think his I'm-a-tough-thirteen-year-old voice would scare Dad away? 'Who is it?'

'It's Eden,' I said.

I heard the locks being opened and the bolts being drawn back. I still didn't know where my mother had found them, as I didn't know anyone else who'd even heard of bolts, but they made an ordinary wooden door a step closer to the fortress we required. I dove inside. My brother closed the door and locked it behind me.

I looked around the living room. The larger section of the old couch we'd found had gone, probably sold in exchange for food, leaving only the single lounge chair Jed had picked up somewhere. There was a new hole in it and Lenny was pulling the stuffing out and giggling as he threw it in the air.

'I'm so relieved it's you,' said my mother from the lounge chair. She had her computer on her lap before her, her eyes fixed on it. 'I've got to get these budgets done for the furniture company or they won't pay me.'

Kathleen raced over, her flaxen pigtails streaming out behind her. 'I'm so glad to see you.' She threw her arms around me and I put mine around her. She didn't like it when I kept my distance.

Jed stood before me, arms folded. One blue eye gazed steadily at me. The other was hidden behind a black eye. 'When did that happen?' I asked.

'This morning.'

How had Dad got in this time? The door seemed undamaged. Probably Mother had given in to his pleading. I think she was trying to keep the anguished look off her face as she glanced up. 'How did it go?'

'I got the job.' It was strange. I should be glad. It would help them. It would help me. But I could hardly look at anyone.

Kathleen burst into tears. We hadn't told her or Lenny of our plans. She would have blabbed it to Dad in no time. She threw her arms around me again. 'No. Where are you going? You can't leave us!'

Mother looked resigned. But like me, she was also practical. 'When do you get your first paycheck?'

'I'm not sure.'

'I set up the account,' she said, keying in her link and pressing it to mine. 'Those are the details. Now, I don't expect you to give us everything.'

'I think you'll need it. I mean, those government units, they're fully furnished and everything. I'll get meal vouchers.'

She pressed her hands to my chest. 'You still need some for you. You need to live, maybe meet a nice guy.'

Finding a man wasn't high on my list of priorities. It only led to black eyes, broken ribs and wretchedness.

I pushed past my crying sister, trying not to trip over the hole in the threadbare rug we'd fished out of a dumpster in the middle-class sector, and headed for the room Mother and I shared.

Jed followed me. 'So it's the job at the Archives?'

I grabbed a bag from under my bed. It wasn't very big, but then, I didn't need much, especially now I knew I'd be given uniforms. I began piling my belongings inside. 'Yes, I'm the new junior keeper.'

'I guess Izrod did us a favour.'

I didn't like him talking like that but before I could rebuke him, I heard a fist slamming on the front door. 'Marge, open up!'

There was the sound of scrambling in the living room. Mother appeared at the bedroom door, her eyes frantic, the computer in her hands. 'Quick, Jed. You know what to do.'

Jed snatched the computer from her and fell to his knees beside my bed, pulling the covers off to reveal a large slit in the mattress. He slid the computer inside.

Still Dad pounded on the door. I raced back out to the living room to see it shaking, my mother pleading for him to go away, Kathleen sobbing, Lenny whimpering. Jed moved in front of me. I appreciated it, but I wouldn't let my little brother take a pounding for me. We'd just have to hope the locks did their job.

'Jim, please,' my mother said. 'I gave you something earlier. We don't have anything else.'

'What you mean you don't have anything? You're lying to me again!' my father roared. 'And I saw that good-for-nothing daughter of mine come home. Let me see her!'

Mother continued pleading, then yelped, jumping back. I heard a splintering sound and the tip of a bottle appeared through the door. My father's hand reached through the gap, his eyes scanning around. 'Let me in!'

With shaking hands, my mother opened the locks. What else could she have done? He would have got in anyway, and then we'd need a new door on top of everything else.

My father appeared in the doorway, weaving as he gazed around. His belt hung even lower than usual, his pants barely staying on his hips. He lifted a beer bottle to his mouth and took a swig. I could smell stale beer and urine wafting toward me. The beer would have been bad enough. The other meant that we were in for a hell of a ride.

Mother jumped back from the door after she'd unlocked it, arms crossed in front of herself. Father reached over and grabbed her, dragging her towards him for a kiss. Even though she didn't object, he still threw her into the wall. 'You never want me here, do you?'

Kathleen was shaking, tears streaming down her face. She wasn't old enough to control herself yet. I could see him turning towards her, but before I could say anything, Jed spoke up. 'No, we don't want you here. Go away!'

What the hell? Isn't a black eye enough?

But my father laughed. At least, I think that's what that bleating sound meant. 'Finally, my son is becoming a man. You speak your mind. And make sure no one ever treads on you.' He straightened up, adjusting his shirt like he was some kind of suit, then grabbed Jed by the shoulder, fixing his hair a bit for him. My brother shot him a look but said no more. I was glad he'd decided not to push his luck.

Then Dad turned to me, his face millimetres from mine, his breath hitting me full in the face. I made myself continue breathing and stared back at him.

He stared. He sneered. He looked me up and down. 'Still just like a rock, aren't you? No man would ever want you.'

Good.

I knew Kathleen was trying to be helpful, but she wasn't old enough to know any better. 'Eden's got a job,' she said.

Mother gasped and picked Lenny up from the floor, hurrying as far away as possible. Jed put an arm in front of me, but I pushed him back.

'A job.' He hitched his pants up a little, straightening once more, his voice quiet. 'Doing what?'

I said nothing. I knew what would happen if he knew.

'Doing what?'

Silence.

'DOING WHAT?' He raised his fist.

'She's a keeper!' Kathleen shrieked. 'A junior keeper. I heard her tell Jed.'

Mother groaned and shifted Lenny to the other arm, grabbing Kathleen and dragging the two of them into the second bedroom, where the kids slept. She didn't shut the door, though, kept it open a crack. Jed's arm trembled but again extended in front of me. I shook my head at him, but he didn't move.

'You're going to be a keeper?' Dad's bloodshot eyes blinked. 'For government.' His face turned scarlet, his vein throbbing in his neck, but then he took a deep breath, calming himself. I didn't know that was possible. But it was easy to guess why. I could almost quote the lines that were about to spew from his mouth. 'That's good money. Did they give you an advance?'

'No.'

'But you'll get one. And you'll share some with your father, won't you? Give me your new address.'

'No.'

A dark cloud passed over his face. 'No? You said no to me? After all I've done in raising you?'

You mean the times you beat Mother? You mean the times you snatched money from her link while she begged for it to buy us food? You mean the times you let us lie around sick without medical attention because we didn't have enough money? And why? BECAUSE YOU DRANK IT AWAY!

His eyes bored into mine. 'Nothing. No life on that face of yours. Just like a rock!'

I ducked the fist, which wasn't hard, given how drunk he was, but I came up too quickly and was struck by the bottle he was holding in his other hand. It glanced off my cheek and I gasped, bending over and putting a hand to my face.

'Finally a peep out of you. You'll be screaming by the time I'm done!'

'No!' Jed jumped in, fists flying, pummelling him all over. 'Leave her alone. Don't touch her!'

'Jed, don't!' I dragged him away and to my surprise, Mother grabbed Dad from behind. She hardly ever interfered. She pulled him back, but he flung his elbow at her, catching her on the side of her face. At least it gave me time to pull Jed to safety.

He turned back to us and flung the bottle. We dived out of the way and it smashed against the wall, stale beer trickling through the wooden slats.

I couldn't tell what was louder—Lenny's crying, Kathleen's shrieking, my mother's hysterics or my father as he continued to rage. 'Look at what you've done. All that beer wasted. You'd better pay me back!'

But he'd finally reached it, the point I'd been waiting for. His voice died mid-rant. 'Oh well.' He hiccupped. 'I guess I'd better go get some more.'

He hit the floor with a thud, groaning as his body levelled out, unconscious.

Mother wiped the tears from her face. 'Took him long enough.'

'Come on,' I said to her and Jed. 'Help me with him.'

Jed and I grabbed a shoulder each and Mother his legs, and we carried him to the door, throwing him outside. He'd sleep out there for a good nine hours before waking up and going back out onto the street and doing it all over again.

Mother shut the door behind him and leaned against it. 'But there's a hole in it now. He'll see in. He'll know what we're doing!'

She sank to the floor and gathered Lenny and Kathleen in her arms as they emerged from the bedroom, all of them sobbing together. I looked at Jed, who was sniffling himself, although his eyes lit up. He raced into the bedroom he shared with Lenny and Kathleen and came out with a piece of board.

'Look, Mother,' he said, 'I found this yesterday. We can use it to fix the door.' He beamed at her.

She grabbed him and held him tight. 'My poor boy.'

I went into the kitchen. The cupboard under the sink held a hammer and nails left over from us boarding up the windows. I took the wood from Jed and began to affix it.

'No, Eden,' Jed said. 'It's okay. I'll do that. You take care of your face.'

I had forgotten the lump I could feel on my cheekbone. But at his words, Mother began fussing over me, even though the cut on her cheek had left a scarlet crescent on her face. 'My poor darling, let me fix you up.'

I shrugged her off and went to get the dustpan and brush. 'I'll clean up the glass before the kids stand in it. Kathleen, can you get a cloth to clean the stains off the wall?' She may have only been five, but she'd already learnt how to help put the place back together after Dad pulled it apart.

By the time I'd got the glass cleaned up, my mother had a wet cloth and dabbed it on my face. I could smell disinfectant. I wondered when she'd hidden it. If Dad had smelled it, he would have drunk the whole thing.

'You should have someone look at this,' she said. 'Now you have a job, you can probably get someone really decent to stitch you up.'

I moved her hands away from my face. 'I'm fine. You don't need to worry.'

'At least he didn't find the computer,' Jed said.

Mother put her hand on her heart. 'No, he didn't. That would have been the end. I don't have any money to buy it back from the hawker.'

It looked like they were on their way to recovery, which meant it was time for my long-overdue exit. I finished packing my bag, shoving in everything I could, slid the strap over my shoulder and came back out into the living room, looking at my shell-shocked family.

Kathleen was crying. Jed looked crestfallen. Mother looked bereft.

Lenny was playing with the couch stuffing again.

I kissed my brothers and sister and smiled at Mother as I passed her. 'My salary should start being paid into your account in a week or two.'

'The other account, remember.'

As if I would forget?

Guilt raked over every corner of my soul as the door shut behind me. It was all right for me—I was going to a new life, a new home, with money and security. My family would be left here, securing deadbolts, barricading the door, hiding their valuables and tidying up in the aftermath. I wasn't naive enough to think that just because my money was being paid into a separate account that my father wouldn't be able to get some. He always did, cajoling, wheedling, blustering, threatening until some ended up in his wretched hands.

But I couldn't stay.

I stepped over his body and headed off.

CHAPTER FOUR

'It's not much, I'm afraid, but it will mean you don't have to go far to get to work.'

The supervisor of my building, a woman in a purple suit with a name tag that identified her as Rachel Hammond, smiled as though the proximity to my workplace was what I should like most about my new home. I smiled back but knew she couldn't see behind it. She didn't know how overwhelmed I was that this bright, sparkling new place was *mine*—mine alone. Even the shiny lobby downstairs had smelled of new fittings, although I imagined they weren't the upmarket ones where people like the governor lived.

In this building, there were twenty floors with four units on each. Mine was on floor fourteen and as I stepped into the entryway, Rachel opened a door just beside it. 'Your bathroom's in here.'

The bathroom had the most amazing cream-coloured tiles on the floor. And the taps sparkled. I bet the water ran hot in under twenty minutes.

Just a few steps down, we entered the living area, with its standard couch and single armchair. It flowed into a small kitchen area. 'All the fittings and everything is new.' She looked like she expected me to grumble and groan but it was just as big as the one in our old unit had been. The one that had burnt to cinders, that is. It was way bigger than the one in the shack.

My heart clenched as thoughts of my family flashed before my eyes. I quickly stomped on them, making sure my face stayed neutral.

The bedroom was accessed through a door that led from the living area and as we walked through, Rachel's smile wavered as she looked at the bed. 'I'm so sorry it's only a double, but you know, on your level … It will be different once you get a few promotions.'

'It won't be a problem.' My previous bed had been so narrow I'd had to sleep on my side or fall out.

'Well then,' she said, with a not-so-subtle look at her link. She probably had more important people to fawn over. 'I'll leave you to settle in.'

Once she was gone, I ran my hands over the back of the lounge and opened the refrigerator several times just to enjoy the cool air. I was in my own place, somewhere just for me, somewhere my dad couldn't invade. But I knew that Jed, Kathleen and Lenny would be crowded into Mother's bed right now, ready for her to rock and comfort them when the nightmares came—terrors of a dark figure with a bottle of amber liquid.

I should have been there to console and calm. I usually would have been, even though my heart would have been bloodied and bleeding. But what could I do? If I went back now, I'd have to get through three separate checkpoints before I even left the government sector, and when I reached the shack, Mother would just shoo me away.

But it meant I spent much of the first night in my new home lying in my bed, staring at the ceiling, wondering if they were okay.

In the morning, I shoved those thoughts into the vault in my mind where I kept my life behind lock and key. I tried to drape my hair over the bruise on my face so no one could see it. It wasn't too obvious, and I hoped that if anyone noticed, they'd be too polite to ask questions.

The lobby in the building that housed the Archives was bustling when I entered. As heels clomped over the wide tiles on the floor, hurrying this way and that, it seemed as though there was a purpose behind everyone's rushing. Whatever it was, it had nothing to do with me.

I made my way over to the elevator, only to see Derek point a long finger at me. 'Not here. You have to go to the main assembly room on the ground floor. That way.' He indicated to my left.

'Is that where I get my uniform?'

'No, there's a meeting there. New employees are required to attend.'

'Oh.' Did they always do this for newcomers or was it something to do with the urgency in everyone's step? Derek was chewing his nails. A sign of tension or bad grooming?

He didn't seem inclined to talk anymore. I'd need to find out where to get my uniform later.

I headed in the direction he had pointed. A woman sat at a table near one of the carved wooden doors that led off from the lobby. I took a place at the end of the line and watched her check names off the list in front of her.

Eventually, it was my turn. 'Name?'

'Eden Fittell.'

She ran her finger down the list on her screen until she found me. 'Here.' She gave me a security disk on a chain. I put it around my neck.

'This disk can only be used today,' she said. 'In future, when you go to meetings, a code will be sent to your link. Go through the doors and to your right.'

A couple of other suits hurried through the doorway, security running a device over their links. As the guard scanned my disk, I followed them.

At the end of the corridor, double doors stood open and I could see scores of employees inside the bright room, and not just new employees, either. I could see some of the workers who had been in the Archives the day before. There was no furniture to get in the way, the scuff marks on the tiled floor bearing testament to the fact that it had been hurriedly removed.

I caught snatches of conversation in the hubbub around me. I heard 'Izrod' and 'gone' and 'when?' over and over again, accompanied by frantic glances.

Okay, so this wasn't normal.

'People, can I have your attention?'

The murmur of voices subsided as everyone turned their attention to a man standing in the middle of the room on a raised dais. It was the second suit who'd come down to the Archives during my interview. He looked calm and controlled, even as the crowd around me continued to hiss and whisper.

'I'm sure you've all heard by now that another employee has disappeared,' he said.

The murmurs increased and the man raised his voice. 'While the security sector is investigating, they have yet to come to any firm conclusions about what happened. The employee in question has some family outside the city and he may have gone to visit them. He could also have been a victim of a mugging. We're checking the medical sector for him.'

Murmurs sounded around me again, rolling in like thunder in an approaching storm. I couldn't make out much more than 'Izrod', 'Izrod', 'Izrod'.

'I know you're all worried about what this might mean, but please don't assume the worst has happened until we have a better idea of what's going on. Make sure you check your link regularly for updates. Don't go out too late and stay in the government sector whenever possible. If you need to leave it for any reason, let security know.

'Let me assure you that we will do our best to keep you safe.

Follow the instructions of your sector leaders and together, we'll all get through this. Thank you. Please go about your work. Your sector leaders will have additional information.'

As he stepped down, everyone huddled in groups, their eyes frantic as they let out streams of agitated whispers. I could see a knot of Archives employees but decided not to invade.

I headed back to the elevator, my head spinning after what I'd just heard. *Another* employee gone missing? I knew that people other than government workers had disappeared but it looked like Izrod was favouring them over others, at least at the moment. Would this one reappear or never be seen again? To my knowledge, only two people had ever returned, and they'd been crazy. I didn't know of anyone who picked up the threads of their old life after being snatched by Izrod.

As I left the room, I passed a door with 'uniforms' emblazoned on the front. At least I wouldn't have to ask Derek where to go, especially since I could see him crowding into the elevator with the other Archives employees.

It didn't take long to get things sorted out in the uniform store, and I shut the door behind me only fifteen minutes later, dressed in my new uniform, another two and my old almost threadbare clothes tucked under my arm. Should I keep them or throw them away? Maybe I should put them in a dumpster in the poor sector. Someone else might need them for an interview.

When I reached the elevator, Derek was talking to the man who'd been on the podium. Derek held his hand out as I approached. 'You'll have to wait. Official Hensen needs to be taken down first.'

Official Hensen frowned at him. 'There's no need for that. There's room for three in here.' He turned to me. 'You must be the new junior keeper. I'd heard another had been taken on.'

Yes, replacing the last victim. Not that it mattered to me. Izrod could kidnap every other worker in the government sector and I'd still turn up for work the next day.

We boarded the elevator and the grinding and groaning began as we descended.

Hensen looked down at me. He didn't seem like the usual stiff suit I'd seen strutting the streets of the government sector. His face was open and friendly, and his eyes twinkled. I couldn't tell how old he was. Forty? Fifty? Something like that. I thought I saw his eyes pass over the odd lump on my cheekbone but he didn't say anything about it. Derek didn't seem to notice.

'And your name is?' he said.

'Eden.' I didn't want to mention my last name in case Derek started with his 'famous Fittells' joke.

'You were at the briefing, I take it?'

'Yes, sir.'

His eyes were serious but kind. 'I don't want you to worry. Every step is being taken to ensure the protection of all employees in the government sector.'

'It was Izrod, wasn't it?' Derek put in.

Hensen shifted uncomfortably. 'That hasn't been confirmed.'

'But it was him the other times, wasn't it? Otter, Karen, Evan, Jane, Andrew. And the others.'

The official glowered at him. 'That's enough.' He looked down at me again but seemed relieved. Maybe it was because I wasn't banging on the elevator doors, demanding to be let out. But I couldn't deny I was a little disturbed.

The doors opened and we entered the Archives. I welcomed the close, musty atmosphere. It had an air of protection.

Susan appeared, her hands folded gravely before her. 'Official Hensen, I heard you were coming. I have everything set out ready for you.'

'Thank you,' he replied. 'The others will be here soon.'

Susan turned to me. 'I'm sorry, Eden. I had hoped to do your orientation with you today, but I'm afraid our guests will require my assistance. Adriana can guide you. This is your desk.' She led me to a small desk in the corner. It had an ancient, tiny computer on it and printed forms as well. 'Please fill out the documents on the computer. They should be self-explanatory. After you've done that, Adriana will be ready to assist you.'

I filled in my personal information, making sure I included a request for half my salary to go into Mother's account. I wondered what would happen if I disappeared. Would they give Mother a payout? It might be best to ask.

As I was finishing up, the elevator doors opened again and a woman charged out. I recognised her instantly—Governor Jerrill. She looked every bit as formidable as she did in the media sector shorts. She had a broad waist and curled black hair tied back in a knot.

In her wake came a tiny woman, older than me but smaller. Her darting eyes and hunched shoulders reminded me of the little mouse that sometimes ventured out at my mother's shack, only to scurry away again if one of us moved. She carried a bundle of papers under one arm and a small computer under the other.

Three others joined them—the same three who'd been with Hensen the day before.

Governor Jerrill looked around and her eyes landed on me. 'Where's the head keeper?' she demanded.

I pointed down the corridor just as Susan appeared. 'Madam Governor, a pleasure to see you. Please come this way. We're ready for you.'

'I don't think "pleasure" is the right word, Keeper,' grumbled the governor.

I watched them go as a woman approached my desk. She assessed me with cold eyes almost buried in wavy blonde hair.

'I guess I need to show you what to do.' But her eyes were fixed on the crowded corner with its distinguished guests. I could see she had no interest in doing this and the other keepers were already wheeling their carts towards the gathering, as they had the day before.

Adriana waved her hand vaguely to the left. 'Susan showed you the digital records yesterday. City blueprints and stuff. Then there's infrastructure, plants and history and things. Further down there,' she pointed at the awkward crossway that cut over most of the aisles, 'are paper records that follow the same pattern. There's no point in me detailing them for you. It'll take at least a month before you can navigate this place and remember where everything is.'

She continually turned her head toward the low murmur coming from the officials, but she heaved a sigh and led me through a maze of shelves right to the back of the room, where the ceiling was much lower. The back wall was devoid of shelves, instead containing large pipes, a trickle echoing from within. There was also large throbbing machinery with huge rectangular conduits running along the top of the wall. They were so big I could have crawled through them with ease. I guessed what they were as Adriana confirmed it. 'The air conditioning is run from down here. It services the entire building.'

I wondered why they needed conduits so large. Maybe they made it easier for a worker from the maintenance sector to crawl through and find a problem.

'And these pipes'—she pointed to the sloshy ones—'carry water, but more importantly, they supply water to this.' She uncoiled part of a large hose from the wall. 'If there's ever a fire down here, this is what we need.'

I felt a rush of fear as I remembered the choking smoke that had filled my throat only a couple of weeks ago. 'What if the fire's at the front of the room?'

She rolled her eyes and pulled it out a bit more. 'It's big enough to make it down there. We've also got sprinklers in the ceiling.'

I looked up to see water spigots embedded in the ceiling at regular intervals. 'So what do we do if there's a fire?' I asked.

'Grab the hose.' She waved it at me again.

'What if we can't get to the hose?' Would we be able to find it if the Archives went up? What if the spigots didn't work? I knew how little we'd be able to see if there was a fire, especially with all the shelves looming over us.

'There's also an axe on the wall there,' she said.

An axe? 'What's that for?'

'No idea. But apparently, they used to have them as part of a firefighting kit in old plans of the city from before the conflict, so they put one in.'

She started heading back towards the others. I kept up. 'So if there's a fire, we just grab the hose and hope the sprinklers come on?'

'That's the idea.'

I looked up again. 'Do they actually work?' It was a fair question; most of the services in our city were intermittent, at best.

'Well, we're only supposed to use the hose if the sprinklers don't come on. And in any case, they'd rather we tried to get out.'

'How do we do that?'

'The elevator.'

'In a fire? Isn't that a bad idea?' I was sure they'd taught us that in the learning sector.

She scowled, still heading back to the others. 'There's a trapdoor in the ceiling of the elevator. We go through that and climb up a ladder in the elevator shaft. There's a trigger that lets us manually open the elevator door in case the power's out, but you'll need to get Derek to show you that.' She folded her arms. 'Happy?'

Not really, but she'd already turned away. 'Get a cart.' She grabbed the nearest one and shoved it at me, taking a book from the top and showing me a code on the base of its spine. 'The first number is the category, the second is the row, the third is the shelf, then the following letters will tell you which order it's in. Everything is alphabetical according to title.'

She flounced off, back to the others.

I would make sure I found out from Derek how the trigger worked. I didn't like the idea of being trapped in this basement, fire all around me. A ladder? For all of us? There were seven people who worked down here, judging by the number of desks.

I trundled my cart around, doing my best to put things in the right place. It was harder than it looked, especially for someone short like me. There were ladders to reach the higher shelves and I made the most of them. However, like everyone else, I found myself being drawn to the meeting in the corner.

Soon I was trundling my cart up just behind Derek, who was standing furthest back. 'So do you want to tell me what's going on?' I asked.

He looked upset that I was dragging his attention from the officials, but then his eyes lit up. I got the impression he liked an audience as he bent over, like a wizened old man. 'This isn't the safest place to work.'

He seemed disappointed by my lack of reaction so I put on my I'm-really-intrigued face. It must have been enough for him because he launched back into the tale. 'It all started about nine months ago. You must have heard about it from the media sector.'

'About the disappearances?' And reappearances of crazy people.

'That's right. At first, they were from other sectors, so no one important.' He thought anyone who didn't work for government wasn't important? Good to know. 'Then a guy who worked in logistics disappeared. His name was Otter. I chatted with him sometimes when he came down to the Archives. Security had a record of him going into his unit for a few days' leave, but he never returned to work. They went to check on him and no one was there. There were no signs of a struggle or anything. It was like he'd just ceased to exist.

'And then he turns up, two days later, babbling like he's crazy and throwing his arms around. He was only little. Not as little as you, but still small, and he managed to get one of the security guys in a headlock. They arrested him and took him away somewhere, but ...' He shook his head. What had happened? Had he died? Stayed mad?

'Now, you'd be excused for thinking that that was just one of those things, right? Nope. A few weeks later, a girl, Karen, who was a proper official, disappeared. She had a day off and didn't come in. Again, no signs of a struggle or anything like that. And no one ever saw her again.

'So people started getting a little nervous. Otter and Karen wouldn't have done anything more than pass one another in the hallway, so it wasn't like there was any reason for them both to disappear.

'And then another guy, Evan, also disappeared. But he was a big guy and this time there were signs that something had gone on at his unit. It looked like someone had tried to tidy it afterwards, but there were things out of place. No one ever saw him again, either. Some others went after him, but I didn't know them at all.

'By the time Jane went, everyone was getting frantic. They were talking about not allowing anyone any days off, but instead, we have to check in with security every day we're off work so they know we're okay. They've been doing that for the past month, and I guess they thought they had it all figured out, but then Andrew and now this latest guy went missing.' He looked at the officials. 'I'm guessing they're trying to work out what they can do to keep people safe.' He hooked his hands like claws. 'But how can they keep us safe from ... Izrod?'

He extended the name out and I suppressed a shiver. 'But how do they know it's Izrod?'

He held up a finger. 'Aha, that's what these guys have been figuring out. They don't often catch him on security visuals, but they've seen footage of him in the area at the time of a couple of disappearances.'

'But was he carrying anyone or dragging them along?'

'No.' I guess he hadn't thought of that. 'But maybe they just didn't get footage of it.' That seemed to cheer him up.

He must have felt the tale was told because he craned his neck to see what the officials were doing and wandered towards them again. I followed, but there wasn't much to see, especially since Susan kept shooing us away.

Eventually, I went back to my cart. It wasn't like I could hear anything anyway. But the fact that I worked without the constant hovering everyone else was doing brought me to the head keeper's attention. At the end of the day, while the guests were packing up, she came over to me.

'Eden, I'd like to thank you for putting in such a stellar effort today. I can see you're going to be an asset to the Archives.'

As she spoke, Official Hensen came to her side. 'We're going now, Susan.'

'Do you have everything you need?'

'Yes.' He gave me a friendly look. 'I hope your first day wasn't too frightening. Don't worry, we'll get Kore and all his gang.'

His smile wavered at the end but he managed to cling to it, like someone might cling to a ledge before they fell.

Fear aside, it was nice to know some people cared.

CHAPTER FIVE

'Eden, can you put the digital files away for me?'

I looked over at Susan, who stood leaning against her desk. She had one of her spindly hands on her back, the other on her forehead. But as she turned to me, her gaze was still steadfast.

I went over the fetch the files and put them on my cart. 'Sure. I'll do it right away.' I guess it had been a busy time for her lately. Or was it always like this?

'I'm glad I hired you,' she said. 'You've definitely proved your worth over the last month. You're a hard worker.'

I saw a couple of the other junior keepers turn their noses up at her words. I had noticed a sting in their behaviour toward me lately, probably because I emptied five carts in the time it took them to do one. They thought *I* was to blame because *they* were slow?

Derek gave half a smile, sidling over, shoulders hunched. 'Yeah, you're a better worker than most of the other bozos, including me.' He gave a nervous chuckle.

He stood way too close. Then he put his hand on the small of my back. My spine stiffened. 'Keep your hands to yourself,' I snapped. I hoped one warning was enough. I didn't want to start doing the keep-just-out-of-reach dance with him. I did it often enough when my dad's fists were flying.

His eyes widened in surprise. 'Man, give a guy some feedback. Don't keep him guessing until the last minute!'

I wasn't sure exactly what that meant. I shoved the question away in the same place where I locked up thoughts of my family.

Derek was called to the elevator, still grumbling about my rebuke as the doors shut. Ten minutes later, he returned with Official Hensen and Elena Gregor, the governor's mousy assistant.

'Good morning, Eden,' Hensen said as he passed me. He called out greetings to a few other keepers he knew before heading for the head keeper's desk. Miss Gregor gave me a slight smile as she slipped past.

I wondered what they had come to the Archives for this time. There didn't seem to be much urgency, so it couldn't be another attack from Izrod. No government workers had been taken since the man who'd disappeared the day before I'd started work. Not that any of the stringent security measures had been relaxed, as a few people had vanished from other sectors.

I went about my work, aware that everyone was craning their necks to see what Hensen and Miss Gregor were doing. I could see Reggie O'Neal looking around the corner of a bay as he stacked some papers in place. As he wandered away, I went over to check what he'd done. Yep. They'd been put in the wrong place. I followed him up the aisle, correcting all the mistakes he'd made.

Adriana Michaels gave me a withering glare over her trolley. 'Keep your hands on your own work,' she whispered.

'That would be fantastic, wouldn't it? Reggie goes and puts the most crucial piece of intel we've got about Izrod where no one can find it.' I couldn't work out whether she was worried I'd hurt his feelings or if she wanted him to be caught out and sent packing.

'No, idiot.' She pointed to the electronic log on the cart. 'That tells us what's been on the cart so if we can't find a file it can be tracked.'

I looked at the readout. Did she think I hadn't noticed it in all this time? But that was just for the digital records. The logs for the paper records were kept only on Susan's computer. 'That only lists the digital ones. And isn't it better just to make sure everything's in the right place the first time?'

Her eyes blazed. 'Don't try and play smart, you stupid poor sector nitwit.'

She called that an insult? It was hard not to laugh in her face. She'd have to try a lot harder if she wanted to get under my skin.

I turned back to my work. Adriana's cheeks turned red, but she kept her mouth shut. Her cart's wheels let out a shrill *eee-eek-eek* as she moved it away, reminding me of the high-pitched squeal of her voice. It was more annoying than her attempt at provoking me. She kept looking at Hensen and Miss Gregor too, but neither of them showed any hint that there had been another kidnapping or some other nefarious crime.

The lights flickered off and everyone groaned.

'Now, now, people,' said Susan. 'They should be back on in a few minutes.'

My work had taken me close enough to hear Miss Gregor's low voice. 'You'd think we could at least do something about the power grid.'

Official Hensen's voice was calm and easy. 'I know they're working on it but you know how difficult things have been since we rebuilt the city. It only takes one circuit break to cause a problem. We'll get it all working in the end.'

I could understand Miss Gregor's frustration. I'd been surprised that the power outages even impacted the government sector. Could they really not give the government stuffed shirts enough light to work by?

The lights flickered back on before long, and at the end of the day, our two guests packed up their work, taking the files they needed with them.

'We'll be out of the city for a few days,' Hensen told Susan. 'There's a conference at Reacher's Pass.'

'I hope you found what you needed.'

'Yes, it's just about some trade route changes, nothing special. But I think we've had enough excitement for a while, don't you?' He turned to me. 'And how are you, Eden? How long have you been here for now?'

'About a month, sir.'

'I hope you haven't found all the security restrictions too arduous.'

Sure, if you like trudging through three security checkpoints every time you have to walk ten metres. 'No, sir. It's fine.'

'Eden has three days' leave as of today,' Susan said. 'She's done so much overtime she's already built up an extra day.' Usually, we only had a maximum of two days off at a time. But I wished Susan hadn't mentioned it. I could feel the glares of all my fellow employees hitting me in the back of the head.

He nodded. 'That'll be good. You can go and catch up with family and friends.'

The smile stayed on my face. 'Yes, sir.' I had already planned to go and see my family. I just hoped it would be a drunk-free visit.

By the time I'd finished these thoughts, Hensen and Miss Gregor were getting in the elevator. 'Stay safe, everyone,' he said as the doors shut. Miss Gregor had time to give us a slight nod.

When I'd finished my work before everyone else, as usual, I headed for the elevator. Maybe I shouldn't work so hard or so fast. It would help me blend in better.

Derek was silent as he took me up to the ground floor. No comments about famous Fittells and only a grunt when I said goodbye. I left the building and walked the three blocks to my unit, through a checkpoint just near Archive Central, another at the end of the first block, then the third. At each point, I was asked the same questions.

'Name?'

'Eden Fittell.'

'Position?'

'Junior keeper in the Archives.'

'Are you headed for your unit?'

'Yes.'

'How long are you expected to be there?'

Finally, I made it to my unit building. Here, it was at least a little more personal. Jenny Johnson was on duty and she touched her cap as I approached, her frizzy hair sticking out from under it. 'Hello, Eden. Heading home?'

'Yes. Do you have long to work this shift?'

'No, I'll be relieved in half an hour or so,' she said as she scanned my link. Her hands were so large, my wrist was buried in them as she held it steady and ran her scanner over it. 'I hear you've got an extra day off?'

'Yes.'

'Make sure you check in every twelve hours. Touch your link to the scanner in your unit if you don't want to go out just so we know you're in there and okay. And if you do go out, make sure we know where and the duration of your absence. No changing plans on a whim. Okay?'

'Sure.' I wondered if she appreciated my extra time off just because it gave her something different to say rather than just parroting the 'every twelve hours' line.

I scanned my link at my door, pushing hard on it to make it swing open. I didn't know why they made them so heavy. I let it thud shut behind me, taking a deep breath as I adjusted to the cool solitude.

I still hadn't tired of my beautiful unit, enjoying the feeling of the plush carpet. I liked that my toes sank in and I could wiggle them in the soft fabric. The lounge might not have been flash, but at least there were no holes in it. And I would make sure it stayed that way.

After I'd changed out of my uniform, I checked my small refrigerator, which I'd stocked with the bare essentials over the past few weeks. What was there for dinner? A bowl of noodles and some faux fruit? It was impossible to get real fruit. I couldn't remember ever having it before. Even in the government sector, it seemed scarce.

After I'd eaten my meal and cleaned up, I noticed how stuffy it was and went into the bedroom to make sure the air conditioning was functioning. The air conditioning duct sat quietly in its corner, a gentle *shhhhh* coming from it, confirming that it seemed to be working. But I could still taste staleness in the air.

I bent over and looked at the duct, putting my hand against the grill. The air breathed against it, a gentle waft washing over me, but it didn't seem as strong as usual. Maybe something was blocking it. I didn't think I'd be able to get the vent off by myself; I'd probably need maintenance to do that, so it would have to wait. They wouldn't like being dragged up at this time of night because of a faulty vent.

I went back into the living room and looked at the window. There was a time when it could have been opened. Security had justified that too. 'It's just until they catch Izrod and round up the rest of Kore's gang. Once that's done, we'll all have fresh air again.' But some people said that the air still contained poison from the bombings during the Unbidden Conflict, so maybe it was better that the windows were shut.

The unit still felt stuffy. I knew it was unlikely I'd be able to budge the window, but I pulled at the latch and although it took a bit of huffing and puffing, it opened halfway.

What? I shouldn't be able to—

I felt the depression on the carpet under my feet the same moment I heard the footfall. I didn't have time to turn before something heavy and hard slammed into my head. I collapsed to the floor, twisting as I fell, my surprise churning into fear in my stomach as I saw a hulking form with a distinct mane of sandy hair standing over me.

Then he faded away into the blackness that overtook me.

CHAPTER SIX

Is someone standing on my head?

I put my hand up to it, finding a huge lump on the back. I inhaled the stale odour of sweat and urine. I gagged and tried to lift my head out of it, only to find that my neck was another point of misery.

Izrod.

I pushed through the pain and snapped myself upright. Where was I? My head was still fuzzy and at first, my eyes wouldn't focus properly. Then finally, I saw my surroundings.

I was sitting on a bunk with a fetid mattress on it that looked like it pre-dated the Unbidden Conflict. The squeak of springs sounded under me as I stood up. This bed had springs? I'd only heard about spring beds in the learning sector.

I put my feet over the edge where they were met with a cold floor made of large concrete blocks. I looked at the walls. More thick concrete on three sides. But it was the fourth that sent my heart into overdrive. It was made of iron bars with a gate in it, a gate with an electronic lock.

Despite the ache in my skull, I stumbled over to the gate and pulled on it. Nothing. I pulled harder, yanking with all my strength. It stayed put. I put my hands on the bars and tried them. They weren't going anywhere.

I was in a prison.

I looked down to the right from my cell only to see another. To the left was the same, and across from me. The electric lights over my head flickered, which wasn't unusual, but the momentary blackness made me see ghosts in the hallway. I blinked, and they were gone. Maybe if I blinked hard enough, all of this would melt away into the crypt of nightmares in my mind.

I squeezed my eyes shut and opened them. Iron bars were still staring me in the face.

Then I noticed the sounds. Someone was moaning, a long discordant *eee-ooo-eee-oooh* that went on and on, increasing in volume before drifting away, only to start again. Someone else was shrieking. Was it a human? It was difficult to tell. It didn't sound like any animal I'd ever heard but even Dad at his drunkest hadn't sounded so manic. I heard the sound of a thud and the shrieking cut off.

In the cell across from me, a figure was on the bed, wrapped up in a blanket, the sound of despairing sobbing echoing across as the blanket shivered and trembled in time with the sobs.

Where *was* I? How had I got here? What was—

'Oooh, she awakes.'

A man came sauntering along the passageway, rattling the bars on each cell by running a metal truncheon along them. It was tied to his belt by a cord, hanging next to what looked like a master link—the kind the head keeper had that opened multiple doors, except that this one was much larger than Susan's.

That made me glance at my wrist, as it suddenly occurred to me that something was missing. I was right—my link was gone. No one was supposed to be able to remove a link unless they cut your arm off, so how had they got it off me? And where was it? I had no hope of anything without it. I could buy nothing, get no transport, I didn't even officially exist without it.

I stepped back as the man came up to the bars and ran his metal prong along them, the sound echoing down the hallway. His grin revealed an unhealthy display of rotten teeth and putrid gums. His eyes reminded me of the man I'd seen with rabies once on my way to the learning sector. The security sector had shot him but he'd still screamed and foamed for a minute or two before the light of life had finally left his eyes.

This man was very much alive and looked me over greedily.

'Where am I?' I hoped I didn't sound afraid.

'Welcome, my lady, to your new home, at least for the next day or two.' He bowed mockingly. 'We've only got the best company for you, as you can see over here.' He pointed at the quivering blanket. Then he went over, took the truncheon and ran it across the bars of the cell opposite me. I stopped myself from covering my ears as the clang reverberated off the walls.

'Come on, buddy. I know it's a bit too much for you, but we've got a lady here.' He turned back to me with a rotting grin. 'I guess he didn't see much of the last one. She wasn't here long.'

This kind of taunting I knew all too well. My father had taught me how to respond to it—with nothing. 'Where am I?' I said again.

I heard the sound of more footfalls. 'She's woken up, has she?'

I looked up and braced myself. *Show no emotion.* But it was difficult when looking into the eyes of the most feared creature in this city.

Izrod was way more than a head taller than me. He towered over the other man, who looked at Izrod as though he'd been caught swiping merchandise from a vendor.

But this towering hulk paid him no attention, his eyes boring into mine. They were a verdant green and so intense it was difficult to look into them. But I'd trained myself to meet gazes just as intimidating as this. I wasn't going to give him the satisfaction of seeing any terror on my face.

I was surprised at how much was in his expression. The media sector had told us he was a brain-dead Neanderthal who lumbered around blindly following instructions. But his eyes were sharp and forceful. And even though his hands were too big for his arms and his shoulders were bigger still, his face looked like any other face I saw on the street—two eyes, a nose in the right place, a serious and uncompromising mouth. He wasn't the hideous freak everyone said he was.

I thought back to that video footage I shouldn't have been watching. It had been dark and grainy, but he'd looked like a monster, walked like a monster. Was this really the same man? He'd had a lumbering gait, but now he stood straight and tall, no sign of deformity, nothing grotesque.

He looked me up and down. 'That's a relief. I was worried I'd hit her too hard. We don't have time to waste.'

The little man beside him let out a haunting chuckle, dancing from foot to foot. He moved out of the way as Izrod stepped in front of him, waving his link over the door. It buzzed and unlocked. He grabbed both of my wrists in one meaty hand and yanked me out into the corridor, dragging me behind him. I considered protesting but what good would it do? And yelling or—heaven forbid—doing something like begging was out of the question.

But through the throbbing pulse of my headache, I knew I was out of my depth. Sure, living with Dad had taught me a thing or two about surviving bullies, but he could always be depended on to pass out eventually and wake up and stagger out to find more booze. That kind of reprieve was unlikely to be offered here.

I could hear the resident of the other cell sobbing as I was led away.

Izrod dragged me down a corridor of stone with a barred cell on either side. I tried not to cringe away from the figures in them. One person was doubled over on the bed, clutching her stomach—she was the screamer I'd heard. Another lay twitching on the floor.

We reached the end of the corridor abruptly and passed a thick concrete door like the one to my unit. I could almost feel the weight of it. Was that an escape route?

I turned away from it to see a pair of green eyes fixed on me. 'Don't even try it,' he growled.

But rather than turn and continue dragging me, he stopped and gazed at me. I tried to keep the mask in place that I'd used on my father for so long but this was no drunken binge that would end in a deep sleep and loud snores. I didn't even know what they wanted of me, much less how to fight against it.

After a moment of reflection, he continued dragging me.

We went through a set of double doors, both thicker than the door of my unit, which Izrod opened with the gentle push of one hand. The other still held both my wrists. Then he threw me inside before coming in after me and closing the doors.

I used a deep breath to disguise my trembling as I looked around me. It was a cold room—more concrete everywhere—with dilapidated plastic chairs and tables around. At each one sat someone who might have been human once. Now they resembled Izrod—bodies out of proportion, hands too big for arms, arms too long for bodies, unnaturally large shoulders. Men or women, it made no difference. Some of them looked way more monstrous than Izrod.

There were ten or so people in this room, all lolling back, drinking. The stale smell of alcohol relieved me in a strange way—at least it was familiar—and terrified me in others.

A man stood at a set of shelves at the far end of the room. Lined up before him were numerous vials filled with viscous liquid. He picked up each in turn and held it up to the light, which flickered, causing him to scowl.

He glanced up as we approached, taking a second look at me. He had to be the oldest person present, probably in his mid-thirties or maybe forty, although his jet-black hair was untouched by any signs of ageing. His gaze penetrated me, my stomach curling uncomfortably.

I didn't need to be told that this was Kore.

Kore's mouth twisted and he put down the vial. 'And this is the latest acquisition? You didn't have any trouble obtaining her?'

Izrod snorted. 'Please.'

His boss seemed amused. 'Even you occasionally strike trouble, Leon.'

Leon? Izrod has a name?

'Not in the government sector.'

Kore tittered. 'Fair enough.' He looked me over again and I held rigidly still.

'And you really think she's the best option?' I loved the way they talked about me as though I wasn't there.

'She's a junior keeper,' Izrod replied. 'You don't want someone too high up in the chain. And unlike the last one we took, she's relatively new to the job so they haven't gotten the chance to get to know her too well, so any small personality changes won't be noticed. She also keeps to herself, so again, few are likely to notice changes.'

I could feel my face paling. Were they going to make me insane, like everybody else? But that would be a pretty major personality change, so maybe not.

Kore stood before me, appraising me like I was chattel for sale on someone's cart. 'It had better work, although I'm fairly sure about this formula. Anyway, let's pay our informant and get on with it. I'm tired of having him around.'

He looked at a woman at a door on the far side of the room and she opened it. 'Come on, in you come,' she said.

It was difficult to hold my face in check, probably harder than anything I'd ever done, because in walked my father. He was sober—as sober as he got, anyway—and he spared me a guilt-ridden glance as he sidled past me and up to Kore. 'So you got her okay, then?'

Kore went back to examining the vials on the shelf. 'Clearly.' He gestured at Izrod. 'My compatriot here seems to think she'll be an asset to my program.'

Dad's eyes lit up. 'I knew she would be. As soon as I heard, I knew she'd be perfect. She's in the government sector, but still new. Just what you want.'

'Very well.' Kore held out his link and my father put his against it. I heard a beep—a clear sound of a financial exchange.

He'd sold me. Sold me out to them for money that he could drink away. How many drinks had he got for me? Probably not more than a day's worth, if that. Was I really worth no more than an afternoon binge?

Dad's eyes shone as he examined the lifeline he'd just received. 'I've got three more children. It won't be long before—'

'Don't you *dare* touch them!' I spat.

Every eye in the room turned to me. Some of the abettors around the room chuckled, glanced at each other, gloried in my downfall. But my father's eyes bugged out and he took a step back.

Kore laughed. 'Hm, I'd started to think she had no emotions at all. Good to know, good to know.' He turned back to Dad. 'Thank you for that.'

My father licked his lips. 'Perhaps a higher fee—'

Kore's humour turned into a snarl. 'Don't push your luck.' He pointed at the door. My father hunched in on himself, and without another glance at me, turned and slunk away.

As the door shut behind him, Kore's gaze returned to me. 'What's your name, girl?'

I clenched my teeth shut.

'It's Eden,' said Izrod.

'Well, Eden,' Kore sauntered up and walked around me, 'you're in luck. We're not going to make you insane with this one. At least, I hope not. There's a good likelihood you'll survive. And I think you'll find that, once you get to know us, we're not so bad.'

Laughter broke out around us. I held myself still to stop myself from shaking. *Don't let them know. Don't let them in.*

Kore handed Izrod a few of the vials and the big monster grabbed my arm and hauled me away. I looked back at Kore's impassive face. Did I beg? Would it do any good? It had never worked with my father and he was supposed to have loved me. Kore had no reason to care.

Izrod dragged me out of the room and back down the corridor of cells. I passed by the screamer on one side and a woman moaning and rocking on the other. But he led me past the one I thought was my cell and kept going, past another set of cells, some occupied, some awaiting their next victim.

At the other end of the hall, he opened a door and dragged me in. This room was clean and white, every surface polished, shining and white. There were no windows and only one door. There were cupboards with drawers lining every wall, with a multitude of medical equipment spilling out of them.

A woman in a medical coat sat in the corner going over something on a computer. She looked up as we entered. 'Another one?'

In the middle of the room was a pillar with a slab on top of it. Manacles were attached at either end. Izrod lifted me up and placed me on it, snapping the manacles around my wrists and ankles. 'Yep. This is the latest.' He handed her the vials Kore had given him.

'The new stuff? Hopefully it works,' she said.

I couldn't keep the fear at bay any longer. I thrashed and fought but I might as well have been hitting a bag of rocks for all the effect it had on this beast.

Once he was satisfied I wasn't going anywhere, Izrod turned for the door. 'Let me know when it's done and I'll take her back to her cell.'

I can't beg. I'm not going to beg. But my breaths came faster and I struggled with the manacles. I could feel them bruising my flesh.

It won't work, you fool! Don't do it! But I couldn't keep the words in any longer. 'Please ... please ...'

As I'd expected, the woman ignored me, selecting a syringe and putting the vial into it. She brought it over and without any this-won't-hurt-a-bit garbage, she thrust it into the vein in my arm.

I gasped and groaned as the liquid left the syringe and entered my bloodstream. I could feel a cold burn as it travelled up towards my neck. As it spread further, the burning increased, followed by agonising pain.

My right arm sought to escape its bonds to try and rub the pain away, but it was no use. It wasn't long before the burn and then the agony spread through my head, down my other arm, through my chest, all the way down to my toes. I screamed and thrashed and begged some more, only to see the woman loading more syringes. It made no difference to her if I thrashed around; she thrust the needles in wherever she could find skin, one after the other, until another three had been inserted. Then she retreated to her corner with her computer, eyes flicking over it, while I continued to writhe and scream.

A sour taste rose in my throat. I was going to vomit and choke on it like my father nearly had once. But although I retched, nothing came out. My body spasmed and I shook uncontrollably. I gasped for breath, my throat raw from the burning and the screaming.

Then a weariness settled over me. I could feel my eyes shutting. Bizarrely, I fought against it. *Wouldn't it be better to pass out? Then you won't feel anymore.* But I was sure I would never open my eyes again, or if I did, I'd have a different body, one with huge arms and stumpy fingers, someone who was an empty shell of me, someone who would do whatever Kore wanted, like Izrod.

But the weariness possessed me and I was powerless to stop it.

CHAPTER SEVEN

Darkness swirled around me and I fought to escape it. I stretched out my hands, searching for something in the mist, but they only clenched air. I tried to pull myself out, hand over hand, struggling every moment.

I can't breathe!

My hearing cleared of its water-logged timbre and I sat bolt upright.

I was back in my cell. That realisation hit me with a depressing thud, while at the same time, I felt relief. I still had all my fingers and toes. My arms and legs looked normal, apart from being covered with purple and red streaks. They throbbed, but nothing else seemed to hurt.

I felt my shoulders. No huge mass of muscle, no deformity that I could feel. I felt my face. It felt fine, but I couldn't see it. Was there something wrong with it? Something I didn't know about?

And I couldn't sense any fog in my brain. Every thought of Kore, Izrod and their cronies was filled with hatred.

I was still me.

Maybe it hadn't worked. Kore had seemed doubtful. I hoped beyond anything that I'd be his biggest disappointment.

But I could guess what happened if you disappointed Kore.

As I heard footsteps approaching, cold dread washed over me. Was this when I found out what happened to failed experiments?

Izrod's hulking form appeared in the corner of my eye as he stopped in front of my cell. Then I looked into his eyes and everything changed.

Or rather, *he* had changed. His face … it was so … so indescribable. It was noble and powerful and trustworthy and everything good all rolled into one. I couldn't take my eyes off him.

It was impossible to stay where I was. I gasped and raced to the bars, reaching out to him.

A look of alarm crossed his features and he angled his body to the side, covering me with his shadow. He moved his face close to the bars and his mouth barely moved as he said, 'Control your face.'

That snapped me out of whatever trance he'd put on me. I *had* been brainwashed. I was seeing him as trustworthy and good because whatever they'd put in me *made* me see him that way. I stepped back from him, my shoulders bowed in disgust at both of us. And he'd known. He'd clearly seen my feelings. *How could I be so stupid?*

I reconstructed the walls around me. No one else would know. I wouldn't let them see how I felt. I wouldn't let myself feel that way.

'So she's awake?' It was another voice—my regular jailer, the little man who seemed to take great delight in rattling the bars and grinning senselessly at everything.

I braced myself. How would he look?

As his eyes met mine I felt shock again, but this time I kept it locked inside. This man didn't look trustworthy or good. He looked pathetic, more frightened than frightening. His eyes were shot through with fear and seemed to widen with greater terror the closer he got to Izrod.

He gave a gleeful jig at the sight of me. At least, I think it was meant to be gleeful. Given how scared he looked, it was difficult to tell. He ran his metal truncheon up and down the bars of my cell but I felt nothing greater than embarrassment. It was ridiculous rather than threatening.

'Do you think it worked?' he said. He seemed terrified of a negative response.

Izrod looked me over. 'Hard to tell. I can't see anything different, can you?'

'Yeah, but this one isn't supposed to be something we see, is it?'

'I guess not.' Izrod huffed. 'I'll go and tell Kore.'

My jailer looked like he was about to blubber. 'I hope for your sake that something's changed, little girl, or it's …' He ran a finger across his throat.

It was hard to see him as dangerous.

I heard Izrod returning, someone with him. I carefully schooled my face to keep it expressionless. What would Kore look like?

He came around the corner and surveyed me. I gazed back, hoping I was revealing nothing as I catalogued every aspect of his face. Of the three of them, he seemed the least different. His eyes were still cunning, his face hard and calculating. Although there was something new about him, something a little unhinged, not that that was a big surprise. Then there was the way he looked at Izrod. It made me think of a teacher I'd liked in the learning sector.

Disappointment passed across Kore's features. 'So there's no change.'

'There doesn't seem to be,' said Izrod.

Kore scowled. 'There *should* be. I'm absolutely certain I got the formula right.' He leant closer. 'So, Eden, talk to me.'

I wasn't exactly disposed to be cooperative, but I thought I'd better at least answer before they stuck me with more needles. 'What about?'

He narrowed his eyes, trying to see below the surface to peer inside me, I imagined. 'Do you feel any different?'

'Apart from where you stuck me'—I showed him the bruising—'no, not at all.' I couldn't keep the sarcasm out of my voice.

He examined me, discerning what he could. 'There's nothing different?'

'Should there be?' I figured a question was better. Anything to keep him guessing.

The excitement left his eyes, disappointment swirling in their depths. 'I don't know what went wrong.'

'Maybe she's hiding it,' the jailer said. 'You should give her Alpha-D, just in case. Once she's loyal to you, she'll tell you everything.'

'It could be that it's taking longer to show up than we thought. Maybe you should wait another twelve hours,' said Izrod.

'Give her Alpha-D,' the little man begged, 'just in case.'

Kore turned a scathing glare on him. 'It's too precious to waste on a failed test subject.' He looked back at me. 'The dosage must have been incorrect. I thought because she was small … Never mind. We'll just have to try again on the next one.' He walked away. 'You know what to do.'

The jailer smacked his lips in terror. Or was it excitement? 'I'll do it. This is my favourite part.' I got the feeling he was threatening me.

Izrod held out his hand. 'No, we'll give it a couple of hours. It's only been ten since she underwent the procedure. Get her a meal. You never know, feeding her might make a difference.'

'That's not what Kore said,' the little man pleaded. But it was clear he wasn't going to contradict Izrod. 'Humph. And I suppose he'll do it himself,' he grumbled as he walked away. 'I never get to have any fun.'

I was left alone then, looking at the cell opposite, which was now empty. There was a small trail of blood leading from the cot to the door. Had they killed its occupant there, I wondered, or dragged him away to do it?

Because it was clear what was going to happen now. It hadn't worked … as far as they knew, anyway. There was only one conclusion after that. Would they inject me with whatever had made the others mad or just slit my throat?

But *had* this formula worked? People looked different to me, well, two people, anyway. I didn't know why or what it meant. Maybe it was just a temporary thing. Kore hadn't looked that different. If I saw the rest of his crew, they might be the same.

But why see Izrod and the jailer differently at all? What had happened? I cringed at the thought of how I'd reacted to Izrod. I thought I'd destroyed my ability to show feelings like that years ago. My father had trampled it to dust.

What if I called them back and told them I saw things differently? Would they keep me alive? Maybe I would have a chance to escape. But what was Alpha-D? No, I couldn't risk it.

The jailer returned in about half an hour with a tray containing a crust of bread, water and what looked like broth of some kind. It smelled foul, but I was too hungry to refuse it.

He pulled down a small gate in the bars near the floor and pushed the tray in. 'Enjoy your last meal,' he said with a chuckle, then bolted out of sight, running from me in terror.

How sad.

Would they really kill me? Of course they would. But I couldn't let the fear overtake me. I dampened it down, making sure I crushed it between bites of the stale bread dipped in the broth. It tasted better than it smelled, or maybe my standards were lower now I knew this was probably going to be the last thing I ate.

As I picked up the cup of water, I noticed something flapping on the bottom of it. I put my hand under it and pulled away a piece of paper. It was folded into a small square and there was something written on it. I held it up to the feeble light, which chose that moment to flicker off. Fortunately, it flickered back on again a few seconds later, and I was able to read what it said.

Next time the lights go off try the door.

I scrunched the note in my hand, watching for the lights to flicker again. They stayed on.

What did this mean? Was someone trying to help me get out of there? Why would they do that? Who could it be? Had someone taken pity on me?

Maybe this was a trap and they wanted me to try the door and make my escape. Was it a test, some kind of follow-up to their procedure? If I escaped, would it be a sign that it had actually worked? How was I to know? Did I trust whoever had written this? Could I believe that they wanted to help me?

No. Absolutely not.

As much as I told myself to ignore this suspicious note, my attention was riveted on the lights. They stayed on. What difference would it make if they did go off? It wasn't going to cut the power to the locks on the doors. If it did that, everyone here would have escaped in the first five minutes.

Eventually, I sat back down on the bunk. Did I try the door or was it too risky? Even as I vacillated between the two, I knew that when the lights flickered out again, I would try it. It was too tempting not to. My fingertips itched. Maybe if I tried it now …

Wait.

It was another long hour before they flickered again, and when they did, everything was black for a solid minute.

I fumbled my way to the door and pushed on it. At first, I thought it wasn't working, but then it creaked open. It was hard to see where everything was, but I'd spent the past hour memorising which way to turn after getting out of my cell and how many steps it was to the door at the end of the corridor—just two cells down on the right.

To my relief, that door was also unlocked. But now came the problem—I didn't know what was on the other side of it. For all I knew, it was Kore's bedroom.

The lights came back on. There was nothing for it—I pushed the door open and stepped through, shutting it behind me as quietly as I could.

I was in an antechamber. It had several doors and I could see light shining around the edges of a door at the end.

Sunshine. I hurried over to it.

'Hey, stop her!'

The door at the other end of the antechamber slammed open. Izrod raced towards me. I yanked on the door and raced out into an alleyway. I had no idea where to go but as far away as possible seemed like the best option.

I'd always been a good sprinter—I'd used it to avoid Dad more than once. I bolted around the corner, relieved to see people at a crossroad up ahead. It looked like the poor sector. My old burnt-out unit block home wouldn't be far away.

I yelped as something hit my arm. I looked down to see a knife clattering to the ground. It felt like it had just caught the edge of my flesh. The shock drove me faster.

'Hey! Hey!' I waved my arms as I ran. The more people who saw me, the more it would put Izrod off my tail. He couldn't launch himself into a throng of people and drag someone away without causing a riot.

Finally, two figures turned my way. One was a cart vendor—fortunately, not vending drinks, as I wouldn't have trusted him—the other his customer.

I fell into her arms. 'Please, please help me,' I gasped.

'What—?' she began, then sucked in a breath when she saw the blood dripping from my arm.

The cart vendor darted to the far side of his cart. 'I don't want anything to do with no trouble.' Had other escapees charged towards his place of business, begging for help? I could tell by the fear and fickleness on his face that he wasn't going to put his life on the line for me, or anyone else, for that matter.

'Come on, don't be ridiculous,' the woman said. 'The girl's been injured, for crying out loud!' Her hair was in strings and I could feel her long fingernails digging into me. But although her face had severity embedded in every corner, I could see a sense of justice there as well.

'Who are you, girl?' she demanded, scowling as the vendor picked up his cart and trundled it away. Soon we were surrounded by others, people with dirt on their hands and fear on their faces, but as I looked around, most seemed genuine in their curiosity. One or two slunk away—one with terror in every feature, the other looking treacherous—but I didn't dare call them out. What if people realised there was something different about me and told Kore? We were still virtually on his doorstep. And what if people thought I was corrupted, brainwashed, a potential traitor?

'Please,' I said again, 'I work in the government sector. I was kidnapped. Call the security sector. There'll be people looking for me.' I could see fear in a few eyes, so I didn't stop there. 'There's bound to be a reward.'

Everyone exploded into action. The woman who cradled me told me everything would be all right. The man who lived in the hovel across the street pressed the security contact on his link. Hands passed me cups of water, food, fighting for the right to help me.

By the time two members of the security sector arrived, they had to beat their way through a horde, everyone asking for codes so they could send their link numbers for the reward, making sure the officers knew they'd helped me.

'We haven't left her side since she got here.'

'Look, we gave her food. That's all my family has left to eat for the week!'

'Hey, I'm the one who saw her first,' said my rescuer as the officers reached her and she released me into their arms.

I looked up at the two of them. Both seemed disinterested, but neither looked deceptive. The female's face made me think she aspired to greater things, but her companion just seemed bored. I couldn't detect any sign that either of them worked for Kore. But could I really have told if they did?

It made no difference anyway. I was exhausted. Blood was leaking from the wound on my arm. I could barely stand, but I wasn't sure it was from blood loss, although I couldn't stop staring at the wound the knife had left behind.

They took my basic details and didn't even blink when I said my name and told them I thought Kore had a base less than a block from where we were standing. They raised their eyebrows when they saw my link was missing, though.

As they loaded me into their security car, I glanced back in the direction of Kore's lair. It was invisible behind the crush of people.

CHAPTER EIGHT

'It's not often we have to do this,' the security officer said as she fastened the new link on my wrist. 'I can't remember the last time I gave a new one to someone above two years old.' She laughed. 'Theirs are only rubber and they have a habit of pulling on them for the first couple of years.'

I gave her an absent chuckle, but I didn't like this woman. She was nice to everyone on the surface, but her face was like a shifting shadow—one minute there was sunshine, the next it was plunged into the abyss of anger.

Nurse Grimway took my vitals again. 'Well, I'm glad to say that your little adventure doesn't seem to have harmed you, Eden. I'm sure your family and fellow workers in the government sector will be relieved.'

'Thanks. That's good to hear.' And it was good that, physically, everything seemed to be fine. I'd been in the government wing of the medical sector hospital for the past twenty-four hours and they'd barely stopped the tests long enough to allow me to sleep. They'd patched up the wound left by the knife, which hadn't required more than a few stitches. They'd run my bloods and checked my heart, lungs, all organs, scanning everything. They'd even scanned my brain. The tech had laughed and said at least I had one, not like some of his patients, but it was difficult to appreciate his joke when his face reminded me of a boy in the learning sector who'd gone home one day and killed himself.

That was the most disturbing thing about all this. While I'd never met any of these people before, I was sure I wouldn't have picked up this much about them with just a casual glance before I'd been taken. What had Kore done to me? And what was going to happen when I met someone I knew?

Whatever the case, I needed to keep quiet about it. But I knew how to do that.

The nurse straightened the bed in my private ward. I hadn't expected a room of my own—most wards held twenty—but they said it was because I was a valued government employee. They'd even kept a straight face as they'd said it. But would they really do so much for a junior keeper in the Archives? No, they were worried I was going to pick up a knife and start slashing. There was even a guard on my door to 'make sure you're safe'. Yeah, right.

They wouldn't let my family visit either. I'd had to send Mother messages via the staff here since I had only just got a new link. I did my best to assure her I was fine.

Two security officers entered my room. They looked like marshals, higher up in the chain of command than anyone I'd seen yet. The woman stepped forward, smiling, but her face held a shrewish look, like she'd sell me to Kore herself if it benefited her. The man's face was a little more open. Not much deception on it, as far as I could see, but I still wouldn't risk it by telling him any more than I'd told the others.

This new skill of mine was a real pain. Would I ever trust anyone again?

The shrew was still smiling as she spoke. 'Miss Fittell, I'm Marshall Donovan and this is Marshall Avery. We need to ask you a few questions about what happened to you, if that's all right.'

The nurse put her hands on her hips. 'She's supposed to be resting.'

'We just need a few minutes,' Marshall Donovan said, curling her lip at her. Or maybe she didn't because Nurse Grimway didn't seem bothered as she turned and left.

The two marshalls got chairs that were leaning against the wall and brought them over to my bedside. Marshall Donovan looked imperious as she sat down but her voice sounded friendly. 'Now, I'm sorry to have to ask you about this, but we need to know as much detail as we can about what happened to you.'

'I told the other officers already.' Why did officials always want everything repeated six times? 'I was in my unit. As far as I knew, I was alone. Then someone hit me from behind and I woke up in a cell.' My hands always started shaking at this point, so I slipped them under the sheet on my bed. 'I was taken to a man named Kore who gave Izrod a vial of something. Izrod took me to another room and they injected me with whatever it was. It felt …'—*terrifying, spine-chilling, horrific*—'unpleasant. But I woke up, I don't know how much later, and I was …'—*different, all-seeing*—'normal. That seemed to disappoint them. I'm not exactly sure why. I got the impression they were going to kill me.' *Don't let your voice quiver!* 'But the power went out and I thought I'd try the door. It actually opened and I managed to escape.'

Marshall Avery looked at the medical patch on my arm. 'Not unscathed, though.'

'No. Izrod threw a knife at me. But I kept going.'

He looked approving. 'Very brave.'

Marshall Donovan patted my hand, her face impatient. 'We're glad that you've come through what must have been a terrifying ordeal. Now, just some more questions about this procedure they put you through. You don't know what was in the vial?'

'No.'

'You don't know what they expected the result to be once you'd recovered?'

'No. All I know is that they expected something and seemed disappointed that I ... wasn't what they'd been hoping for.' I threw in what I hoped was a casual laugh. 'Maybe they'd wanted me to grow another head.'

She didn't look surprised at that. 'We have reason to believe that Kore has been responsible for the recent spate of ... disturbed individuals.'

That's what they were calling them?

'You're *sure* there was no mention of the results they were hoping for?'

I don't know if she saw something on my face that made her distrust me, but her question was ludicrous. 'They were hardly going to tell me their plans, were they?'

Her eyes sparked. 'Don't be disrespectful.'

Avery leant forward again. 'I understand how hard it is for you to go over all this, but it would be of great help if you could tell us anything that would give us some idea of what they're planning or trying to do.'

I was starting to think he was genuine, but that didn't mean I was going to tell him the truth. *What will they do to me if they find out? They'll shut me up in another cell and poke and prod me for the rest of my life.* I could see it now—the tests, the never-ending questions. *I* didn't even understand this! I didn't want to know about it either.

I kept my face under control. 'Like I said, they told me nothing. They just did what they wanted to me.'

Donovan looked annoyed, Avery disappointed. 'Thank you for your assistance,' Donovan said. 'We'll confer with your medical team and see when you'll be released. Once you're cleared, Marshall Avery will escort you home.'

She marched out. Avery gave me a farewell nod.

I *think* I'd convinced them. I'd say whatever I needed to get them to take me back to my unit so I could go back to work and to the way it was supposed to be. I would keep my head down and put all this behind me.

But would I ever really be able to do that when I saw the truth lurking behind everyone's smiles? What would I see when I looked at the governor? At Derek? At the head keeper? How long would I be like this? Seeing all this stuff, it was exhausting! Would I spend the rest of my life as some kind of freak?

Like the man who'd kidnapped me. Well, not exactly. He'd got super muscles. I'd just got clarity. That was all I could think to call it.

It was a few more hours, a few more tests, a few more rounds of being careful about everything I said before Avery returned with the good news. 'I'm going to escort you back to your unit as soon as you're ready.'

Nurse Grimway quickly obtained the necessary permissions and we were on our way.

It was evening by the time we left. I sat in the back of the security vehicle, Avery in the front. He was quiet for most of the trip, which was fine by me. I was too busy looking out the window to see if anything familiar had changed.

The buildings didn't look any different, but then, they didn't have faces. And fortunately, we travelled quickly and smoothly so it was difficult to get a good look at anyone. I also didn't see anyone I knew, and that would be the real test. How could I tell if it was this clarity that made a random vendor on the street look like he'd rather murder his customers than serve them?

It wasn't long before we arrived at my unit building. To my surprise, Marshall Avery didn't drop me off at the door. Instead, after speaking to Jenny, who was the security officer on duty, he took me upstairs. I was grateful that he didn't pay too much attention to me as we entered, as one look at Jenny's face had made me glance away. It looked like she desired him as … more than a friend. I hoped it was just him and she wasn't going to look at everyone like that. Fortunately, she didn't have the same reaction when she looked at me.

The door to my unit was already open when we arrived and there was a hustle of activity within, several security officers coming out as we entered.

'We've put in some new security measures,' Avery said, as he led me inside. 'There are now panic buttons in a few key areas of the unit. There's one here,' he pointed to a small button tucked under the kitchen bench, 'another in your living area, and another near your bed. If anyone breaks in or you feel threatened in any way, press one of the buttons and we'll come straight here to help you.'

Avery led me into my bedroom and seemed a bit embarrassed to be there. 'I just wanted to show you what we've done to the windows,' he said. He went to the window I'd noticed earlier. 'We're pretty sure Izrod got in this way, so we've sealed this and every other window in the unit permanently.' He pointed to where the latch used to be. 'It seemed safer. And the last thing we want to do is give him an easy way to get to you.'

So Izrod *had* come in the window? I knew what the side of the building was like. 'How do you think he climbed it? There aren't exactly footholds or anything, are there?'

'No, but it's concrete slab so there are grooves. We've already seen what a climber he is, so I'd say he used the grooves and worked his way up.'

How strong did you have to be to be able to pull yourself up a twenty-storey wall with nothing more than your fingertips? Although I could see one major problem with this idea. While Izrod might have been able to do that, and while he might have been able to squeeze his huge frame in my window, could he have really carried me out the same way without anyone seeing?

But Marshall Avery was looking at me and smiling, waiting for some kind of response. I think he wanted to see me relieved. He might have been lying to me, saying these things to make me feel that there was no way I would ever be a victim again, but I already knew how easy it was for the safety around me to shatter.

I don't think I'd ever really been safe in my life. I'd thought coming to work in the government sector would change that. Apparently not. Maybe it was my destiny or some sort of curse. Some spell or power had me in its grip and let me get a few steps outside before it slammed the chains on again.

But I slapped happiness on my face and Avery seemed satisfied. 'Right,' he said. 'I'll leave you to it. I'm told that you want to go back to work tomorrow but my understanding was that you had another day's leave.'

And spend twenty-four hours here alone, cowering in my bedroom, constantly seeing Izrod out of the corner of my eye? I would feel safer at the Archives. 'I would like to work tomorrow,' I said, just as I had when this same question had been put to me earlier. 'To give me something to do.'

At least he didn't give me a derisive look. He didn't insist that I needed more time or that he knew best. That's what they'd said in the medical sector. 'Okay. If you need longer, just send word to the Archives.'

'Thank you, Marshall,' I said. I kept the happy look in place until he went out the door and closed it behind him.

Silence. I breathed deeply. The security team had left all the lights on and I pressed them off, mellowing the light in the living room. I sat on my couch and tried to relax.

But there was a space behind me. Empty space. Was someone …? I snapped my head around. No, no one was there. I breathed again, before hearing a dull thud. My heart leapt. Was it …? No, everything was quiet.

This was ridiculous. How long had it been since Marshall Avery had left? Ten minutes? Less? He'd checked the entire unit and found nothing. The windows were sealed. I was alone.

But I couldn't rest. I went and checked every window, one by one, yanking on them, fiddling with them, doing everything possible to move them even a little. I couldn't.

I turned the lights back on. I had learnt to love them off—it was easier to hide from a drunk when there were shadows—but now I was frightened of what was in the shadows. They weren't hiding me anymore. Izrod was there. He had to be. I kept seeing a hulking form, but when I turned …

It was nothing. I was imagining things.

The lights were on. The windows were sealed. I went around the unit again and found nothing. And again.

There *was* nothing.

I needed to relax. 'I'll make something,' I said to the empty room. 'When was the last time I had something to eat? I'll put something together.'

I went to the refrigerator, trying to remember if anything was in there. Then I realised I'd only been gone about forty-eight hours, not enough time for anything in there to perish. I got out some bread and made myself a sandwich, trying to concentrate on the taste, especially compared to the meal I'd had at Kore's, and reassured myself that I was okay. I chewed slowly and thoroughly, forcing myself to relax with each bite. My unit had been checked. The windows were sealed. I was safe.

I cleaned up and washed the dishes I'd used. There was a creak somewhere. Probably building movement. Happened all the time. I'd been around the whole place more than once.

'Building movement,' I told myself. 'Perfectly normal.'

'Sorry about the knife.'

My heart leapt into my throat as I saw the figure standing in the bedroom doorway. I launched myself sideways, whipping out a knife that was in a rack there, brandishing it in front of me.

Izrod came into the living room and raised his hands. 'Eden, please put that down. I have no intention of hurting you, but if you come at me with a weapon, I'll have no choice.'

I wasn't doing anything he said. 'What do you want? How did you get in here? Get out!' I resurrected my walls to keep from showing fear and I *did* feel afraid of him, the man who'd kidnapped me, who'd taken me to that place, who'd strapped me down and let them do …

But I also felt that ludicrous sense that he was safe, that he was trustworthy, that he was noble and good. There was no way this man could be anything but evil! This thing Kore had put in me was manipulating my emotions. Despite what my head told me, there was no way I could trust him.

Although I had to admit that the media sector had definitely played up his deformities. Even while I was forcing my brain to hate him, my eyes had to acknowledge that his blond mane fell around his head attractively and his shoulders weren't big enough to make him look disfigured, just well-built. Then there were those deep green eyes. They demanded I look into them, intelligence and wisdom swirling in their depths.

That was annoying. It would be easier to hate him if he wasn't so damn hot.

Wait, did I really just think that?

He took a step towards me, hands still raised. 'I only want to talk. I swear I won't hurt you, and I certainly won't take you anywhere you don't want to go.'

I still couldn't believe he could talk so rationally. Or at all. Wasn't he supposed to be primitive? Brainless? Ignorant? But there he was, standing before me, forming perfect sentences, a knowing look in his eyes. It made me feel so insignificant. How could an uneducated girl like me possibly outthink someone like him?

I still gripped the knife in front of me but it didn't seem to bother him. Maybe he didn't think I'd use it. Well, he'd find out how wrong he was if he took one step …

He changed direction and headed towards the couch, taking a seat. He waved at the armchair. 'Please, come and sit down. As I said, I have no intention of hurting you in any way. But I think we need to talk. And please, don't hit the panic buttons. It would make things unnecessarily messy.'

I'd forgotten about the panic buttons. One was just beside me. I could reach it … But there again was that unreasoning sense that I should trust this man.

I shuffled my feet, moving into the living area, my back hugging the wall, the knife held in front of me. My legs shook with every step. I had to still them. I knew the only way I could do that was by sitting down.

I sat gingerly in the armchair, still brandishing the knife.

'Please put that down. I've said I won't hurt you. And honestly, if I wanted to, a knife that size would make no difference.'

My fingers were cramped from clutching it, and I knew he was right. Was a little knife like this going to stop a hulking form of muscle like him? What's more, it was trembling in my hand, revealing the fear I was sure I was successfully keeping off my face. I needed to look like I was calm, act like I was calm. As if having a monster in my home was an everyday occurrence.

It was the story of my life, really.

I laid the knife on the arm of my chair. 'It isn't much different from the knife you used on me.' He expected me to trust him after what he'd done to me? No, but *I* did. Everything in my head told me he was trustworthy. I felt like banging it into the wall until it worked properly.

He dipped his head. 'I said I was sorry about that. I had to make it look like I was trying to stop you. Even then, Kore was suspicious. He knows I usually score a direct hit on my targets, not a glancing blow.'

So what was he trying to say? 'Are you telling me you let me get away?'

'Of course. Who do you think left that note for you? Who do you think made sure the power was cut to the door? Who do you think made sure your cell was almost the closest one to the exit?'

'You deliberately put me in that cell just so I could escape?' That would mean that he'd wanted me to escape from the beginning.

He leant forward, his elbows on his knees. 'Eden, if what Kore gave you has worked, you had the potential to be a game-changer for him, especially if he decided to extend that operation to others as well.'

I wasn't giving anything away. 'Pity it didn't work.'

He gave me a long, searching look. 'You're good. That's one of the reasons I selected you. I knew you could hide evidence of any change.'

His words filled me with rage, not to mention confusion. 'My father gave me up to Kore. Or did you put him up to it?' Had he gone looking for Dad, seen how weak he was, and made him the offer? But how would he have known who I was without Dad?

At least he had the decency to look uncomfortable. 'He came to us. You'd be surprised how many family members do. The government sector shouldn't employ people from the poor sector. Their families are too susceptible, too desperate. Kore's people put the word around that they can make money betraying anyone they know who works in the government sector and yes, they do it. It's one of the reasons the government keeps all their workers close by, but it doesn't solve the problem entirely.'

It was typical that my father would be one of the lowlifes who'd gone for it.

'Part of my role in Kore's establishment is to look for the best candidates,' he continued. 'When families bring us this information, I find out whatever I can about the individual, then take that information to Kore with a recommendation on who's best to target.

'You were, honestly, like a gift.' He looked lighter as he spoke. 'I watched you for a while and it was difficult to get any idea about how you felt about anything. It was ideal, given what Kore was planning, to offer you because I knew you could hide the results.'

So I was a pawn in a power struggle between Izrod and Kore. For what? To see who could rule the streets of the city? Why was Izrod trying to undermine Kore?

'I'm sorry for doing that,' he said, 'but you've no idea how important it is to stop Kore from advancing any further. We need to do whatever we can to slow him down.'

'Who's we? What is this? I'm just someone you're using? What for? Why wouldn't you want Kore to succeed? Do you really expect me to believe this?'

He got out of the chair slowly, trying not to scare me, I think. I made sure I didn't flinch, but I could almost feel his strength as he approached. Close-up, his arms seemed thicker than a concrete beam and exuded power. If he wanted to do anything to me, I couldn't stop him.

'I knew you'd have trouble believing this,' he said, 'so I need to show you the answers to your questions. I think it would be better—'

I put my palm out. 'Stop right there. I'm not going anywhere or doing anything with you.' Even though my mind told me I really, really wanted to. 'And definitely not until you tell me exactly what's been done to me. How do you know it worked? Maybe I'm just another failure.'

His eyes were steady. 'I could tell by the way you reacted to me that something had happened. I was expecting a reaction of some sort. Unfortunately, it was a little stronger than I anticipated, but at least you managed to control it in front of the others. Can you tell me what made you react that way? What did you see?'

How did I explain it to him? That my brain told me he was

noble? That every look made me trust him more? Even as I thought of it, my rational self rebelled against it while the rest of me wanted to reach out to him.

I couldn't tell him that. Apart from the fact that it would give him too much power over me, he'd think I was insane.

'No, tell me first what you did to me,' I said. 'What was that thing supposed to do?'

'Tell me what you can—'

'I don't understand what I can do!' I said. 'I can't make any sense of it. Please, tell me what it is.'

'All right.' He set himself back in the chair. 'Kore has an incredible gift for understanding the human body. He understands our chemical, biological and anatomical makeup. As you've probably heard,' he held a hand out before me, fingers spread out; it was huge, out of proportion with his forearm, 'he excels at engineering our physical selves. But more recently, he's also learnt to use chemicals to change parts of our minds. You've seen the result, haven't you? Or at least heard about it. The people driven mad.'

'Mistakes?'

He looked sombre. 'Unfortunately, no. But a while ago, he started experimenting with how to make people reveal their true selves. He wanted to develop a formula that would allow a person to see the truth in everyone else. He intends to take it himself when he's sure it works successfully. But he needed to try it on a test subject first.'

'Like me.' How nice to be treated like a learning sector experiment.

'Yes, although he's interested in giving it to certain promising individuals too. People who can access areas he can't, like the government sector.' He leant forward again. 'You were a great starting point. As a junior keeper, you have access to the Archives, something he wants anyway. But that also gives you access to a lot of people he can't reach. You could tell him who's corrupted and corruptible.

Who's weak and who's strong. Who's too moral to be of use to him.

'So tell me,' he said, 'did it work?'

At least that explained why people looked so different to me now. But had it worked? Was I seeing what people were *really* like?

If Izrod was right, then he was amazing and noble and true. I didn't know if I could deal with that. But he was clearly double-crossing Kore. Shouldn't I be able to see that?

He must have taken my silence as doubt. 'Why don't I help you? Tell me how you saw me. I can tell you if you were right or not.'

I couldn't sit here and tell him that he was all kinds of awesome! I didn't know if I could tell anyone that. But he was waiting for an answer. I had to say something. 'I saw ... you looked like someone I could trust?'

'That's right. You can.' Something shone in his eyes. I didn't want to examine it too closely.

'But shouldn't you have looked shady?' I said. 'I mean, if you always intended to get me out of there, aren't you double-crossing Kore? Shouldn't I be able to see that?'

'Hm.' It looked like he hadn't thought of that. 'Perhaps his formula is still too centred on the individual. Or maybe that problem would have been overcome if he'd given you Alpha-D.'

That's what he'd been talking to the jailer about. 'What's Alpha-D?'

'It's a brainwashing formula. It binds the subject to whoever they see first when they open their eyes after receiving a dose. Kore uses it on his people to ensure obedience.'

'So he used it on you?' If so, how could he be betraying Kore?

'He did, but the strong-minded can resist. He doesn't know it didn't work on me. But he's working on it all the time, refining it, improving it.'

That made no sense either. 'Then why didn't he give it to me before the other thing? I would have told him the truth.' I wouldn't have been able to stop myself. What a horrific thought—losing my mind to Kore so he could do what he liked to me.

'Because it's expensive and hard to make. He can't afford to waste it on subjects who might not prove valuable.'

Easier to kill me if I didn't prove useful.

He cocked his head. 'Please tell me what you're thinking. You're so hard to read. You give virtually nothing away.'

I still wasn't sure I trusted him enough to do that, despite my bizarre reaction every time I looked at him. 'I'm just trying to understand it all.'

'Okay. But I think I've answered all your questions. So we need to be going.'

'And where do we need to be going?'

'I want to introduce you to the people I work with, the people who are fighting against Kore.'

'Do they work in the security sector?' I was pretty sure what the answer would be.

'No. The security sector is either ineffective or corrupt, although it's been difficult to tell which … until now.'

So that explained why he wanted me. I was useful to him and his friends, just as I would have been useful to Kore. But I wasn't being used as a pawn in anyone's game. Did he think I owed him for getting me out of there? If it hadn't been for him, I would never have been in there in the first place. He should have chosen someone else, someone more compliant, if he thought I was just going to agree to anything *he* said.

Perhaps he read that on my face because he said, 'You know, if Kore's allowed to continue, the damage he could do to this city will be immense. No sector will be safe. We could lose everything.

'Eden, I know you have no reason to trust me except a thing in your head that you're scared of, but I promise you I'm on the right side here. We need your help. You are under no obligation to help us, but I'd like to introduce you to the ones trying to make a difference for the better, to help people like your family. We can probably do it without you, but your insight would be invaluable.

'Will you let me show you?'

CHAPTER NINE

I wondered what Izrod would do if I refused. Probably nothing. But I knew I wanted to help him. My instincts told me it was the right thing to do. Shouldn't it be the opposite? Shouldn't I be scrambling for the panic button as I threw the knife at him?

'Fine,' I said eventually. 'Who do you want me to meet?' And how did he expect us to walk out of this building together without being stopped? There was no way I was letting him climb me down the wall. And even if he could hide in shadows or climb down by himself, I would have to walk out past the supervisor and she wasn't going to let me go anywhere. I was supposed to be recovering. There was no doubt she'd tell Marshall Avery. She'd jump at any opportunity to talk to him.

'Follow me.' He turned and walked towards my bedroom.

Were his friends hiding in there? Was I so out of it that I hadn't even heard them? Or did he have something else in mind? I prepared to be outraged.

To my surprise, he walked over to the air conditioning vent and removed it. I hadn't realised how big it was. Half of it was painted the same colour and texture as the wall, hiding its size.

I walked over, a memory rising from the terror of the kidnapping. 'Were you hiding in here the other night?' I could hardly choke the words out over my heartbeat, which climbed up my throat as I remembered hearing the thud of his footfall behind me and feeling the panic and pain as his fist collided with my head.

And now you're entertaining him in your home, Eden. Want to offer him some refreshments before he drags you back to Kore's for more needle-poking fun?

The big creature folded his hands in front of him and bowed his head, looking up at me contritely. 'I thought you might have seen me when you put your hand on the grill.'

So something *had* been blocking the air conditioning. A pretty big something, as it turned out. Did everyone's unit have a huge vent like this? A convenient entry point so Izrod could pick and choose his victims, slipping away with the air. 'I thought you climbed up the walls.'

He smirked. 'I can do that, but it's a little difficult when you're carrying someone.'

'Why are they this big? Do they need to be?'

He didn't seem to find it strange. 'When they rebuilt this city, there were apparently loads of these left over from the Unbidden Conflict, or maybe before it. Not sure what they used them for. And in the rebuild, they used anything they didn't have to create from scratch. Great for someone like me.'

He motioned for me to crawl inside and he came in behind me, pulling the vent back in place and fastening it. 'We can't talk much. I'll tap you on the shoulder to indicate whether we need to go left or right.'

Still wondering if I was insane for agreeing to this, I started shuffling along on my hands and knees, feeling his presence right behind me the whole way. Most of the time we just slid along the chute. Despite how roomy it was, it was still tight on his shoulders. He tapped left or right if I needed to turn and we said nothing, not that I had anything to say to him.

Then I had to stop as the shaft took a steep dive. I couldn't see the bottom.

'Excuse me.' He tried to squeeze past. It wasn't easy in that space. I flattened myself against the wall while he tried to drag his wide shoulders past me. In the end, I practically had to slide underneath him, which made me feel like blushing. I hoped it didn't show on my face.

He didn't seem disturbed, producing a thin line from a notch on his belt. He attached it to a clip embedded in the side of the chute. I wondered if he'd put that there or if the designer of this air conditioning conduit had been an unwitting accomplice.

The wire looked too thin to support the weight of a feather, but he swung out on it, hanging suspended by one hand as he reached for me with the other, gathering me in his arm, holding me tight against his chest. I felt myself stiffen. Being in his arms was … weird. It had to be something to do with the thing Kore had done to my brain.

I felt stiff as a board at his closeness and he looked down at me. 'It's all right. You're perfectly safe. I won't drop you.'

I was glad that was what he thought I was worried about. And I was sure that was all it was. Well, I wasn't sure, but I hoped that Kore's formula wasn't going to make me like this guy. I ignored the tightening of his muscles where I gripped them as he pulled out a device hooked to his belt and attached it to the wire.

'Hold on tight.'

His thumb pressed down on the device and my stomach leapt into my throat as we whizzed down the wire. I didn't want to hold him tighter than I already was, but it wasn't like I could help it. It was hard enough not to scream at the rush of wind and the feeling that we were going to slam into the floor at any moment. But he slowed us before we hit the bottom and then it was back to crawling through the conduits again.

Before long, we arrived at a panel, which he unscrewed, going ahead of me this time, before reaching back to help me crawl through it. I had to jump and slide down to ground level.

He pulled me into the shadows. 'This is where it gets a little more tricky,' he whispered.

We crept along the side of the building, our backs to the wall. Two days ago, this same man had dragged me out of here, unconscious, his prisoner—a hopeless victim. Now, I was willingly sneaking away from safety, following his every direction, heading into darkness and any imaginable number of evils. Maybe Kore *had* brainwashed me, linking me to this hulk of a man instead of to himself.

For someone so large, Izrod was whisper-quiet. I could hear my steps more than his as we sneaked through the shadows. I knew there were security personnel at the base of each building, but Izrod seemed to know where they weren't and headed for the space between their patrols.

But I knew there were also cameras out here. He'd been caught on them several times. I'd seen the footage myself.

'Aren't there cameras out here?' I whispered.

'They can only get me if I want them to.'

I wondered why he'd want to be caught on camera. To scare people? To make sure everyone kept thinking of him as a lumbering moron?

Soon I was lost. I wasn't used to travelling after dark. Most people didn't do it often, mainly because you weren't sure who you'd be walking past and the streetlights were likely to flicker off the moment they leapt on you.

Eventually, Izrod headed towards a large structure at the end of a filthy street coated with grime and lost papers. I couldn't make out anything except that it loomed above me, wide rather than tall.

'Here,' he said, opening a door that was half-embedded in the garbage that was littered around it. I hadn't even realised it was there until he reached for it. Was that intentional? With one more glance at the deserted street, I ducked inside, pleased that a little light was coming from within, creating a feeling of warmth that I hoped wasn't misplaced.

Izrod shut the door behind us and I looked around. We were in a small atrium. The walls were reminiscent of Kore's lair, but the light was brighter and felt warmer, or maybe it had been my terror that had chilled me at Kore's.

We headed for a desk a few metres from us. A man sat behind it, guarding the way to a large set of double doors. There was a metal canister with a flickering light on the desk, something I'd only read about in books in the learning sector. I think they'd called it a lamp. It was old, stains tarnishing the inside of the glass.

'Is this her?' said the man. His hair was matted and stuck out from his head in stiff strands. His face was gruff, shaggy eyebrows pulling together as he looked me over with dark, suspicious eyes. 'She doesn't look like much.'

Neither do you, I wanted to retort. I could tell he didn't trust a soul, keeping to himself as much as possible. How about that? We had something in common.

'Neither do you,' Izrod said. I was surprised that he'd guessed what I was thinking. Maybe it was just a coincidence. I hoped so.

The eyebrows nearly buried his eyes as he grumbled, 'Well, it's not me that matters, is it?' He pointed his thumb at the doors behind him. 'She's waiting.'

Izrod indicated I should go before him but opened the doors for us.

The next room was about twice the size Kore's lair had been and while most of the people within were severe with sharp eyes, there was a smattering of elderly and even a few children darting in and out. There were tables strewn with the remains of a meal on either side of the room, with a path down the middle. Izrod and I walked along it, subject to the stares of everyone we passed. Or, at least, I was subject to them. It was weird that I drew more attention than he did, but I guessed this was his crowd, so I was the curiosity.

At the top table, there was another group of men and women

who lolled about with a sense of importance, occasionally barking commands at the people my age. As we approached, the woman with the loudest voice turned toward us. I was immediately struck by the severity of her face. And not just that, either. This stern face, grey hair pulled back in a braid, was instantly recognisable.

'So this is her, is it?' she said to Izrod.

'Yes,' he replied. 'Eden, I'd like you to meet Sasha, the leader of the Underground. Sasha, this is Eden.'

I wasn't sure she'd know who I was. We'd never really met that terrible night of smoke and flame. For this was the woman who had led us to our new homes.

'You're the one,' I said.

She gave me a blank look. 'Excuse me?'

'You. During the fire.'

'Which one?'

'The one a couple of months ago at the unit block in Savey Street. You took us to those shacks.'

Some kind of recognition appeared on her face. 'You were there?'

'Yes. My family lost our home.'

She gave the glimmer of a smile. 'Good.'

Had she just said that she was glad we'd lost our home? What kind of woman was this? I held still as she circled me. 'And can she do it?' she said to Izrod.

'It seems she can, yes.'

'Follow me.'

She led us to another room. It was far smaller, containing only a few chairs scattered around and an ancient table. 'Please, sit.'

Izrod pulled up a chair for me and one for himself.

'What's your name, girl?' Sasha barked.

'Eden Fittell.'

'Hm.' She poured some drink into glasses in front of us. 'And your family, they're settled into their new home?'

'Yes.' *Such as it is, anyway. It's not exactly a palace.*

She laced her fingers on the table in front of us. 'You have us to thank for that, you know.'

What did she mean by that? 'I thought you worked for government.'

She let out a snorting laugh. 'Government? I know *you* work for them. You should know by now that they don't exactly go out of their way to help anyone in the poor sector. They just hope that we'll look after ourselves or die of cold or starvation so all they need to do is bury us.'

Sasha looked me over again. 'She is impressive, isn't she? Just like you said. Most people who had been left in that kind of accommodation after a traumatic fire would either be thumping on the table, demanding more help or have burst into tears by now. She doesn't look troubled at all.'

I wasn't sure if she was complimenting me or insulting me. But while we were on that subject ... 'So why did you leave us there?'

Her eyes were derisive. 'Where else were you going to go?' She gestured around her. 'We have some resources here, but not enough for thirty homeless people, especially when there's a new fire every other week. Thirty, fifty, one hundred. Where are we supposed to put them?'

She stood up and sat on the edge of the table. 'We do what we can. We are the ones who got those shacks into a state where people could at least live in them. We are the ones who made sure they were hooked up to the power grid. We are the ones who made sure they had running water and appropriate plumbing. Or did you think those hovels just magically stayed working all these years?'

I could feel rage biting, as well as shame. She was right—it hadn't entered my head to think about why those tumble-down little shacks still had functioning utilities. I'd just assumed that government had taken care of it.

'So who are you, then?' I meant 'you' in the collective sense. She seemed to get it, but she didn't answer straight away.

'Has Leon told you what we want you to do for us?'

The name threw me for a moment until I realised who she was talking about. 'You mean Iz—' I sucked in my words as her eyes narrowed. 'You mean ... using this thing I can do?' This was not the place to call him names.

He hadn't told me much more than that they wanted my help. I wasn't sure I trusted Sasha, but was it just because of the severity of her face? The longer I looked, the more I could see an openness behind her scowl. But open to what?

'Yes. If we can find allies in the government sector, it will benefit our work,' she said.

'Why? Do you need supplies to link up more shacks for the homeless?'

She gave me a withering look and turned to Izrod. 'Did you tell her nothing?'

'There hasn't been a lot of time to get to the specifics.'

She turned her sharp gaze back on me. 'We help the poor, yes, as much as we can. We have people—usually in lower positions—in each sector, helping us access what we need. But we still need to keep our headquarters mobile so we can move whenever it's required, mainly because government doesn't like us, but also because of Kore. We try and combat him as much as we can.' She nodded towards the room we'd just left. 'The people out there are our own—family members. It's safer for them to be here with us, but not everyone can be. Kore has been known to find our hideouts, and that's never ended well.'

She smiled at me. It lightened her face a little. 'And government doesn't like us because we're more inclined towards ... other activities.'

She didn't seem happy with my blank look. 'We don't obey

government directives,' she went on. 'Quite often they're ridiculously limited, hemmed in by bureaucratic restriction and incredibly slow in any response they give. The free rein they've given to Kore is testament to that. His organisation grows in strength every day and they don't seem to care, despite the government employees who go missing.' She shrugged. 'Maybe if someone as high as the governor disappears that will change, but who knows? Someone else would probably step in the moment she was gone.

'We do what we can to combat Kore, but we need more resources. Some of them will have to come from the government sector but we don't have time to wait for them to talk about it, budget our request, tell us the scope of our powers and give us what they can spare, if they even think it's worth bothering about.'

'You need me to tell you who might be willing to help without going through the proper channels.' I shot a look at Izrod. I should have expected this.

She seemed pleased that she didn't have to spell it out. 'Yes, there are bound to be some individuals who aren't happy with the status quo and who are more worried about Kore than they let on. Your job is to identify them for us. Then we can make contact.'

'So you don't want me to set up meetings or whatever?'

'No, that would reveal you. We need to make sure your participation remains a secret.'

It wasn't as bad as I'd thought it was going to be, but I worried they were expecting a little too much. 'What if I can't do it? I don't even know how to use this thing in my head. How am I to tell someone who's …'—*corrupt*—'willing to help you from someone who's not?'

She glared at Izrod. 'You said she could do this. You *promised* she could do this.'

He was unperturbed. 'She's still learning what she can do and I never made you any promises. You know this isn't an exact science.

Kore wasn't one hundred percent sure it would work at all.'

She grumbled and turned back to me. 'Fine. Just do what you can. And remember, we didn't have to help your family. We could have just left them there, shaking on a corner. You owe us.' She went over to the door and opened it, gesturing for us to go out. 'Leon, show her around so she can see what we're trying to achieve here.'

She slammed the door behind us. If she thought her biting words and suggestion that I was in her debt was going to see me fawning at her feet, she should get lessons from my father. He'd mastered the art of that kind of manipulation years ago. Although I did acknowledge that she had helped my family, so maybe I might be swayed enough to help … if I could.

'Come on,' Izrod said. 'I'll show you around.'

The place he called the Underground was made up of a group of rooms, all set in the basement of a large building.

'This building used to house a community hub that serviced the local area before it ran out of resources. It's ideal for us, giving us both shelter and keeping us incognito. But we won't be here for more than a few months. It's not safe to stay longer than that. It's a shame because it's an ideal setup.'

I didn't see what was upstairs in the building—Izrod gave me the impression it was units—but he showed me rooms dedicated to fighting training and housing an impressive array of knives. There was also a storeroom with stocks of food. Some they kept but some was handed out to the needy. There was also a busy kitchen, clearing up after the evening meal and laying things out for the morning.

'This is our medical sector,' he said, waving his arm around the latest section of the basement. It was grey concrete and, unlike the other rooms, not warmed by any heating equipment. It was also much cleaner than the others. There were several pristine beds made up with spotless sheets, a small set of drawers beside each. Some were occupied, a couple with children who hid their coughs behind tiny hands as we approached, a couple with the elderly—one lady in particular who seemed to be nearing the end of her life, if the rattle of her breathing was any indication. Fleetingly, I was reminded of Mr Ivanov.

A woman looked up as we passed, Izrod catching her eye. Actually, she gazed at him with so much desire I felt like I should leave them alone for a while. But there was no reaction from Izrod at all. Either he was oblivious to it or he was as good as me at hiding his feelings.

'Eden, this is Aurora,' he said. 'Aurora, this is the girl I was talking about.'

Aurora looked at me with unnecessary envy, her blue eyes flashing as she tied her red hair in a ponytail. 'You're Eden.' That was as much acknowledgement as she gave me, turning back to Izrod eagerly. 'And can she do what you were hoping she could do?'

'We're still exploring the extent of her skills, but she can definitely do something.'

Aurora shot a look between us. I got the feeling she would have rolled up her sleeve and begged for Kore's formula if it meant she could spend more time with Izrod. 'Let's hope she doesn't disappoint us.'

'And I hope we don't disappoint her either.' Izrod looked at me. 'Aurora is our medic. She makes a big difference to our people, as we can't get help from the medical sector without being reported. She also runs a clinic above ground, treating some poor families.'

Aurora's face flushed. 'I do what I can. It's a healer's calling.' She gazed up at him as though he was the only source of light in the room.

'Uh, yeah. It's great.' Aurora shot a glance at me, so I instilled some enthusiasm into my voice. 'I mean, sure, so many have a lot of needs and anything you can give them is great. I should send my family here next time they need medical care.'

Aurora puffed herself up. 'We don't do this for just anyone, you know.'

What, did she think I was from the rich sector? Did the governor dress in jeans?

Izrod cleared his throat. 'I'm sure your family would be welcome,' he said to me. 'I know they've had it rough. Anyway, I should get you back.'

Aurora shone a smile on him as we left.

We walked up a small set of stairs from the basement area to the street. I finally realised where we were. It was on the border of the poor sector and where the city ended. The hovel where my family lived was only a few streets away.

Once we'd left the building, Izrod didn't seem too concerned that we were out in public side by side. But then, there weren't many onlookers, just a few scraggly street sweepers and drunks. I hoped my father wasn't amongst them.

'Now,' he said, 'tell me what you really think.'

'I think it looks like you're doing—'

'No, I mean *really*. Is Sasha trustworthy?'

Seriously? He was asking me, a complete stranger, to tell him if the people he worked with were going to betray him? How could he be sure I knew? And how could he be sure I'd tell him the truth?

But he simply looked at me patiently as we walked along, waiting for an answer to his question. What could I say? What *should* I say?

'It's hard to tell. I think she likes the power she has. She didn't seem to like me very much. But then, neither did Aurora.'

'What about her? Is *she* trustworthy?'

That was an easier one to answer. 'I don't think you need to worry about *her* betraying you.' Coming on to him was another thing entirely. I cringed at the image of that in my mind and tried to ignore the scene as it played out with me rushing forward to pull her away from him.

He chuckled. 'No, I guess not.' So he knew how Aurora felt. Did he feel the same way?

What did it matter to me?

'So you don't think anyone in there is about to betray me?' he continued.

'No, but they don't trust *me*. As far as I can see, Sasha likes to be in charge and she's severe, but I didn't notice anything that suggested that she might, I don't know, become more like Kore? She *seemed* to be genuine in what she was doing to help people. But I don't know how these things work.' They should have stuck this formula in someone with a bit more life experience.

So he didn't trust his allies, the ones who were supposed to be our only hope against Kore. If so, why was he with them? It felt like I should ask him, but I didn't want to betray my curiosity. Better to keep him guessing.

He said nothing as we travelled back to the government sector, making sure we kept to the shadows. He took me through some basements at one point. I didn't know why. Eventually, we made it back to my unit block and then it was back up the air conditioning ducts. I tried not to react when he gathered me in his arms and walked us up the shafts but being that close to him brought the weird feelings on again.

Then it was back to crawling through the conduits until he stopped and unscrewed a vent. 'Here you are. Home again, safe and sound.'

I crawled through and he stayed in the conduit, looking out at me.

I knew this wasn't the last time I'd see him. Whether I wanted him to or not, he would be back. 'What happens now?' I asked.

'You go back to work tomorrow, is that right?'

'Yes.'

'Take it easy. Everyone you know there will probably look different now, some considerably so. Make sure you don't react. If you can find anyone who looks like they might be interested in working … outside the box, let me know.'

'And how do I do that?'

His massive hand reached out and drew my wrist towards him.

Using another gadget from his belt, he undid my link.

'Hey!' I'd already lost one to Kore. I couldn't lose a second. I could imagine the questions it would raise.

'It's all right.' He put the link against another one, holding it there until the new one beeped, then he slipped the new one on my wrist, fixing it in place. He angled my wrist to the side and used his thumb to slide back a tiny sliver of metal on the link.

'See that button?' he said. 'If you need me, press it. I may not be able to get to you immediately, but you'll be a priority. It has a tracker in it, so I'll know where you are, but try and get back here or somewhere on the streets where you can be alone. Go visit home or something like that if you can.'

He drew his hand away and looked at me.

What now? Did I thank him? Did I tell him I never wanted to see him again? Did I object to him dragging me all over the place? I didn't know. I couldn't work through the maze of feelings I had every time I looked into his eyes.

'All right. Goodbye, then,' I said.

He looked at me, trying to look behind my words, I think. I gave him nothing.

'See you soon,' he said, slipping the vent back in place. A moment later, he was gone.

CHAPTER TEN

Everyone will look different.

Izrod's words echoed in my head as I walked into the government building the following morning. I looked at the official at the desk. It was Annie. Fortunately, she looked just as bored as she usually did. There may have been a slight increase in the vulnerability on her face, but that was all.

I passed her with a nod and headed for the elevator.

There was Derek. I kept my face under control as I looked at him.

'Back again, are you?' he said with a guffaw. But he wasn't fooling me now. He had shifting eyes that were more alert than I would have thought possible. I would have to keep an eye on him. His gaze held desire as it passed over me but he must have remembered my earlier rebuke, as it disappeared almost instantly.

He took me down to the Archives and I stepped out, ready to be assailed by the faces of my workmates. Reggie O'Neal's eyes bugged out of his sockets when he saw me, his face a suggestive leer. Wow. I'd never got that from him before. He'd better keep his hands to himself. Adriana Michaels' face was so imperious and arrogant that I had to make myself stop staring, but she shied away from Reggie. I wondered if she'd seen behind his mask before.

'Eden, it's so good to have you back.'

I turned at the sound of Susan's voice and kept my expression neutral as I spoke. 'It's good to be back.'

'We were relieved to hear you'd survived your ordeal relatively unscathed,' she said. 'Please let me know if you become distressed throughout the day. I'd be more than happy to let you go early if you're experiencing any difficulties.'

Her voice sounded as calm and collected as ever, but her face told a different story. While she'd seemed so confident and steady, now there was panic in her eyes and uncertainty in her stance. She seemed so frail and fragile that I felt like reassuring her. *It'll be all right. Izrod won't get you. He's actually quite friendly.* Although, for all I knew, she was trembling at some ghost of the past that haunted her.

I couldn't prevent a fritter of disappointment. I'd hoped this woman might be able to help Izrod and his Underground crew.

She didn't seem to notice any change in my expression, so hopefully I'd kept it hidden well enough. She was probably too busy jumping at shadows to notice anyway.

'Well, if you're okay, go and get your cart. We've got a number of the old city papers to put back today.'

My cart contained stacks of old papers, some bound in their book covers, some lying loose on the cart. I'd have to put them back in their covers myself. The loose ones dated back to before the Unbidden Conflict. I looked sideways at one as I trundled my cart towards the back of the Archives, where they were stored.

City expansion stalled, said one headline. *Government opening talks* … but I couldn't see who with.

These old records were suddenly intriguing to me. Was there information in them that might benefit the Underground? Or perhaps I could get an idea of someone who could work with them based on what they'd been looking at.

I really shouldn't care one way or another. I resisted touching the new link Izrod had given me with the alert button that led straight to him. I couldn't get tied up in their business. But my eyes kept switching to those files, checking the headline of each one as I put them away.

I heard the sound of the elevator and looked up to see who was visiting us. Out marched our governor with a man I didn't know. I wondered if he was standing in for Miss Gregor while she was away, or maybe he worked with Official Hensen. His eyes shifted greedily as he dissected every corner of the room, giving everyone the once-over. This man was looking for something in the people around him. What was it? Someone who could satisfy something within him? A desire for power? A hunger for something baser than that?

Governor Jerrill's face was less interesting, even though I'd seen her before, probably because she didn't look much different, which surprised me. My father had, in his drunken state, regularly railed about politicians being two-faced. Maybe the governor didn't bother to hide her true self. As she came closer, I could see that there was something a little shadier in her expression, but it didn't fill me with dread. She also looked a little uncertain. Or was I imagining that?

The head keeper came up to them as they approached and I could hear a slight quiver in her voice as she spoke to them. 'I'm glad to be of service to you again today, Governor. What do you require?'

'We need to see the blueprints from before the restoration again, if you don't mind, Head Keeper. There are some additional elements we need to check.'

'Certainly. I think Eden has already put them away.' She went to her computer and entered a code. I felt my link bleep. 'Eden, can you find the files with this number on them? They should be among the ones you just refiled.'

I got the code from my link and searched the shelves until I found a book with the right code on it. I pulled out the papers they needed and a title flashed before my eyes. *City basement levels.*

I wondered why they were looking at that. Perhaps Izrod would want to know. *Stop worrying about what that creature wants, Eden!*

I kept my eyes from looking at the papers as I handed them to the head keeper. She flinched as the governor snatched them from her hands, frowning over them. 'Yes, these are the ones. We'll bring them back when we're done.'

They left and I returned to work. Late in the day, I noticed Reggie sidling over. His eyes bugged out so far I could have stuck my fingers in them. I was tempted to do just that, but I kept my mind and gaze on my work.

A bell chimed on the head keeper's desk. She opened the call line and spoke briefly, then ended the call, turning to me. 'Eden?'

I made my way to her desk. 'Yes, Head Keeper?'

'You have a visitor at the front desk. Unfortunately, we don't allow guests down here, so you'll need to go up and see her.'

A visitor? Visions of Izrod standing in the lobby dressed in a business suit flitted through my brain. But Susan had said 'her'. Sasha? There was only one way to find out.

But when I caught a glimpse of the woman waiting for me, my heart lurched into my throat. It was my mother.

'Eden, thank goodness I've found you,' she said. 'I wanted to see you anyway to make sure you're all right after what happened, but I need your help with something as well.' She came over and hugged me while I controlled my face, seeing what I saw in her now.

I'd always considered my mother weak—weak in picking a husband, weak in defending her children against him, weak in standing up to him in any way. But as my all-seeing eyes took her in, I was overwhelmed by the sense of love that radiated from her face. It wasn't just directed at me, either, although I felt engulfed by it. She seemed to love everybody. And far from making her look weak, her dominating force was strength.

Maybe that was why she'd stayed with Dad all these years. She couldn't give up on someone she loved. Her strength made her keep trying to win him over. I just wish it hadn't put the rest of us in the firing line.

But why had she come?

She took my hands in hers. 'Your brother is missing. Jed, I mean. Not Lenny. Lenny's fine. He and Kathleen are at home and okay.'

Missing? Jed had occasionally scampered off overnight in the past few years. It was difficult to stay at home when at any moment someone might barge in the door and cuff him around the head. It was weird she was so concerned about it. 'I'm sure he'll be back in a day or two.'

'No, you don't understand. He didn't go off by himself. Your father took him away.'

I felt rooted to the spot. My father would never take Jed out for a casual stroll. He didn't want to show off his wonderful children or educate us in the ways of the world or give us some fluffy childhood memories by taking us on a nice trip somewhere. So why had he taken Jed?

I could think of only one reason. He'd sold one of his children, why not another? I could still see the glee on his face at the credit he'd gotten for me.

'How long has he been gone?' I asked.

'Dad came yesterday,' she explained. 'He was sober, for a change, so I didn't think anything of it that he wanted to spend some time with his son.'

Except he never had before, but understanding my mother now, I could see why she had assumed our father had a noble reason for what he'd done. I would have threatened him with a kitchen knife before I'd let him take any of my siblings out of the house.

Not that I'd been there to do it. I'd left them alone to face a father who saw them as a line of credit and a mother who loved too much to see things clearly.

'I went to the security sector to report it when he didn't come back last night,' she continued, 'but they think he's just run away. They won't do anything until he's been gone at least another day. But Eden, why would your dad take him? I can't understand it.' She glanced at the suited officials rushing around us. 'I was thinking that, since you work in the government sector, maybe you could ask someone and they could get the security sector involved. I know you're only a junior at the moment, but I'm sure you've made friends. Can someone help us?'

I didn't know anyone in the government sector I'd trust, except maybe Official Hensen, who was away. But there was someone else who might be able to help. Someone who could probably gain access to my brother instantly. Someone who might already know where he was.

I touched my link, slid back the door to the little compartment, and pressed the button. 'I'll do what I can. Go home and make sure Dad doesn't come back for either of the others.'

Her face paled. 'Yes, I will. I left them with Mrs Murphy. I don't think she'll let them out. I'll go back now. Let me know if you hear anything.' She turned and hurried out of the building.

I went back to the elevator and down to the Archives, trying to look only slightly concerned as I approached Susan's desk. 'Head Keeper, my mother's just been here to say my oldest brother has run off. She wants some help to look for him. Would you mind if I left a little early today? I promise I'll make up my hours.'

She gave me a nervous smile. 'Of course, Eden. You've nearly worked all your hours today anyway. And I'm sure your mother could do with your help. Don't forget to check in with security, though, if you're leaving the government sector.'

I could hardly avoid doing that. They'd want to know where I was going and how long I was likely to be gone. I wasn't sure what to tell them.

I took the elevator back to the lobby and headed to my unit to change out of my uniform. I changed as quickly as I could and went out on the street. Where should I meet Izrod? I passed through the lobby of my unit building, security scanning my link and asking me where I was going and how long I'd be gone. I told them I was going to look for my brother and didn't know.

I got down to the street and travelled to the end of our block of buildings, where I passed through another checkpoint and went through the same thing. I tried not to let my eyes dart right and left, looking for any sign of a hulking form in the shadows, but it felt like there was a sign on my head saying, *I'm looking for Izrod. Try and stop me!*

By the time I'd got through the third checkpoint, it was getting dark, which might be why they took a little longer with their approvals and were sterner in admonishing me to stay in contact and not stay away too long. I wasn't going to promise either of those things.

I'd never been so relieved to reach the darkness of the streets at the edge of the government sector. As I walked along, I began to feel a presence beside me. We should have made a code or some kind of signal. I kept walking until I turned a corner and was out of sight of security. There weren't many people around, so I ducked into an alley, hopefully unnoticed.

Now what did I do? Did I just wait—

'What's wrong?' Izrod stepped out of the shadows, concern mingled with curiosity on his face.

'My brother's gone missing.' He seemed about to reply but he needed to know the full story. 'My mother said my father took him away. He would never do that. I think he's taken him to Kore to try and sell him.'

'Are you sure?'

'Yes. You saw the way he reacted when he got the money for me. Hell, he'd probably sell my baby brother for spare parts—' Images buzzed around in my head. Jed strapped to that table, Jed begging for help, Jed screaming as that uncaring woman pumped him full of

Kore's poison, all to feed my father's addiction.

Izrod's face filled with pity as he put his hands on my shoulders. 'Okay. Go to your mother's place. I'll go to Kore's—'

'No, I'm coming with you.'

His expression tightened. 'Don't be ridiculous, Eden. You can't come with me. It will be virtually impossible to get in and out with you there as well. It will be hard enough to get your brother out.'

'Not having me there won't mean it's easy either,' I snapped. 'Do you think my brother's just going to walk out with Izrod? He'll probably shriek the whole way.'

'Would you rather Kore kept him there? I might be too late as it is.'

No. That couldn't be true. Surely I would be able to tell if my little brother …

I'd failed him. Just walked away, moved out and got a life. What kind of a sister was I? I couldn't abandon him now. 'Please,' I said, 'you've got to let me help.'

His voice was level. 'Eden, if I take you in there with me, it greatly increases the chance that we'll all be caught. Going in there at all and removing your brother is an incredible risk. I want to do this for you, but I can't take you with me. It's too dangerous.'

'Not all the way, then,' I said. 'I won't come inside. I'll write a note that you can give to my brother, like the one you gave to me. He should recognise my writing.'

He sighed, took my hand and tugged me along with him.

For the first few streets, he was careful where we stood—always in shadow, always hugging the wall of a building, ducking at frequent intervals. But after that, he relaxed a little more, hurrying me along streets that were mostly empty, heading for the poor sector of the city. Some streets I thought I recognised but I was soon lost in the maze of backways and alleys until he came to a stop beside an abandoned building. The door was old and broken, all the windows boarded up, but he reached inside the hole in the door and triggered something, making it creak open.

We went inside and he closed the door behind us, plunging us into darkness, until I heard a huff of air and he lit one of the lamps they'd had at the Underground.

I looked around. The room was barely big enough for us both to stand in and only contained the lamp on a small table, nothing else except dust and dirt.

'Now,' he said, 'you're going to wait here. Don't leave under any circumstances unless I'm not back by daylight. Here.' He opened a drawer on the side of the table and pulled out a paper and pen. 'Write a message for your brother.'

He kept talking while I wrote. 'The streets aren't safe around here. If I'm not back by morning, head north for five blocks. By then, you should be back in an area you know. Whether you contact your mother or security at that point is up to you.'

I didn't want to say that I understood. If he didn't return, not only would my brother be lost, but him as well. I hadn't considered the risk he might be taking to help Jed. He'd done a lot to keep his role in Kore's organisation. Getting my brother out could spell an end to that.

And there was something in me that didn't want him to go, didn't want him to do something risky. But he was Izrod. It was what he did.

I gave him the message for Jed and managed to spit out, 'Good luck.'

He went out the door, closing it behind him, leaving a cloud of dust in his wake.

I waited fifteen minutes before opening it. To hell with waiting behind. So what if the streets were dangerous? I should have realised Dad would try again. I didn't deserve to stay safe while Jed was probably shrieking with agony under the merciless gaze of that medic. Maybe it would serve me right if the evil out there swallowed me up. I had to go and find out what had happened to my brother.

CHAPTER ELEVEN

I crept along in the shadows, my heart thundering with every step. Would someone stop me? Was anyone around? How could I hope to find my way to Kore's? I wasn't even sure where I was!

But perhaps this new thing in my head would help me. At least it should let me know truth from fable.

'Hey, little lady.'

A man sidled up to me. His clothes were ripped and torn. I got the feeling he was trying to look threatening, but he looked as scared of me as I was of him. My advantage was that I didn't *look* scared, so unless Kore had stabbed him with a syringe lately, he wouldn't know about my fear, only his own.

I made my voice as light and easy as I could. 'I'm interested in buying information.'

That made him look slightly more at ease, although surprised. 'What makes you think—'

I held up my link. 'I can send you a credit amount straight away.' I selected an amount I thought would impress him and held it up.

The light of greed appeared in his eyes, vanquishing the fear. 'What do you want to know?'

'Where does Kore's gang hide out?'

'You want to *go* to Kore's place? Are you crazy? People usually want to get as far away as they can.' Then he looked me over. 'Hey, you're the one who …'

'Escaped? That's me. But I have business with him and I need to go back.' I hoped I sounded confident enough.

His eyes glittered, but the mention of Kore had allowed the fear to reign on his face again. 'I think you'll regret it.'

'Maybe so. But it'll be my problem, and you'll be all the richer for it.'

Still, he hesitated.

'Look, I'm not asking you to walk me in the front door. Just get me to the street where I got out the other day.'

He scratched his chin. 'Kore's not there anymore. He had to shift. Security was searching.'

'Okay, just get me to where he is.' I couldn't waste any more time on a stupid conversation.

He held his link out. I held mine back. 'Not until I'm sure we're in the right place.' Something flashed across his face that made me scared he would double-cross me, but it was barely there before it was gone again. I had to hope that his greed would keep him compliant.

He started moving up the street and I followed, fear coursing through me. Was I doing the right thing? Of course I wasn't. He could be leading me anywhere, into the dark where he'd do what he liked, to friends who were a lot tougher than he was, to hand me in to Kore himself.

I shuffled behind him down a few streets and just when I was about to prod him with questions, he stopped and pointed. 'See those doors down there?'

I could see a dull light shining from around a set of double doors a step or two down from street level. 'Yes?'

He held out his link. 'That's Kore's place.'

What if he was—

I heard a crash and the doors buckled, then they sprang back into place, looking a little worse for wear. An unearthly shrieking made my ears tingle. It was just like the mournful cries of my cellmates when I'd been a resident in Kore's facility.

I looked back at my guide, who was wide-eyed. 'The money, now!'

I pressed my link to his and as soon as the transaction was done, he was gone.

The doors exploded open and Izrod emerged, carrying a writhing Jed in his arms. My brother pummelled Izrod with his fists.

Izrod started running as soon as he cleared the doors, fortunately, in my direction. He slid to a stop as he saw me. 'What the hell are you doing here?'

'I had to come, I'm sorry.' I turned to my brother. 'Jed, it's all right. He's a …'

My brother's empty eyes stared back at me. His pupils were huge and there was foam on his lips. He arched his back unnaturally, shrieking again and bucking against Izrod's firm grasp.

My heart crashed. He was just like the others, the ones who'd lost their minds.

Izrod ignored Jed's thrashing, holding on even as Jed's fists struck him in the face, his legs swinging violently against Izrod's chest. 'Come on, we need to leave.'

I followed him down the street, hugging the building behind him. Not that it mattered if we kept to the shadows. Jed's shrieking made it clear where we were.

Izrod glanced at me. 'Sorry.'

I was about to ask what for when he struck Jed a savage blow on the head. My brother fell silent, although his body still twitched and spasmed.

'Stop right there, Leon.'

Izrod had been mid-stride, but he halted at the voice, drawing further into the shadows. He dragged me with him, putting me behind him.

I peered through the gloom to see who owned the voice. A man strode forward, clearly one of Kore's crew, as his shoulders were larger than the rest of him and he walked with a rolling gait as he stepped toward us.

'Justin,' Izrod said.

I saw light flash on the blade of the knife Justin held. 'Where do you think you're going with him?'

'Does it matter? You saw what I did in there. This is your chance to join me. You don't owe Kore anything. I know Alpha-D didn't work on you any more than it did on me, so don't tell me it's too hard to walk away.'

Justin gave me a baleful glare. I stared back, trying to get a read on his face. It was hard. He seemed to be shifting around, almost like he was moving but not moving. 'Maybe you have another reason for leaving him. Do you think he's just going to let you walk away with two test subjects?'

'I don't notice anyone trying to stop me. Apart from you, that is.'

I looked back in the direction of Kore's lair. Although there was a lot of noise coming from within, no one else had come out in pursuit of us.

Justin glanced back too. 'Well, you did kind of throw a bomb in there.'

Izrod hadn't killed Kore, had he? No, if he'd done that, I could imagine all the freaks lumbering out and attacking us, like a deformed army. What had he done?

'Like I said,' Izrod told him, 'this is your chance to walk away. You know whatever Kore's planning won't work. And what will it do for you anyway? What will it do for any of us? He doesn't care about us.'

He looked dubious. 'And you're going to bring in a fantastic supply of all good things, are you?'

Izrod met his incredulous eyes. 'You know I wouldn't lead as Kore has done.'

Justin inclined his head. 'Maybe not. But still, going against Kore … And even though some can resist Alpha-D, half of them in there are still under his spell.' He turned at the sound of voices from the double doors. 'Just get out of here. Don't show your face around here anytime soon.'

Izrod grabbed my arm, hurrying me along with him.

'What was that about?' I asked.

'No talking. There'll be time for that later.'

After about an hour of creeping from shadow to shadow, I recognised the ramshackle homes in the dusty street where my family lived. Soon Izrod was outside our house, Jed's twitching body in his arms. I opened my mouth to ask how he knew the address, then realised that he'd probably got it from Dad when he'd decided to sell me out.

He rapped on the door and I heard my mother's timid voice. 'Who is it?'

I moved forward. 'Mother, it's me. Don't be afraid. I've got a … friend with me. He got Jed for you.'

I heard the clatter of the bolts being drawn back and the door unlocking, then my mother flung it open. Her eyes bugged out at the sight of Izrod, but that only lasted until she saw Jed in his arms. She reached out for him, but Izrod pushed her out of the way and hurried inside.

'Shut the door,' he commanded. 'We need to keep this place secure.' He examined the doors leading to the two bedrooms and the bathroom. 'Which room is bigger?'

I pointed to my mother's.

He charged over to the door, opened it and went in. We followed him.

I looked at Mother. 'Kathleen and Lenny?'

'Both asleep in their room. This might wake them up, though.'

'More than likely,' said Izrod, as he laid my brother on my mother's bed.

Mother ran her hand over my brother's forehead. 'Jed? Jed, darling, wake up,' she crooned. 'It's all right. You're safe and home now.' She turned to Izrod. 'What's wrong with him?'

He didn't answer. 'Do you have any rope? I need bandages as well. Cloths will do if you don't have any bandages.'

We had plenty of bandages. The rope was a little trickier, but I eventually found some by digging in the bottom of the cupboard. I must have flung it in there at one point, maybe hoping I could use it on Dad.

He took them from us and draped the bandages over Jed's wrists and ankles. Then, to our horror, he tied him to the bed.

'What are you doing?' I demanded.

'Kore injected your brother with one of his formulas. I'm sure you've heard of others like this. A couple turned up on the street. It not only makes them insane, it increases their strength. I have to restrain him. He'll try and leave as soon as he wakes up and I don't want to have to hit him again. This is the next best thing.'

My mother pressed her hands to her lips, her eyes fluttering, as Izrod pulled her away when Jed started twitching. 'You can't sit next to him. He could very easily kill you.'

I could tell her love wouldn't find that a convincing argument.

Izrod turned to me. 'Eden, do you think you can find your way back to the Underground? It's not far from here.'

'Um, yes. I think so.'

'You need to find Aurora. Tell her we have another chaos case. She'll know what to do. See if you can get permission for us to move Jed over there. It'll be safer.'

After he'd made sure I knew how to get there, I raced to the door, making sure I shut it firmly behind me. The last thing we needed was my father staggering in to steal Kathleen or Lenny away.

No, my father's days of interfering with my family were over. No matter what I had to do, I would make sure he never darkened this door again. And Aurora would fix my brother. She had to.

CHAPTER TWELVE

Izrod had told me to hurry, but I was stiff with anxiety. Had someone from Kore's followed us to Mother's place? There were clearly others apart from Justin. And maybe Justin would decide betraying us was better. Would they invade our home and drag Jed and Izrod away?

Finally, I saw the half-buried entryway to the Underground. Now I just had to get in. I knew it wouldn't be as simple as strolling about looking for Aurora. It didn't seem like the place where friends and family came around for a casual chat. I just had to hope I could get past whatever guards were waiting for me.

I went up and knocked on the door as hard as I could. I soon moved from knocking to slamming my fist down on it. I looked around; no one else was in sight. But the hairs on the back of my neck told me there were eyes on me.

I was about to start yelling when someone grabbed me from behind and held a knife to my throat. 'What do you think you're doing here?'

It didn't sound like anyone I'd met when I'd visited with Izrod. I couldn't decipher anything except menace in his voice. 'Please,' I said, 'I'm looking for Aurora. I need her help.'

The knife withdrew as my assailant stepped around me,

brandishing his weapon in front of me. He was a head or so taller than me and didn't look that much older. I assessed his face—it spoke of darkness and loyalty and not much else.

'There's no one here by that name,' he spat.

I didn't have time for games. 'I was here just the other day with Iz … with Leon. He got my brother out of Kore's. He said he's another chaos case.'

Had he heard of me? There seemed to be some kind of recognition on his face. I mean, how many girls did Izrod bring around for a visit?

'Wait here.' He stepped away from me and back into the nearby shadows.

I counted five interminable minutes before the door finally swung open. Before I could say anything, someone hauled me inside, slamming the door behind me.

There stood Knifer and, to my surprise, Sasha, looking me over scornfully.

'Please,' I said. 'My brother's been hurt.'

She folded her arms. 'By Kore? And Leon got him out for you, did he?'

'My father sold him to Kore, just like he sold me.'

Knifer's eyes widened at that, but Sasha's expression didn't change. 'And your brother, what value is he to us?' she said. 'Leon had no business rescuing him. He has tasks he needs to complete so we can defeat Kore and see an end to the corruption in this city.' She turned back to Knifer. 'Throw her out.'

He grabbed my arm and I reached around him. 'I'll take him to the medical sector if you don't help. They'll hand him over to the security sector!'

She waved a dismissive hand and started walking away.

I glanced at Knifer, who dragged me towards the door. Loyalty. His face was overlaid with it. It might not mean anything to Sasha, but was she the one I needed to convince? 'Leon asked for your help. Doesn't he deserve some kind of loyalty?' I shrieked. 'You're no better than Kore!'

Knifer's hands snapped away from me and he stood back.

Sasha's feet dragged to a halt and she turned back to me. 'We're loyal to the cause. If people no longer support that, they're on their own.'

'Even if they help someone in need? Or is that just about seeing who's useful to you? Did you really help my family because it was the right thing to do or were they potential recruits? Is this all about "the cause" or do you actually care about people?' I hadn't seen anyone from our old unit block here, but for all I knew, several were grateful, dedicated members of the Underground.

Knifer watched Sasha carefully. It looked like she was building up to an explosion, but then the fury on her face melted away. 'Take her to Aurora.'

She disappeared before I could thank her.

I turned to Knifer and he looked me up and down, this time with respect.

I remembered the way to the medical sector, but I let him lead me. He pushed the door open and let me go in by myself. 'I'll take you back to the entry when you're done,' he said.

'Leon said to ask about bringing my brother here.'

He gave me an incredulous look. 'Do you think Sasha would agree to that?'

That ended that conversation.

I walked in and there was Aurora, leaning over someone in one of their makeshift beds. 'What are you doing here? Is Leon here?'

'No, but my brother's been injured. He's another chaos case.'

She looked at me, askance. 'So what?'

'Iz—' I stopped short as she glared at me. 'He sent me to tell you. He's at my mother's place. I can take you there.'

I could almost hear her blood boiling. It leaked through her eyes, which sizzled at me. 'Fine. But let me make one thing clear. If you call him "Izrod" in front of me, I'll take the nearest scalpel and slice open your skull just to see if you actually have a brain. His name is *Leon*.'

She grabbed a few things from various medical stations and headed back to Knifer. 'I shouldn't be too long.'

We hurried out onto the street, the journey much quicker now I was sure of the way. I was afraid someone was going to leap on us and drag us to Kore's, but we hardly saw anyone.

Mother let us in when I pounded on the door. I led Aurora to Mother's bedroom, where Jed was still strapped to the bed, but now he was thrashing, inhuman shrieks issuing from between his white lips.

'Hm,' said Aurora. 'That's going to disturb the neighbours.'

'In this area, it's the norm,' I said.

She turned to Leon. 'What happened?'

'Eden's dad thinks selling his children is a great way to earn money. He sold one.' He nodded at me. 'Why not sell another?'

That brought her up short, some of the fire in her eyes extinguished. 'Oh.' She rummaged around in the bags she'd brought with her, pulling out a vial and a syringe, which she filled before plunging it into my brother's arm. 'That should quieten him down for a bit.'

Moments later, my brother's shrieks softened to moans and the spasming turned to small twitches. Jed's breathing settled, although he still let out whimpers and sobs, his chest heaving. Mother took the opportunity to rush over and take his hand. She turned to Aurora. 'You think he'll be okay?'

It was Leon who answered. 'He'll be okay for a few hours. Then it will start again.'

'How long for?' I asked. Was my brother always going to be this twitching, shrieking wreck?

'It's difficult to say. I've never seen it used on someone so young before. Usually, it wears off in a couple of days, but it could take longer for Jed.'

I wasn't sure I believed him. None of the other people who'd disappeared had resumed their normal lives. Most of them had never been seen again.

The two of them went out of the room. I looked back at Mother, who had started singing softly to Jed, stroking his forehead.

At first, I thought Leon had gone, but he came back in after a few moments. He held up a set of syringes. 'Aurora's gone back to the Underground. She'll update Sasha. These should last us hopefully until Jed recovers.'

'But he *will* recover?' asked Mother.

I didn't like the uncertainty on his face. 'He should. Others have.'

Was he lying? He had to be. 'I haven't heard of anyone else recovering!'

His face stayed patient. 'There were some who stayed at Kore's. They recovered.'

'And what happened to them?'

I could see he didn't want to answer, but then he kicked at the dust on the floor. 'Kore had them killed.'

'What about the two who escaped? Do you know what happened to them?'

'Not for certain, no, but Kore gave me the impression they'd also been dealt with. He doesn't like people examining the subjects of his experiments, at least, not until he's satisfied with the results.'

'But some did die from this at Kore's. That means Jed could die too.'

I could tell he wanted to deny it; his darting eyes bore testament to that, but he didn't.

'We'll just have to wait and see,' he said finally. 'It's all guesswork anyway. Kore's formulas can have odd reactions sometimes.'

My mother's face brightened. 'So he could recover sooner?'

Izrod glanced at her. 'I don't think that's likely.'

'But he's a child,' she said, cooing at Jed. 'They recover more quickly from things than adults do. I'm sure it won't take as long.'

How like my mother to insist it must all work out for the best after years of Dad's fists smashing her face.

I heard Kathleen call from next door. Mother rose from Jed's bedside. 'Eden, can you watch him for me? I need to go and settle Kathleen.'

'Make sure she knows we've got visitors. And to shut up about them.' We couldn't have her blabbing this news to Dad. He'd probably lead Kore's gang straight here.

As Mother left, I noticed Izrod—I mean Leon—watching me. His verdant eyes were careful, as if he didn't want to say too much. Or maybe he thought my family was crazy, with our drunken lout of a father, extra-loving mother, and a quartet of kids stuck in the middle. What did he make of us?

'Your mother is a very caring woman.'

He had no idea how right he was. 'Isn't that what mothers are like?'

'I don't know. I can't remember mine.'

It was hard for me to believe he'd had parents at all. For so long he'd just been some nightmare that had crept out of Kore's laboratory. But yes, I guess he'd had parents. Had they loved him? Feared him? Dumped him? 'Well, yes. They care. Usually.' There were probably some mothers out there who were like Dad. I had seen enough staggering around the drink vendor's cart to know that.

I looked back at my brother. 'I didn't ask Sasha about taking Jed there but I got the impression she wouldn't have been crazy about the idea.'

'I know. Aurora told me. It's a shame. This place isn't very secure. I don't like our chances if Kore's people find us here. But we'd need help to move your brother anywhere while he's like this. I think we'll just have to wait until he's well enough to travel.'

Assuming he would be.

123

Izrod sat down next to me and I flinched. I didn't mean to; it just happened. I immediately felt a swathe of guilt, especially when I saw his face. He looked just like Jed had when he'd first realised his father preferred hitting him to hugging him.

'I'm not going to hurt you, Eden. I thought you would have known that by now.' He gestured at Jed.

I shut my eyes, trying to block out that wounded expression. 'I know. I'm sorry. It's just that … you're kind of big.' Ugh! That sounded so lame! Was that the best I could do?

He held up one of his hands and examined it. 'Yeah, parts of me are.' He had massive palms that could encompass a dinner plate. But they were out of proportion with his forearms. His shoulders were a different matter—they were just as massive.

Red scars ran across the pale skin on his wrists. I'd seen lines like that before. 'Did you try to harm yourself?' Dad had done that once, slashed his wrists to get Mother to let him in. I'd hoped he'd bleed to death until someone in the learning sector told me that he'd done it the wrong way. He must have known that, so it was just another one of his little manipulations.

Leon chuckled darkly. 'No, that's Kore's doing.'

So Kore was abusive? Why was I surprised? 'What did he slit your wrists for?'

He shifted a little further away from me. 'That's where he attached my hands.'

Attached … 'What do you mean?' I held myself still, bracing for the horror I felt was to come.

He held up both meaty fists before my eyes. 'These aren't my hands. Kore gave them to me.'

How did you give someone hands? And did I really want to know? I wasn't sure, but Leon answered before I could change the subject. 'When I first met Kore, I was living on the streets. Not here.

It was in Reacher's Pass.'

'Never been there,' I said, trying not to show I was interested.

'It's about the same size as here, people-wise, but it's much more spread out, so there are heaps of lonely areas. They're also a bit more established than here so it had the kind of resources Kore needed.'

I tried to picture it. Did it have tall buildings leaning in, crowding over the streets? Were there fields where farmers toiled? We'd seen pictures of farms in the learning sector. Were there shacks like this one, left standing silent and decrepit, that Kore had used as a base for him and his creepy crew?

'I was eleven, but already tall. I sprang up pretty young. I was foraging through garbage in a dump when Kore found me. He said he could feed me if I worked for him. Now, I knew no one was supposed to employ a kid that young, but he mentioned food, so I figured I'd do it just for that and a roof over my head.

'So I went with him. I was surprised that he lived in a huge warehouse on the edge of the city. I was even more surprised when I saw how pristine it was inside, like the medical sector, all clean and white. He even had others who worked for him. Nurses and the like. That should have told me what I was dealing with, but I was too busy eating to care. I never saw the others, those that he'd worked on before me. He kept them away until afterwards.'

A sick feeling rose in my stomach. I'd seen what Kore did to people. Had he looked at Leon the same way he'd looked at me— assessing me like I was his latest project? How could a kid Leon's age have known what that meant?

'I'd been there a few weeks when I felt sick after a meal,' he said, with an unconcerned look. I suppose it was just part of his story now—part of the horror. 'I passed out and woke up strapped to a table in his lab.' It didn't matter how much I pleaded and begged for him to release me, he wasn't interested. Said he'd invested in me. Said I'd like what he did.

'Over the next few years, he "refined" me. That's what he called it. I fell asleep and woke up to find new hands on my arms. I fell asleep and woke up to find that I'd bulked up beyond what I'd ever thought possible. I might have been tall, but I used to be skinny, if you can believe that. I'd often take weeks to recover, sometimes months. Sometimes his "additions" didn't work and he'd have to replace them.

'He continued to experiment on me on and off for years, but when he had me looking bigger than anyone I'd ever seen before, he must have figured that was enough. Or maybe he just got bored. He had others he was refining at the same time as me and there were more afterwards.'

A chill crept over me, but I kept myself from shuddering. I wasn't sure if my face was telling him anything. He was certainly studying it hard enough.

But I had to ask the question. 'Are you telling me he gave you hands off some dead body?' That was beyond horrible; it was spine-tinglingly terrifying.

He cleared his throat. 'I don't think he was dead. Not when he took the hands, anyway.'

I could feel my eyes bugging out. What a terrible thing to happen to a boy! Jed was thirteen and I couldn't imagine him living through that horror, a more terrifying nightmare than my father and his violence.

I don't know what Leon saw on my face, but he continued. 'Kore has a lot of enemies. He hunts them down or gets some of his people to, and if they have physical traits he values, like strong hands, he takes them and gives them to his people.'

'But how could he do that?'

Leon took it as a practical question. 'He's a genius at that kind of thing. That's why he had such a good setup at Reacher's Pass. But after I'd been with him for about four years, the government of the pass must have decided to do something about him, because suddenly we all up and moved to Sendirian City. He developed a new setup but it wasn't as elaborate as what he'd had there. It had to be more mobile so that if the government sector discovered him, he could move instantly. He stopped literally adding new body parts and moved to chemical changes, developing different drugs and documenting their effects on people.'

I looked at Jed, who seemed to be sleeping. 'Why make a drug to send people crazy?'

Leon's face darkened. 'I'm not sure. I think he's planning a major offensive but he hadn't gotten around to sharing it with me. Maybe he sensed that my allegiance had moved elsewhere. Maybe he's just fed up with me. I'm hoping he'll tell Justin. Did he seem trustworthy to you?'

'Um …' I thought back to our brief encounter. 'Perhaps. It was hard to tell. Kore won't be suspicious that he didn't bring you back?'

'Justin's good, but he's no match for me, and Kore knows it. I hope that doesn't mean he considers him expendable. We'll never get the information we need if that's the case.'

Mother hurried back and went straight to Jed's side. 'Kathleen's gone back to sleep. Lenny woke up too. I told them Jed's back but he isn't well. I told them we were playing hide and seek and they couldn't tell anyone where Jed was hiding.' Her eyes settled on Leon. 'You might be a little more difficult to explain, though.'

That might not be a problem. 'You won't be staying here, will you?' I asked.

'I'll need to be here most of the time,' he replied. 'I'll need to give him the injections.'

My mother's hands reached out. 'I can do that.'

He held the syringes away from her. 'Not today. He's still too volatile. Maybe tomorrow.'

I yawned. 'What time is it?'

Mother looked at her link. 'About midnight.'

'I'll have to report in via my link at seven so that security knows

I'm okay, then I'll have to be at work by nine.' I looked at Leon. 'I think I'd better go to work or they'll get suspicious.'

'Yes, you need to.'

'I'll make it if I leave here by about eight or so.'

'Then you should go and get some sleep.'

I didn't want to leave my brother. I still felt the weight of guilt from what had happened to him. *That's Dad's fault, not yours.* But that didn't make me feel any better. 'What if you need my help?'

Mother pointed to my old bed in the corner. 'Why don't you sleep there? Jed's been using it, but I don't think he'll need it for a while.'

'It'll probably be a few hours before your brother wakes up again,' Leon said. 'Get some sleep while you can.'

I regarded him. 'What about you? You've had a pretty big night.'

'I'm used to it. I'll sleep when he's not likely to be so volatile.'

From what he'd said, that might be at least a day away. Was he going to stay awake that long?

But as I considered his hulking form, I realised he'd be more than a match for Dad. No one else from this family would become the price of a drink as long as Leon was here.

My mind rebelled against finding security in any man, even as part of me welcomed the feeling. I didn't understand what was happening in my head when it came to Leon. There was such a sense of warmth and security when I was with him.

But it couldn't be anything more than just a fondness and a sense of protection. I wouldn't allow it to be anything more. I would never let myself be vulnerable like that.

But my eyes closed to the sound of his voice as he murmured in conversation with Mother. There was safety in the sound and soon I drifted away.

CHAPTER THIRTEEN

I woke up to Lenny bouncing on my head. 'Wake up, Edie. Time to get up.'

I looked at the time on my link. It was seven-thirty. I had to leave in half an hour if I wanted to make it to work on time, but I was half an hour late to report in.

I shot bolt upright in bed, Lenny tumbling away with a cry. He scrambled up and shoved out his bottom lip. 'I'm going to tell Mother!'

I quickly tapped on my link to check in, sure I was going to be berated for being late when I arrived at work, but at least I'd done it. Hopefully, they wouldn't break down the door of my unit or start scouring the streets for me.

I expected to see Mother crouching over Jed, but she was lying next to him, fast asleep, waking as Lenny started prodding her. Leon leaned against the bed, his head nodding. He blinked himself awake as Jed began to twitch and moan. He turned his eyes to mine. 'You need to make sure your little brother and sister stay far away.'

Mother reached for Jed, but Leon held her back. 'No. Don't touch him. Go and look after the other two.' He turned to me. 'You're still going to work today?'

'Would it be better if I stayed?'

'No, I'd appreciate it if you'd continue to look out for potential contacts. Just come back as soon as you can without it being suspicious and try and check that no one's following you.'

Within moments, Jed's cries became shrieks and I could see his wrists and ankles straining against the cords tying him down. Leon turned and fumbled for the bag of syringes Aurora had left, while keeping his other hand stretched out, ready to catch Jed if the cords snapped. Mother took the syringe from him and loaded it up.

'It's all right,' Leon said to me. 'We can deal with this. You need to get to work.'

He put out his hands as my brother's body jerked higher and higher. He touched Jed gently, pushing him back down, only to have him strain up again. Once he'd managed to get Aurora's drugs into his arm, it seemed to help a bit, but Jed still twitched and moaned.

Mother came out with me, reaching out to Lenny and Kathleen, who were staring at the door to her room with wide eyes at the strangled sounds coming from Jed's throat. Kathleen put her hands over her ears.

'I'll get everyone some breakfast.' Mother glanced at me. 'You should go and have a shower too.'

I looked down and saw dirt and dust everywhere. Damn. I'd need to go back to my unit as well, as I'd need to change into my uniform. I wondered if I could get away with not wearing one for a day but decided against it.

I went and had a shower anyway, shaking as much dust off my clothes as I could. I felt better afterwards, even though the cries and thumps from the next room continued. The noise grated on my nerves. Kathleen dissolved back into tears and Lenny imitated Jed's grunts.

My mother put a bowl of steaming porridge in front of me. 'Here you are, Eden. Hurry up. Don't be late for work.'

***

130

I made it to work on time, even with the detour to my unit, although I received a rebuke from security. I explained to them that I would be staying with my mother temporarily, as my brother wasn't well. As I'd been back a few days with nothing unusual happening—apart from Izrod visiting my apartment, me being recruited by the Underground, my brother being drugged by Kore, and Leon practically cracking the place in two to get him out—they didn't seem too concerned. Probably because they didn't know all that. Likely, they also thought Kore and his gang would prefer a new target.

Work was little different from the day before. The governor came down once and there were a few visitors getting books or papers, I wheeled my cart around putting things back where they belonged and was even allowed to deliver some files to another department. But although I met a few new people, there was no one who I felt would give Leon the kind of contacts he needed. Plenty who probably thought they could, though.

I made sure I stayed past the end of my shift, just as I had before Leon had kidnapped me. Susan enquired after my brother, and I told her he was back but unsettled. 'I'll be going there at the end of the day,' I said, trying to layer my voice with just enough concern. 'My mother may need help with him for a while.'

'You do what you need to do,' she said. She sounded nervous, but she always sounded nervous to me now. It was hard to believe she'd seemed so calm and self-assured when I'd started working in the Archives.

At the end of the day, I said goodbye, kept my pace level, told security where I was going and why, got a bag of clothes from my unit, including a spare uniform, and checked out at all the checkpoints, repeating my story.

When I arrived back at my mother's place, I was relieved to hear silence. Mother was making something in the kitchen. Kathleen wrapped her arms around me and gave me a hug and Lenny toddled over and put his sticky mouth against my face to kiss me.

I glanced at the bedroom door. 'Can I go in?'

'Yes.' She handed me a plate with food. 'You can take this in for Leon. I'm sure he's hungry.'

I looked at the scant offering. I knew we didn't have the money to feed someone Leon's size for long, even with the extra from my salary. 'If you need to go and get some more food, I can watch things here.'

She looked at the plate. 'Yes, you're probably right. There should still be a few vendors trading. I'll pop out now.'

The bedroom was cool and dark. Leon's glance held impatience at first, but that quickly melted away. 'Oh, it's you.'

'Yeah. Just finished work.' I put the plate on the floor next to him and he began picking at its contents.

Jed's ankles and wrists were bruised and bleeding. There was some yellow muck soaking the bandages. The smell reminded me of heart-hammering terror and old wounds. It looked like my mother had been trying to treat his injuries, much as she had all our lives, with soothing gels and murmured love. Jed's eyes were ringed by dark circles that stood out on his pale face.

I sat down beside Leon. 'How's he been today?'

'He's had a few sessions. I'll need to go and get some more treatments from Aurora sometime tonight, but I think he's through the worst of it.'

'That's such a relief.' To my surprise, my hand landed on his. I drew it away and tried to hide my embarrassment. But he needed to be thanked. If not for him, Jed could be dead. 'Thank you for what you did for him.'

He smiled. 'That's all right.'

'No, I know that asking you to do this has meant that things aren't great between you and Sasha.' My conversation with her had told me that much. 'I'm sorry.'

With a moment's hesitation, he laid his hand over mine. Unlike me, he didn't remove it. I stopped myself from snatching my hand away, although part of me wanted to. The other part of me was more than happy to feel his warmth. 'I know how much your brother means to you. And let's face it, if I hadn't taken you in the first place, your father wouldn't have seen him as nothing more than a credit to be made.'

That was hardly something I could lay at his door. 'My father sees everyone and everything that way. You just made it a little easier for him.'

He caught my gaze, his green eyes piercing mine. 'But I've made your life more difficult just by it intersecting mine.'

'My life was never sunny and trouble-free.' I grinned, hoping to alleviate some of the pain and uncertainty I could see clouding his eyes. 'Honestly, I think you kidnapping me only ranks about number three on the scale of the worst things I've been through.'

He frowned. 'I find that hard to believe.'

'I don't.' I kept my voice light, but his eyes were serious. 'I mean, let's face it, I've got a deadbeat for a dad who'd rather sell me than love me. I might live in government accommodation now, but my family lives in this hovel. And I nearly burned to death in a fire just a couple of months ago.'

'I remember,' he said, then brought himself up, the weight of his hand disappearing from mine.

What did that mean? Why did he look so evasive? 'Were you following me back then?' But that was before I'd started working at government. Did he *start* the fire? No, his face didn't hold that kind of guilt.

I dredged up my memories of that awful night—the choking smoke in my lungs, the blind helplessness, the despair as we'd watched the little we had turn to ashes. The shrouded shapes changing the street into a graveyard. The cold realisation that no one would help us. I knew that Sasha had been there. And yes, that was right, Mr Ivanov had seen Izrod.

'You were there that night, weren't you?'

There was confirmation in his silence.

'Why?' I asked. 'Were you tracking someone?'

He seemed reluctant to speak, but something must have loosened his tongue. 'No. I saw the flames and went down to see if I could help.'

'Help?' How was he supposed to do that when he was instantly recognisable to everyone just by his size?

When Mr Ivanov had seen him, he'd been near a pile of protective suits. I remembered how high I'd had to look up when I'd peered through the smoke at the man who'd saved us.

The man in the fire suit. His face hidden, his identity concealed.

'You were the one who got us out, weren't you?'

I could tell I'd hit the mark. 'You have no idea how frustrating it is to look like I do—instantly recognisable as the bad guy. I go to fires because there's usually protective gear I can don to get in and do something, not to mention that the officers from the fire sector have to be ordered in before they can do anything.'

How much would we owe this man? He had saved Jed and me from Kore, and he'd saved all of us from that fire! There was no doubt in my mind that we'd all be smoking corpses if it weren't for him.

I had to find a way to help the Underground. It was the least I could do. And this seemed to cement what my mind told me about him. He was good. He was noble. He was trustworthy.

I was glad when he turned back to my brother. My heart was almost beating out of my chest like it often did when Dad was on the prowl, only I didn't feel scared. There was no doubt in my mind that my feelings for him were becoming more confusing by the day.

Don't start thinking that way. Nothing's going to happen. You don't want *anything to happen. Once you're through all this, you just need to keep your head down and do your work. Trying to help the Underground find people to work with is one thing. A relationship? No way.*

But something in my heart rebelled against these thoughts as I watched Leon watch Jed. 'How long before he wakes up this time?'

'It should be soon.'

'What do we do?'

'The same thing we did before. I'm hoping there'll be a sign of some improvement, though. I need to move your family out of here.'

'Where to?'

'The Underground.'

With Sasha still on the warpath? 'Are you going to be allowed to?'

'Sasha will help your family whether she likes it or not. She knows it's a risk to leave them out in the open like this, with two test subjects in the family. And even though she's played it cool about your talent, she still wants to use it. She'll make a fuss, but she'll take them in and they'll be safer there than they are here.'

'When do you think we should move?'

'As soon as Jed's well enough. Tell your mother to start packing whatever you need but keep it light. We'll only be able to make one quick trip.'

I looked at the threadbare sheets and the three hole-filled dresses hanging in Mother's closet. That wouldn't be a problem. We hardly had anything anyway.

He turned back to my brother and watched him. What would he remember when he woke up ... if he did? How much anguish would he carry with him from his time at Kore's? Had he been strapped to that table, pleading for his life, like I'd imagined? Had Leon ripped his body out of that woman's reach as she continued with her macabre job?

I didn't know that story yet. 'Do you want to talk about what happened?'

He looked clueless.

135

'When you rescued Jed.'

That brought a scowl to his face. 'The less said about that the better.' But after a moment, he continued, 'I tried to get in to at least see if your brother was there first. After all, no point in making waves if I didn't need to, right? But it was difficult. I had to pull rank over Marcus pretty hard.'

'Marcus?' I couldn't remember hearing that name before.

'The weaselly-looking guy who was outside your cell a lot. The one who rattled the bars.'

Oh, the little coward. Had he suddenly got a backbone? He would have had to, to stand up to Leon.

'Yeah, Kore nearly killed him when you escaped. He didn't want to risk anything happening to any of his other prisoners.'

So Marcus was more afraid of Kore than he was of Leon. That made sense. He was capable of being bold if he had the right motivation, it seemed.

'He made such a fuss I barely managed to get a look at the cells before Kore was alerted.'

'So what did you do?'

He shrugged. 'The only thing I could do. I challenged Kore for leadership.'

That made my mouth drop open. 'You *what*?'

He looked ashamed. 'I needed some kind of a commotion, so I challenged Kore for leadership of his gang and then threw a few things around, causing as much of a mess as I could.

'It helped that some of his people wanted this. I'd been approached before, on the sly, about taking Kore's place, so some of his gang leapt to my defence. Eventually, I let my path of destruction take me towards the cells. Fortunately, I knew when the next power outage was going to be, so—'

Whoa, what? 'How could you know that?' Those power outages

were random because not all the bugs had been ironed out of the system.

His smirk told me otherwise. 'You really think they just happen? It's not difficult to hack into the system. I can do it with my link. Why do you think the power was cut to your cell door when you got out? I had to enlist Sasha's help for an outage that big, though. That made the timing a bit tricky.'

Now I had another reason to help Sasha.

He resumed his tale. 'I gathered your brother up and headed for the door. Unfortunately, Marcus decided he was still going to try and stop me. I couldn't let him tell Kore I'd left with a prisoner, especially which one it was, so …'

He wouldn't look me in the eye so I prompted him. 'So?'

'I slammed him into the wall.'

That didn't seem so bad. 'And?'

He wet his lips. 'It was hard enough to kill him.'

'Oh.'

He watched me, his eyes dissecting every expression on my face. 'So how do you feel about having a murderer lounging about in your mother's house?'

'Seriously? You killed a guy who tried to kill you? That's not murder.' Was it? I honestly didn't know. Could I hold Leon responsible if he willingly killed someone? At one time, I might have, when I'd been young and there had still been a small shred of innocence in me. But how many times had I imagined my father falling down the stairs at our old unit? Watching him tumble backwards, his head striking the wall with a crack? I'd been living with the thought of his death for years, trying not to see it, trying not to want it, but I couldn't deny that the thought of it brought relief, not regret.

Maybe that's why I didn't judge Leon for this. Were we both murderers? Did it make a difference if mine was only in my head?

He looked down. 'I'm not sure Marcus really stood a chance

of stopping me. I killed him anyway. And I meant to. Maybe it was because I didn't want him to tell Kore about the prisoner I'd taken, but maybe …'

He gave me a long look and it felt like he was on the verge of something, some kind of admission, but then he seemed to draw back. 'You know, you're the most difficult person to figure out. I'll admit that I didn't think you'd break down sobbing when I told you I'd killed Marcus, but I expected …'

'What?'

'I don't know, some kind of reaction. But it's probably a good thing. I wouldn't want you to kick me out.'

I was about to tell him that he'd have to be drunk to be kicked out of this house when I heard a sound that brought terror to my heart. Some of it must have leaked through my eyes because Leon sat up, alert. 'What?'

He hadn't recognised the mad scrambling in the next room as Mother rushed back in the front door. She hadn't been gone nearly long enough to get all the groceries she needed. I heard the sound of the bolts being drawn and the door locked.

Then came the pounding, the ominous *thump, thump, thump* from the other side. My father's fist crashed against the front door again. I could hear his muffled voice. 'Open up, Marge. I know you're in there. Come on, don't keep me waiting.'

Mother charged through the bedroom door. 'He followed me home. Stay in here.'

But fear of my father was subsiding. In its place was a bubbling mess of fury that he'd decided I was worth no more than the price of a beer and my brother meant no more than a few extra credits on his link. I wasn't hiding in this room.

I raced into the living room, grabbing Kathleen and Lenny and practically throwing them into Mother's bedroom. 'Protect them,' I ordered Izrod. Yes, he was Izrod now. Izrod could keep them safe. I watched my brother and sister huddle around him, trembling, as he looked from me to them in confusion.

I shut the door.

'Quick.' My mother shoved her computer into my hands. 'You remember where to hide it?' She raced around the room, hiding the food she'd just bought, as well as crockery, cutlery, anything of value, anything he could use to harm us. I raced to the bedroom and put the computer in its hidey-hole.

I went to stride back into the living room but she stopped me in the doorway. 'You should stay in there.'

'No.' I wasn't hiding from him anymore. I would stay and defend my family against the man who was determined to use us all until there was nothing left.

She held me in place, but we heard the door splinter. I didn't know what he had this time, but he used it to crack a large fissure down the entire length of the door and he reached through and unlocked it, drawing back the bolts.

He strode in, his eyes bloodshot and streaming, his nose bloated, his face red. Then he saw me and he staggered back. 'What … what … you …'

That's right. He'd thought I was Kore's plaything now. Although the media sector had reported my return, I doubted my father had been sober long enough to notice.

I looked at his face, my new abilities letting me see him for the first time. I could feel my fear flitting away at the sight of this pathetic weakling who looked like he'd seen a ghost. He hunched his shoulders against my mother, a woman who'd only ever shown him love and compassion.

My father was a stinking coward. I should have guessed that long ago.

'Yes, I'm here,' I said, my voice unwavering. 'Jed's here too. And he's staying here. And so are Mother and Kathleen and Lenny.' I stalked up to him, taking great pleasure in watching him shrink back. 'And if you so much as lay a finger on any of them, you will regret it.'

I could see his old bravado rising. 'So you got away, did you? I bet Kore would like you back. Maybe he'll pay more for you this time.' I was pretty sure his chuckle was meant to scare me, but it sounded so weak it was difficult to see him as a threat.

He clenched his hand around my forearm. I planted my feet firmly on the ground. 'I'm not going anywhere with you.'

'No, she's not,' said Mother, much to my surprise. Love for him was still on her face, but I could see love for me overriding it. 'Go. Leave us alone. You won't take any of my children away from me again.'

'*Your* children?' my father spat. '*My* children. *My* property. *My* belongings. They're only valuable if they can be traded. And I can do that now. Put them to use, rather than see them run off and make money, hoarding it for themselves with no thought for the man who raised them.'

He dragged me towards the door but there was no way I was going this time. 'You get your damn hands off me or—'

The bedroom door slammed open, the doorknob cracking the wall behind it. Leon stood in the doorway, his frame filling it, his eyes on fire. He took measured steps towards my father, who turned white and scurried with stumbling steps for the door.

'W-what are you doing in my home?' he said, trying to puff his chest out.

Leon's tread was silent as he approached, his eyes never leaving my father. As Leon reached him, my father took a swing at him, but Leon grabbed him by the shirt and raised him half a metre off the ground, slamming him against the wall.

'This is the last time you will come here,' he snarled. 'This family is under my protection now and if you so much as show your face in this house or even this street, I will tear you apart.' He slammed him against the wall again. 'And don't think I won't do that, or that I'm not capable, or that you'll come back when I'm not around. I can find you and I can take you down. And don't run to Kore either. Do you think he'll welcome you back, knowing he didn't even get to keep what you sold him? You'll be lucky if he doesn't put *you* in a cell.'

Dad's eyes rolled back in his head as he tried to push Leon off. His eyes darted to me first, then to his wife. Mother clasped her hands but made no move to help him. He let out a tiny squeak that I think was meant to sound defiant. He tried again to pry off Leon's fists where they clenched his shirt, but eventually, he hung limp in his hold.

Only then did Leon lower him to the ground. 'Now get out.'

My father staggered back, managed to stumble to the door and fumbled outside. I heard two thumps which were, I imagine, him hitting the ground as he tried to run on unsteady legs. But he must have dragged himself on because the shuffling steps retreated.

The silence he left behind was deafening. I looked at Leon, at Mother, at Lenny and Kathleen peering through the door. Leon was breathing heavily and rolled his shoulders a little.

'Mother?'

Light filled my mother's face. She darted to the bedroom, to her bed, where Jed was blinking and looking around, dazed. Mother wrapped her arms around him. 'My darling! You've come back to me!'

Leon strode in after her, peering over her shoulder. Jed shrank back at the sight of him.

'It's all right, Jed,' I said. 'He's a friend.'

Leon squatted down beside him. 'How do you feel, kid?'

Jed's face was still pale, his voice weak. 'My head hurts. And my wrists. And ankles. Why am I tied to the bed?'

Mother's hands reached for the bonds. Leon seemed about to stop her, then straightened up. Mother released Jed, then Leon helped her lift my brother so he was sitting, my mother plumping up some pillows to support him.

'Do you think he's all right?' I asked Leon in a low voice.

'Maybe. It's hard to tell. He was out of it for much less time than the others, but maybe it's because he's so young, maybe it's because Kore changed the formula. I don't know.'

Jed peered around through bloodshot orbs before looking up at Mother. 'I'm hungry.'

She sat back, satisfied. 'He's fine. There's never anything wrong with a hungry boy.'

As she bustled off to make him something, I raised my eyebrows at Leon. 'Is she right?'

'Well, she does have a point.' He picked up the plate of unfinished food from the floor and started feeding Jed. My brother tried to wolf it down, but Leon made him go slowly.

Within a few hours, Jed's colour had returned and there was no sign of any further episodes. He had a headache and didn't argue when Mother prescribed more rest.

'I think we could all do with a good night's sleep.'

But Leon stood. 'We should leave here and get to somewhere safe.'

Mother looked surprised. 'Not here?' I could see why she thought that this might be the best place for us now, since Leon had scared away the one person she feared.

'Others may come for your son. And your daughter. We shouldn't stay any longer than we have to.'

Mother looked down at Jed. 'He's still so exhausted. Surely it could wait until morning. What if moving him too soon causes a relapse or he has another attack?'

Leon scratched his chin. 'That's possible. But the longer we stay here …' He sighed. 'All right. A few hours' rest and then we go.'

Mother jumped onto her bed with Jed, curling herself protectively around her oldest son.

I could hear even breathing from Kathleen and Lenny's room. I'd put them to bed about an hour earlier. But I wasn't going to leave Leon sitting on the floor by himself, so plopped beside him.

He turned his eyes to my old bed. 'Why don't you get some rest?'

'I think even you need it after all this time.' Surely even he got tired sometimes, didn't he?

He looked the bed over. 'I don't think I'll fit.'

'Here.' I grabbed my pillow and got our spare blanket out for him. He laid them on the floor between my bed and Mother's and lay on his side, facing me.

Mother and Jed were already asleep when I turned the light out but I could feel Leon's gaze, even in the dark, as I climbed into bed.

'Do you usually sleep okay after a visit from your father?' he whispered.

Was that what he was worried about? I let out a laugh. 'If I couldn't sleep after every time he stumbles around drunk, I would probably never shut my eyes.'

I was only joking. Sometimes sleep had proved elusive for days, especially if my father was a daily spectre. But I couldn't get the words out.

It seemed I didn't need to. I felt one of his giant hands enclose mine. 'Trust me, he won't come back.'

I knew he was right. My father, coward that he was, wouldn't face down Izrod. I enjoyed the warmth of his hand on mine, heat passing up my arm, radiating through every part of me.

Could I trust him? Really? I had given up on trust a long time ago, determined just to keep my head down and get through every day. Was this the start of something new that might mean a future I could never have imagined?

No, I couldn't risk it. Memories of Dad's drunken bouts danced in my head like skeletons on a string.

But Leon's hand stayed on mine and I didn't want him to move it, so I laid my other hand on top of it and snuggled down for the best sleep I'd ever had in my family home.

CHAPTER FOURTEEN

I woke with five minutes to spare before my twelve-hourly check-in.

Leon was already up. I thought he might have been pacing and demanding that we get going, given Jed was sitting at the table eating his breakfast, but Leon sat next to him, eating twice as much, reaching out to tickle Kathleen whenever she dared to come too close. She shrieked and ran away but came back moments later so they could play the game again.

I couldn't believe what I was seeing—a man, someone my brothers and sister had been taught to fear—was playing with them, loving them, like the father they'd never had. I'd never seen my little sister look so carefree, as if she'd found her best friend ever. She gazed up at Leon adoringly, any fear she'd had of him long gone. Love shone in its place.

Jed also seemed relaxed, although tired. He didn't look at Leon, but nor was he casting frantic glances or jutting out a shoulder to guard against a cuff, as he might do with Dad.

Leon smiled at me as I came and grabbed a bowl of porridge for myself. 'Sleep well?' he asked.

'Yes.' I stopped short of telling him that it was the best sleep I'd had in years. 'Will we be going to the Underground today?'

He looked at Jed. 'No, I'm worried there could be another episode.'

I looked at my brother as well. I noticed a twitch in his eye and every few minutes a manic look passed over his face. I could see why Leon was concerned. It was surprising he didn't have him back in restraints. Maybe Mother had objected.

'I'll help your mother pack,' he said. 'We'll leave as soon as you get back from work. I'm hoping things will be more settled by then.'

I left for work soon after, trying not to dwell on how pleased I was that Leon would be there when I got back. I made my way through the quiet streets, around the vendors setting up their trades in the poor sector, then travelled through the other sectors. I went through the government sector checkpoints, one security guard enquiring after my brother. I was surprised that he remembered, but I suppose it was their job to keep track of why I was coming and going, and I had no intention of staying in my unit until everyone was safe at the Underground.

The grinding elevator took me down into the Archives and I stepped out into the musty scent of the papers mixed with the metallic smell of the digital files. I was early. Even Derek wasn't on duty, although Susan was behind her desk and looked up as I entered. 'Good morning, Eden. How are you today? Is your brother any better?'

'He's still a bit unsettled, thank you, Head Keeper. My mother's having quite a time with him.'

'You're a good girl to be such a help to her.'

I headed for my cart. It was full to overflowing.

Susan noticed me eyeing it. 'Yes, Official Hensen and Miss Gregor returned after you left yesterday. They were going through several files. There's some new project at the planning stage, I believe.'

I looked at the files in my cart. Most of them were paper; not on the ancient papers and books that had been used before our society had been rebuilt, but new ones from after its rebirth. They seemed to be related to infrastructure, some to the electrical grid. Maybe they'd found a way to stop all the power outages. I'd have to tell Leon; it might not be the best thing for the Underground. Other files related to some building project and something marked 'waterways'.

It wasn't long before the other employees turned up and we all got on with work, filing what had been used the day before and pulling out the new requests.

Susan called me over halfway through the day. 'Eden, can you take these files up to the governor's office? They've put in a special request.'

'Certainly, Head Keeper.' I hadn't been allowed up there before. I wondered why they weren't coming down into the Archives to view them.

'Here,' she said, pressing her link. My link beeped. 'That's a special one-time authorisation you'll need before they'll let you in. Just hold up your link at the checkpoints so they can scan it.'

I glanced at the files as I travelled up in the elevator. It looked like more infrastructure stuff, blueprints or plans on some buildings or other. I couldn't work out what it was, except that one of them had a lot of pipes in it.

I had to go through three internal checkpoints before I got to the governor's office. Each time, I was asked my business, looked over, scowled at, and had the code on my link scanned. I wondered if they'd always been this fussy about security or if they were afraid of Leon. Try as I might, I didn't think I'd ever be mistaken for him.

I examined the faces of the security guards as I passed. Most of them looked like your standard no-nonsense guards, but a couple looked furtive, their eyes darting around. Were they afraid of something or someone? Another couple of them had greedy faces that dissected everyone who came near. I wondered if they took bribes. I made a mental note of their names in case they came in useful later.

Finally, I was at the governor's office. My feet sank into the carpet from the moment I left the private elevator. While the other floors in this building weren't shabby, this one was furnished with deep blue walls and contained two desks of the richest red wood. I was pretty sure they weren't plastic replicas. As I came nearer, I could smell a tangy scent on them.

A woman sat at each desk, the plaques before them labelling them junior assistants. Both had blonde hair piled high and wore exquisite makeup and clothes that looked like they cost more than our old unit. They looked up as I approached with the guard who'd travelled up in the elevator with me.

'Eden Fittell here with files from the Archives for the governor's conference,' he said to the one on the left.

She flicked her blue eyes at me and rose from the desk. 'Follow me.'

I walked obediently behind her as she approached a door at the back of the room. She scanned her link on the lock and opened it, gesturing for me to go in ahead of her.

She shut the door behind me, leaving the guard outside. The large room was filled with desks, all of them looking as polished and slick as the ones in the first room. At each desk sat a man or woman, all with computers in front of them, tapping away, writing, sorting, tossing remarks back and forth. My appearance didn't seem to register with them. One or two had the same greedy look as the guards, a few looked more than a little nervous, and another was so scared I was surprised she wasn't cowering under her chair. I reminded myself that only I could see that.

As we walked to the end of the office, we passed through another door into the next room, which was smaller, holding only a few desks. Miss Gregor was at the nearest one. She looked up as we approached. 'Ah, the files we've been waiting for. Good. The conference will be starting shortly. Thank you for bringing them up, Eden.'

Miss Gregor had seemed so timid when I'd first seen her, before my eyes had been opened, but now she looked the opposite. There was something bright about her face, with strength shining through. I wondered why she hid it. Maybe it had something to do with the touch of deviousness I could see as well.

'Oh, hello, Eden. How are you?' It was Official Hensen.

I turned to face him.

Control. Get yourself under control!

I plastered what I hoped was my usual smile on my face as I replied. 'Hello, Official Hensen. I'm fine, thanks. Did the conference at Reacher's Pass go well?'

There was no sign of the pleasant friendliness I'd always seen on Official Hensen's face. It was a seething mass of hatred and evil, with the most dangerous eyes I'd ever seen. They exuded corruption and malice. Even Kore had looked safer than him.

I think his smile was meant to be pleasant but his lip curled too much. 'It was very constructive, thank you. But I'm more concerned about you. I heard what happened. Are you all right?'

I struggled for the words, especially now I distrusted everything he said. Was he working with Kore? With someone else? Was he working for nobody and was just a real creep? I quelled the panic as I considered the best way to answer. If he was already working with Kore, he probably knew what had happened. He might even know that Leon had broken in and taken Jed. What if he knew Jed was my brother? Would he be suspicious?

My answer came a fraction later than it should have. 'Yeah. It was … kind of scary. I was worried that something bad might happen, you know, that I'd never get out or I'd go crazy, like the others. But the power went out and I tried the door and it opened, so I just ran out.' I hoped I wasn't shaking. I hoped the fear that coursed through me wasn't written in my eyes.

Miss Gregor didn't seem to notice anything. She stood calmly by, waiting for Official Hensen to finish.

Again there was that creepy smile and this time he put his hand on my shoulder as well. It took everything I had not to flinch.

'Well, don't push yourself too hard,' he snarled. 'Make sure you take it easy. If work gets too much for you, you should take some time off. And if you need to talk to anyone, we can arrange something for you, I'm sure. We always take care of our employees.'

From the look on his face, he ate them.

'Certainly, sir,' I said, handing over the files. 'Here are the things you requested.'

'Thank you so much.' He came so close that I had to stop myself from taking a step back. 'And remember what I said, don't overdo it. Make sure you take the time to recover.'

'I will, sir. Thank you.'

I turned around and made sure my steps were measured, unhurried, as I left. Everything had to be normal. But I was already cataloguing every file I'd delivered to them. There had been ones about the power grid. Was he planning to destabilise it further or destroy it completely? And what were the others? More infrastructure. Roads and buildings. I wished I could remember which ones.

I sleepwalked back down to the Archives, barely noticing the checkpoints and scowls of the security guards. Was Official Hensen planning something? Maybe not. Maybe he was just a hideous person. And even if he was in league with Kore or something like that, he wasn't necessarily going to be using the files I'd just delivered to the governor's office, where he was going into a conference with the governor and Miss Gregor and probably a dozen other people.

I needed to talk to Leon. Maybe he'd have some idea. Perhaps he'd heard the official's name when he'd been at Kore's.

I stayed there the full day, refusing to leave early or even glance towards the elevator, my only escape route. When the day finally ended, I went through all the checkpoints, explaining again about the problems with my brother, and made sure I walked steadily through the government sector. Even after that, I calmed myself and walked to Mother's. Granted, I was quicker than usual, but I didn't scamper in terror.

Kathleen let me in. 'Eden, I love having you home.'

I put my arms around her. She deserved it. She'd been through a lot, especially the past couple of months. 'Glad to be back.'

I glanced around the room. It was a hive of activity, with Leon and Mother bundling things into packs. Jed sat at the table, watching, his eyes tired. Kathleen went over to help too, although I wasn't sure how much of a help she was, while Lenny played on the floor with some of his toys.

'Edie!' he said and toddled over, wrapping his arms around my legs.

'Hi, Lenny.' But I looked at Leon over his head.

He assessed my face and stopped packing. 'Did something happen today?'

Damn. He'd picked up that something was wrong that easily? Wasn't I supposed to be an unreadable mask? What if Hensen had picked up on it as well? 'How did you know?'

'Just a guess,' he said.

'Yes, something happened today.'

'Did you find someone that we can use?'

'No. More like the opposite.'

He looked intrigued so I launched into my explanation. 'Official Hensen and Miss Gregor came back a couple of days ago. They were away at a conference. You know who they are?'

He nodded. 'What have you discovered about them?'

'Miss Gregor always came across as timid and small, but now I see her as much more confident than I ever would have thought. But Hensen ... it was hard to believe I ever thought he was a nice guy. He looked just about the evilest person I've ever seen. Even Kore didn't look as scary as him.'

This seemed to be a revelation. 'Official Hensen? Are you sure?'

'If this thing Kore put in my head actually works, then yes.'

He pondered that. 'I had suspicions that Kore has a contact in the government. I thought it was just some low-level bureaucrat, but if it's Hensen … What did he say to you today? Did you mention anything about your brother?'

'No, he seemed mainly concerned with me being kidnapped.' It was amazing how easy it was to talk about that to the person who'd done the kidnapping.

That seemed to relieve him a bit. 'That's old news. Have you mentioned your brother to anyone?'

'Yes. Every day. I have to tell them why I'm leaving the government sector. They need to know why I'm not using my unit. I told them I was coming here to help my mother with my brother. What else could I say?'

'Damn it. If he's as dangerous as you say, he'll definitely have asked them what's going on, especially if he's already working with Kore and you're the only victim who's returned to tell your tale. And that means he may know that Jed was at Kore's. Especially if he realises that I was the one who got Jed out.'

Mother emerged from the bedroom, her computer tucked under her arm.

'I'm not sure you can take that with you,' Leon said.

She looked uncertain. 'What about my work?'

'We'll have to discuss that with Sasha. I don't think you'll be able to continue it. It might be best to tell your employer that you're moving to Reacher's Pass or Twin City. Say you've got family there and need their help with the kids, anything to explain you leaving town completely. It's better if everyone you know thinks you're far away from here.'

152

Mother clutched the computer. 'Moving cities doesn't mean I can't continue to work for them.'

That didn't sway him. 'We'll see what Sasha says. Your computer could be traced to the Underground. I don't think she'll want to risk that.'

Fortunately, most of the packing had been done already, so in five minutes, we were ready to go. I helped Kathleen put a pack on her back, put one on my own and then grabbed Lenny's. Jed carried his own and Leon picked up two others, one in each mighty fist.

As we stepped out onto the dark street, I kept looking left and right, my eyes piercing every shadow. Were there spies there? Security? Would Official Hensen send someone to arrest us? Would he even see me as a threat?

We hurried along, Leon constantly trying to urge us to go faster. His head twitched from side to side, alert to every sound. 'Someone may come at us,' he said to me in a low voice. 'If they do, get everyone else there and I'll take care of them.'

He expected me to leave him behind? 'Absolutely not. I'll stay with you.'

'No, Eden. You need to get your family to safety.'

I felt something tear in me at his words. He was responsible for my family's safety more than I was. He'd got us out of that fire. He'd got me away from Kore. He'd gone in and rescued Jed at great personal risk. He'd scared my father away. If he thought I was going to leave him while he took another risk for us, he was crazy.

'Yeah, like they'd let us in if we left you to fend for yourself.' I tried to make my voice sound as dead as it usually did, but something leaked into it, some kind of desperation that frightened me.

Kathleen's scream lanced through me like a dagger. I turned to see her held by a misshapen man, his face dark in the shadows. Then Lenny's wail rang out as he struggled in the grip of another who grinned wickedly, revealing an ugly gap in his teeth. He had a knife at Lenny's throat.

Adrenaline pulled me in both directions, my hands shaking with each moment of indecision. Which way did I go—to help my little brother or my sister? And how was I going to do either?

Mother didn't hesitate. 'Let them go!' She pummelled Lenny's assailant with her fists, but he shoved her to the ground and held her down there with his foot as her shrieking turned to begging.

Jed looked at me, white-faced, just as Leon lurched away from me. 'Put them down.'

I looked in every dirty corner of the street. There had to be a weapon I could use. A stick. That would do.

But there was something else I could do. I turned to Jed. His eyes had glazed over and I was worried he wouldn't even hear what I was saying, but he turned to me at the sound of his name.

'Run to the end of the street. Turn right. Go …' How many doors was it again? '… Three doors down. There's a set of stairs that lead to another door below street level. There's a lot of garbage in front of it, so you have to really look for it. Go tell them what's happening and who we're with.'

I thought one of the men might try and stop him, but they were both watching Leon warily. I guess they didn't see the rest of us being able to take them down, and they were probably right. Mother was still struggling on the ground. She started to pinch and scratch Gap-Tooth's leg. He rammed his foot harder into her, Lenny swinging around as he did it. 'Quiet, witch.'

Leon grabbed his extended leg and twisted it around until we heard it crack. The man shrieked and slid to the ground, Lenny and the knife tumbling away. Mother scampered to her feet and picked up my sobbing baby brother.

A knife. That was a lot better than a stick. I dived on it, clutching it to my chest, nearly stabbing myself in the process. Now what could I do with it? I waved it in front of Gap-Tooth. 'Stay where you are!'

I stood in front of Mother and Lenny. No one was getting through me … unless they knew how to fight with a knife. My hands started to sweat. It didn't matter. I would last as long as I could.

Gap-tooth rolled around groaning as Leon turned to face Kathleen's assailant, who had produced his own knife. My sister shook in terror, her big eyes begging me to help her, but Leon was closer and stood a better chance of getting my sister out of there unscathed.

'Put her down, Hedley,' he said, his voice rumbling with growing ferocity.

The other man finally stepped into the light. I thought I recognised him from Kore's gang. He wasn't quite as big as Leon, but he was close, the cords of muscle on his shoulders looking even more massive. He grinned evilly. 'You know, Leon, I might have listened if it wasn't for her.' He nodded at me.

Leon charged at Hedley, who threw Kathleen to the ground and thrust the knife at Leon, but he snapped his hand out and grabbed him before it connected, holding Hedley's hand high and tightening his grip. Hedley dropped the knife but kicked Leon in the knees.

I jumped forward and waved the knife at him. He looked amused, fortunately not realising that while his attention was on me, it wasn't on Leon. He charged at Hedley again, wrestling him to the ground.

I kept one eye on them and watched Gap-Tooth with the other. He was trying to struggle to his feet. 'Don't even think about it,' I snarled.

'Go on then,' he said, 'Stick me, little girl.' He gathered himself up, preparing to spring.

Great. He was going to call my bluff. Well, if he was going to kill me, I wouldn't make it easy for him. I clenched the knife to try and hide my trembling. *Remember, no one can see who you really are. If you look confident, you could still beat him.* Okay, so that was probably being a bit too optimistic.

A hand appeared beside mine. 'Here, let me.'

I looked up into Knifer's eyes and the frantic feeling drained away, making my knees turn to jelly. I managed to stay upright as Knifer took the knife from me before flinging his own at Gap-tooth's leg. Gap-Tooth screamed and crawled around on the ground before being picked up by a couple of people I recognised from the Underground. They took him away, moaning and groaning.

I looked over at Leon. He knelt before Hedley, who was foaming at the mouth.

Knifer looked at him. 'What happened?'

'I think he took something.'

Knifer snorted. 'Typical of Kore. Make sure everyone's dead so no one gives the game away.' He turned to another man who was with him. 'Go after the others and make sure they don't let the other guy kill himself. He could be a mine of useful information.'

The man took off, only to reappear a moment later. 'Too late.'

'Damn it,' muttered Knifer. He put out his hand and helped Leon to his feet. 'Looks like we arrived just in time.'

Leon raised an eyebrow. 'What, you don't think I could have handled that?'

'Never mind,' said Knifer, looking around at my family. 'Who are these?'

'My mother, brothers and sister,' I said.

'Kore's after them because of the boy. Having him survive, and her as well, could be a liability.'

'Okay, let's not stay out in the open any longer, then,' said Knifer.

He picked up Mother's pack and put it on his back, waving them forward. Mother was still sitting on the ground clutching Lenny, whose tears were drying but his eyes were wild. Kathleen sat next to her, tears rolling down her cheeks. Jed had an awkward arm around her.

Leon looked at me. 'You help your mother. I'll take Kathleen.' He scooped my sister up in his arms.

Jed got to his feet, rubbing his eyes. I thought I saw a trace of tears on his cheeks. I went over to Mother. Her eyes were wide as she rocked Lenny back and forth. I got her to look at me. 'Mother, we need to get going. There's safety just around the corner. Come on.'

She blinked up at me. I usually only saw this shadow on her face after Dad had visited. It broke my heart to see it taking up residence there when I'd hoped we were fleeing to safety. Was she finally broken?

But although her eyes remained shadowed, she took my hand. 'Yes, of course.' I helped her to her feet while she still clutched Lenny.

I felt a rush of relief as we turned the final corner and were ushered in the door to the Underground.

CHAPTER FIFTEEN

Knifer led us through to the main assembly area. Several people were milling around, some working at one of the tables, others eating with their families. There were more children this time, maybe because it was earlier in the evening.

We got lots of curious glances as we weaved our way through everyone, but some looked furious at the sight of us. Why, because we'd take their food or units? I had to remind myself that it was likely I was the only person who could see this. Most people probably kept a generally compliant face for everyone else's clouded eyes.

Knifer took us over to a corner. 'This is Jackie,' he said, gesturing to a woman with a no-nonsense haircut and a face to match. She was the oldest person I'd seen in the Underground if her white hair was anything to go by, but she looked like she could hold her own with the rest of them, judging by the thickness of her arms. I wondered if she was another leftover from Kore's experiments. Her face contained total loyalty to the Underground.

'Jackie, this family needs refuge,' Leon said. 'Kore's after them.' He indicated Jed. 'The boy here has been at Kore's and he did something to him.'

She cast a probing eye over my brother. 'Something new?'

'I think it's just chaos but I can't be sure.'

Her dark eyes bored into him. 'I told you a while ago I thought you were compromised. I wouldn't be surprised if Kore has been keeping things from you. You should have got out of there a long time ago.'

'Tell that to Sasha. She wanted more intel.'

That made Jackie screw her mouth up. 'What's the point of intel if it's fake? Anyway, I'll settle the others and then take the boy to Aurora and see if she can figure out what Kore's put in him.' She turned to my mother who, to my relief, greeted her warmly. That was more like it. Her eyes were scanning around and she seemed reassured by the sight of so many families. Maybe she'd thought everyone here would look like Leon.

Leon turned to me. 'Let's go see Sasha.'

Sasha was already in the same meeting room where I'd met her the first time. She had a stack of files and a computer beside her. She spared us a glance that reeked of disappointment, then looked back at the screen. 'You expect me to take in another dependent family?'

'If you want my help you will,' I snapped.

She rose to her feet. 'How dare you? Let me remind you that you haven't exactly been of great use to me so far. Don't assume you're invaluable.'

'Am I?' said Leon.

She seemed a little more surprised by that and looked between us. 'If you've gone and become emotionally involved then maybe not.'

I didn't believe a word of it. Leon had told me earlier that she would grumble and complain, and it seemed she was going to try, but despite the fire in her eyes, her expression held more resignation than anything else. He was right—she still wanted my help, even with the inconvenient appearance of the rest of my family.

Leon reflected Sasha's fury back at her and her eyes quickly cooled, although she tilted her chin up. 'You've been an assistance in many areas, Leon, it's true, but you've got to learn to keep your head in the game. You're not the only source of intel on Kore. And no longer useful at all in that regard, I hear.' Her smouldering eyes flashed to me. 'But we have other avenues of intel and they've proven useful.'

'What have they told you?' he asked.

'That Kore is planning a major offensive. That he intends to infect the entire city with whatever he gave to those people. He wants to throw the city into chaos.'

Leon's eyebrows pulled together. 'I can't see how or even why he'd do that. He can't very well inject a large portion of the population with his latest drug. When I was with him, he seemed more interested in trialling the drug he used on Eden.'

'Maybe he gave that up when he thought it didn't work on me,' I said.

'I don't care what you say, Leon. This is new information I've received,' Sasha said. 'And not just from one source.'

That gave Leon pause for thought. 'If he does want to do that, how's he planning to administer chaos? He'd have to find a way that's quicker than injecting the drug. He can't just go out and stick needles in hundreds of arms.'

But would that be his game plan? Kore was innovative and more than a little unhinged. Maybe he had another idea. Even if it didn't work completely, it would still be catastrophic. I imagined hordes of people foaming at the mouth and raging through the city. A mob no one could control.

But that gave me an idea. My brother might be the best source of intel we had on Kore's latest plans. 'Do we know if he injected Jed? Maybe Kore gave it to him another way.'

'We need to talk to him,' said Leon.

Sasha waved her hand at an attendant standing by the door. 'Go and fetch Eden's brother, Jed. He's with the new family that just arrived.'

A few minutes later, Jed entered. He looked sheepish and was wiping crumbs from around his mouth. At least they'd fed him something. His eyes were wary as he saw Sasha but he didn't seem overly disturbed by her. What did she look like through normal eyes? I couldn't remember. A stern-faced but kind woman?

At least Sasha smiled at him. 'Jed, we've brought you here so you can recount for us what happened to you when you were in Kore's possession, up until the time Leon rescued you.'

He paled and his voice shook a little as he spoke. 'I don't want to talk about that.'

I could see that Sasha's limited patience was waning. 'We need to know.'

'Jed, don't be afraid,' I said. 'We just want to see if it gives us some idea of what Kore might be planning.'

He shifted from foot to foot and looked at Leon. 'Can't you tell them?'

Sasha's eyes started to smoulder again, but Leon didn't even glance at her. 'How about we try and remember together? I got there at about nine or so. Do you remember how long you'd been there when I arrived?'

'No,' he said morosely. 'I don't even remember you being there. I only remember waking up at home.'

I got the feeling Leon had anticipated that. 'Can you tell us the last thing you remember? Do you remember seeing the time? Did someone come to your cell?'

Jed looked down at his hands. I could see his legs trembling and quickly pulled up a chair for him. I knelt down next to him. 'Come on, Jed. You've always been good at remembering details. What about that creepy guy, the jailer? What was his name, Leon?'

'Marcus.'

'Yeah, Marcus. You know, the one who ran a stick down the

bars and looked crazy.'

'There were no bars on my cell.'

That's right. Kore had moved. Jed's hell was a little different from mine. Maybe one day we could compare notes.

But he had connected the dots. 'I think I know the one you mean. The crazy little one. He was the only person I saw once I was in the cell.'

Sasha leant forward. 'You don't remember anything else?'

'No. That weird guy would open a chute on the door and yell and taunt me.' I could see tears gathering in his eyes. 'I just wanted him to leave me alone.'

'Did he?' asked Leon.

'For a bit. He didn't come back until mealtime.'

That caught my interest. 'What did they feed you?'

'Just some bread and a bit of water. It was all stale, even the water, but I was hungry and thirsty so I finished it off.'

'And afterwards?' said Sasha.

'I remember waking up at home. Nothing else.'

Leon put his hand on Jed's shoulder. 'That's fantastic and so helpful. Thank you, Jed. You can go back to your family now.'

As soon as the door closed behind him, Leon turned back to Sasha. 'It's in the water.'

'You're sure it's not the food?'

'It's too risky. What if someone didn't eat everything or not the right thing? How could you even put it in everything? But put it in the water and it gets to everybody.'

'So they're going to poison the water,' Sasha said, drumming her fingers on the table. 'All the water? At the city's source?'

'And when?' Leon stroked his chin.

'Could he have done it already?' I asked.

'I can't imagine he would be able to organise it that quickly,' Leon said. 'He wasn't working on this when I was last there.'

'That you know of,' said Sasha.

'If he's planning to poison the whole city,' Leon continued, 'I think he'd need to stockpile quite a bit of the drug before he could.'

I hoped that was the case. We'd studied the desalination plant in the learning sector. It was on the border of the city, right near the ocean, taking the salt out of the water and making it drinkable. There had been talk about the learning sector touring one at some stage, but it had never come to pass.

'There should be security there,' I said. I remembered that from our almost-visit.

'Kore could get around that, especially if he has someone on the inside already.'

'Hm,' Sasha steepled her fingers. '*We* need someone on the inside.' Her eyes accused me. 'You were supposed to be helping with that.'

Yeah, yeah, whatever. But I did have some intel for her, although I wasn't sure she'd find it helpful. 'Whoever it is, make sure it's not Official Hensen.'

'Why not?'

It was uncomfortable to say, especially since before Kore's treatment he'd seemed nice, approachable, open. That version of him was like a mirage that had faded away. 'Let's just say that by the look of him, I'm not sure Kore's the bigger threat.'

Was that trust on her face? Maybe a thread of it. 'Are you sure about that?' She glanced between us before fixing her eyes on Leon. 'I'm putting a lot of faith in this girl, or should I say in Kore's abilities. What if what she does is nothing more than an emotive parlour trick? It would be nice if she could deliver something other than desperate family members.'

'Fine,' I said. 'If you want to trust anyone, I think Miss Gregor might be the way to go.'

Her eyebrows shot up. 'Gregor the Mouse?'

I'd thought that once too, but just as with Official Hensen, clarity had changed that. 'I don't think she's as mousey as she wants people to believe.' Of course, that didn't mean she was trustworthy either.

Sasha pondered that. 'Interesting. Very well, we'll see if we can make something out of that connection. In the meantime, try and find the blueprints for the water treatment plant. They must be in the Archives somewhere.'

'I can find them, but if you want me to get you a copy that could be a little difficult. However,' I continued before her face defaulted to disappointment, 'I can try and find out if anyone's had those files out recently. If Official Hensen has, it might be a sign that he's working with Kore.'

Sasha seemed at least reasonably satisfied as we left and I took a quick look at my link. 'It's so late. I need to get back.'

'Will you go back to your unit now?' asked Leon.

'I'll have to.' Would the government sector know my family had left their hovel? I didn't even know if they'd kept track of their whereabouts after the fire. They would probably have been happier to forget they'd ever existed. But what if they knew they'd disappeared? Would they ask me where they'd gone? What if Hensen found out?

'What's wrong?' Leon asked.

'What do you think I should tell them about my family?'

'Say they've moved to relatives at Twin City or Reacher's Pass. You've been telling them your mother's struggling to cope with Jed anyway. You could say she has relatives or friends there, whichever's the most plausible, and they've gone so she has some support.'

That might work. 'But what if Hensen finds out?'

He sighed. 'He's going to anyway, if he's the danger he seems to be.'

After I'd said goodbye to my family, I was surprised when Leon accompanied me to the door. 'I won't walk by your side,' he said, 'but

I won't be far away. I want to make sure you get back safely, especially if there are any more of Kore's people around.'

Why did that make me feel so good? I knew why, and it filled my whole body with warmth. 'Thanks.'

'And don't be surprised if I'm in your unit when you get home from work tomorrow night. I don't want you shrieking if I sneak up on you. Someone outside might hear.' He grinned as he melted away into the darkness of the street.

'Thanks for that,' I said through my teeth. But my feet were light as I walked, despite the dark streets and the occasional dangerous glare. I would see Leon again tomorrow.

CHAPTER SIXTEEN

The next day, the security guard at the first checkpoint enquired after my brother. Given the events of the past few days, I wondered if it was casual interest, professional concern or suspicious investigation.

'My mother's still struggling. She's gone to visit some friends in Twin City and taken my brothers and sister with her.' I'd decided that was the best answer. We had no family to speak of, but Mother had said once that she knew someone in Twin City. As long as they didn't ask for details, that would do.

After that, it was down to the Archives. In spite of my assurances to Sasha, I knew it wouldn't be easy to find out who had been looking at the plans for the water treatment plant. The head keeper kept the records of who'd borrowed what on her computer and they couldn't be accessed by anyone else. I might be able to see it on the logs that were kept on our carts, but only if the records were digital. And the digital records were only borrowed if they needed to see intricate details or update the file to match changes they made online. I was hoping that the plans for the water treatment plant would be intricate enough to be required every time.

I looked around the Archives. They were quiet that morning. Even Susan wasn't at her desk. Was anyone else there?

I wandered through the dark shelves, poking in every corner. Did I dare try and access Susan's computer? I didn't have the necessary codes so the system might flag me if I tried. For the moment, I would make do with the carts.

I started with my own. I wheeled it down the walkways, as I normally did, moving to a corner that was dark and unseen. I brought up the records. Was there anything relating to the water grid? There were a couple of records that talked about pipes running under the city. I'd heard a casual mention that some needed replacing. Was that how they planned to get Kore's formula in?

I heard the familiar groan of the elevator. The doors slid open and I resumed my work, only to realise I was in the wrong place to put away anything that was on my cart.

The doors opened to reveal Official Hensen, Miss Gregor and Governor Jerrill.

'I don't know what we do now,' the governor said, heading over to Susan's desk. 'Does anyone know how to do her job?'

'I'm sure someone here does,' said Hensen, sneering, but I was sure only I could see that. He looked up, peering into the dark corners of the Archives. I wheeled my cart out into the light. 'Ah! Eden! Do you know how to access the head keeper's files?'

Seriously? He was inviting me to do the very thing I wanted to do? But while I was the only one there yet, I was hardly the most experienced after the head keeper. 'Where's Susan?'

Hensen looked gleeful although I thought he was aiming for sorrowful. Miss Gregor looked noble and strong. The governor looked disturbed.

Hensen came up to me and put his hands on my shoulders in a gesture I used to find comforting. I made sure I smiled, at least until he said, 'I'm sorry, Eden. She died last night.'

'What? How?' Shock was all right. Shock would be expected. I allowed it to fill my face. And then to further throw them off, 'Was it Izrod again?' It felt so weird, so wrong, to call him that.

'No. She had a bad heart,' said Miss Gregor. 'It gave out last night. At least, that's what the medical sector told us.' The look on her face was guarded, but what against? Did she think Leon might have slipped Susan something, something ultimately from Kore? But why would Kore switch to causing a heart attack rather than just using chaos? Maybe that was more difficult now Leon was no longer with him. But if so, how had Kore gotten to her at all?

I did everything I could to keep my eyes away from Hensen. Could he have been involved? He certainly didn't seem troubled by her death, but given what I knew of him, I wouldn't have expected him to break down and wail.

Fortunately, he moved away from me. It had been difficult not to flinch under his touch. 'Do you know how her computer system works? Can you access it?'

I knew that there were keepers more senior than me who would have more of a right to do just that, but they weren't there. I hid my glee, also wondering if I could hide any snooping I needed to do for the Underground. 'I'll try. I'll need an override code to get in without a security flag.'

I sat at Susan's desk and brought up the system. The lights flickered off for a few minutes, but the power stayed on to the computer. I allowed the screen to scan my retina, thankful it had been put into the system in the last few weeks. Miss Gregor had an override code on hand for me.

I entered it and Susan's confidential screen came up. 'What are you looking for?' I asked.

This led to a flurry of whispers between the three. It was clear the governor didn't want me to know what was going on. I could hear Hensen trying to placate her.

'We have no choice,' he whispered in the end, before turning back to me. 'Any logs showing what files she might have accessed in the past twenty-four hours.'

That was easy enough. And again, it was something I wanted to see. I hoped I could memorise it or print my own copy if they wanted something to take back upstairs with them. Maybe I could accidentally print two.

But to my surprise, all the file information from the past week had been wiped. I searched as much as I could throughout the system but couldn't find anything anywhere. There were records from the previous week, but nothing more recent than that.

This revelation didn't go down well. Again, Hensen didn't seem too troubled, but I wasn't sure if that was because he'd caused this, because he liked the mayhem, or because it suited his plans. It was difficult to interpret the motive behind the evil on his face.

As the three of them hissed at each other, I went back to my cart and began to put files away, keeping my face as neutral as possible, although I felt so much for Susan. She had been jumping at the shadows of shadows. Could she have known this was going to happen? Had someone threatened her? What did it mean if they had?

Some of my fellow keepers started arriving. They murmured at the sight of the officials, their mouths dropping open when Official Hensen told them what had happened to Susan. He pretended to comfort them briefly before returning to the place he really wanted to be—next to the governor.

I spent the rest of their visit with my head down, doing my work, my ears constantly attuned to snatches of conversation. They stayed at Susan's desk for an hour before they started roaming the rows of files.

'The file on the Osten Bridge Treatment Plant seems to be missing,' said the governor. She was standing near me but I wasn't sure if she was talking to me or not.

'Ma'am?' I said.

She turned her eyes on me. 'Eden, am I right in saying that the master digital files should all be in this area?'

I looked at the shelves before her. There were rows of thin drawers, each one holding numerous small digital files. 'If it's not being updated by the tech department or borrowed it should, yes.' I brought up the call number for the Osten Bridge Treatment Plant plans on my cart's system. Once I had that, I went straight to the drawer where it should have been located. She was right—it wasn't there. Four other files were missing from that drawer alone.

'Which ones go in these spaces?' she asked.

'Um … it looks like other plans.' All for treatment plants and water grids. And not just our city's either. I didn't realise we'd had anything to do with the water grids in Reacher's Pass or Twin City, but apparently, we kept copies of them. Or had, at any rate. They were gone.

'They must be being updated or borrowed,' I said.

'They're not,' she replied. 'I've already checked.'

'But surely they have copies online.'

I could tell from her face that if they'd had any, they didn't now. What had happened to them? She was obviously unnerved by it and I didn't blame her. Had Hensen done it or someone else? Maybe he was covering Kore's tracks so no one could stop him.

Once it became clear that the masters had gone, Governor Jerrill gathered all the keepers together. 'The files of the plans for several key pieces of infrastructure are missing.' I could see sweat beading on her upper lip. 'These files need to be found. I want everyone here to check the records on your carts for who might have had these files last. Also, try and recall the last time you were asked for them and who wanted them. I want a list sent to me via your links by the end of the day.'

She then turned to Adriana and began hissing at her. I could see her shaking her head, growing more and more wide-eyed as the governor snarled at her.

To my surprise, Adriana turned to me. 'Eden, we need to help the governor find any paper copies of the plans. Do you know where they might be?'

She was asking me? She'd worked there for five years. I'd been there for weeks! But I quickly realised her plan, as she retreated from the governor until she was behind me, then scampered off.

I became the focus of the governor's fury. 'Well, do we have any or not?'

'I don't think so.'

I spent the next few hours leading her around the Archives, looking for anything that resembled paper plans. But although we managed to find some for the old pre-conflict water system, there was nothing for the new.

By the time they left, Governor Jerrill looked despondent, Hensen both gleeful and annoyed, and Miss Gregor calm and composed. While I could interpret the governor and Miss Gregor's looks, I didn't know why Hensen would look simultaneously disappointed and delighted. I'd have to report it to Leon to see if he had any idea.

As I finished work for the day, I touched the secret button on my link. Hopefully, Leon would come to see me as soon as he could.

I made my way back to my unit for the first time in days. I picked up some groceries on the way; I was pretty sure everything in my refrigerator would be spoiled and my guest was usually ravenous.

I arrived to find my unit cool and quiet. I'd been worrying that someone might have done something to it, but it seemed untouched. I cleaned out the old food and put in the new, hearing a step behind me before I turned.

It was him. Who else would it have been? 'You called?'

I quickly told him about Susan's death and the disappearing files. 'The head keeper's dead? That can't be a coincidence.'

'I know,' I said. 'But how was she killed? Something from Kore? If so, how did he get it to her?'

'Through Hensen? Did you pick up anything from him today?'

'He looked happy about something but also annoyed. I'm not sure why. Is he happy the keeper's dead and angry about something else or the other way around?'

The missing files also concerned him. 'The governor was beside herself when she realised they were missing,' I said. 'And not just the ones for our plants, either. The ones for Reacher's Pass and Twin City as well.'

That puzzled him as much as it had me. 'We had theirs too? That seems strange. Maybe they were designed by the same person.'

I hadn't thought of that. 'So someone here? I guess they could have been.'

'And why would Governor Jerrill be so upset? Unless she knows what Kore's planning.' He sat down in one of my lounge chairs, stroking his chin.

I leaned against the arm of his chair. 'Couldn't she stop him if she knew that? Beef up security? Change things around to make sure Kore can't get in?'

'Maybe it's not that simple. Or maybe that's why she needs the plans, so she can ensure every angle's covered. Kore's resourceful; he tends to plan for every contingency. He wouldn't have decided on taking this action if he hadn't considered that someone might try to stop him. Maybe that's why the plans have conveniently disappeared. Maybe what he's planning is imminent.'

'Then we've got to imminently stop him!' I said.

'But without plans, how the hell do we get in? We have no idea what the inside of the treatment plant is like or even if it's a good idea to put the drug in there or somewhere else along the chain, or even if they're going to do it at all.'

He was right. We needed more information. 'What if I could find something else in the Archives? Maybe there were articles or podcasts, even shows, when the plants were first designed. They could mention something that would help us at least get in.'

His eyes lit up. 'That's a great idea. See what you can find. But be careful. You don't want Official Hensen or anyone else to guess what you're up to. We've just got to hope they don't get the same idea.'

While as a keeper, I was allowed to look up articles and information, if I took anything specific out of the Archives, it was logged on the main system, so people would know what I'd taken. Occasionally, I could catch a glimpse, especially with the old-fashioned paper records, but I wasn't sure they would be of any help.

'Are you all right?'

I looked up from my musings to see him looking at me quizzically. 'Oh. Yes. Just worried about spending another day under Official Hensen's beady gaze.'

He looked relieved, which surprised me until I heard his words. 'I'm glad I guessed right.'

'Guessed what?'

'That something was wrong. It's getting easier to read your face.'

That filled me with dread. 'I hope it's not for everyone. The last thing we need is for Official Hensen to guess I'm onto him.'

'Don't worry,' he said, 'it still takes a lot of work. Unless he spends a few days chatting to you while your brother writhes under Kore's formula, I don't think he's got much of a chance.'

He'd learnt a lot about me there, had he? Seeing me where I'd come from? 'You saw me in my natural habitat.'

'Your what?'

'That's what animals have.' At least, that's what I thought they'd called it in the learning sector. 'It's where they live.'

He watched me carefully. 'Where they feel most at home.'

In that case, I didn't think it was my old home, with the spectre of Dad. But if it wasn't there and it wasn't this new unit, where was it? The Archives? It was the only other place I could think of that meant anything to me.

'You know if he comes back, I'll make sure he never does again.'

I didn't realise what he meant at first. Then it clicked. My natural habitat. It was the place that was supposed to be safe, a hiding place, somewhere creatures allowed themselves to be vulnerable. I had never allowed myself to be vulnerable anywhere, especially not with Dad constantly trying to beat us into submission, but at home, I had felt defenceless. Exposed.

I laughed, but it sounded thin. 'I don't think he'll dare come back. You made it pretty clear you would do terrible things to him if he did.'

That didn't alter the steadfastness in his eyes. 'I still wanted you to know. He has no right to do anything like that to you or your mother, or your brothers and sister.'

I was getting uncomfortable with the direction of his thoughts but tried my best to hide it with another laugh. 'Tell him that.'

One of his huge hands folded over mine. 'Eden, I don't know exactly what kind of a life your father's given you, but I just want you to know that you're worth so much more than he's shown you. That you all are. Keep that in mind. Don't let him taint you. I promise he'll never bother you again.'

His gaze stayed on mine, probably the kindest, most tender look I'd ever seen on a man's face. I felt my eyes start to go misty. *Remember—vulnerable means defenceless, weak.* But it was different, under his gaze. I might have felt vulnerable but I also felt a surge of strength, much as I had when I'd broken out of Kore's cell.

Could I rely on him? Could I allow myself to feel vulnerable, having seen the security he offered?

But Dad was inventive. He would try and find a way around Leon. 'You can't be sure—'

'Yes. Yes, I can.' His mouth quirked up. 'Being Izrod's got to be good for something.'

I tried to withdraw my hands. To my relief, he let me go, but not without another long look.

'I should be heading back,' he said. 'I'll need to update Sasha and see what she's found out. She's got people on the ground looking for information as well.' He turned and headed back towards the bedroom, to his exit. 'Let me know if you need me.'

I would, and I was starting to think that I did.

CHAPTER SEVENTEEN

I braced myself for another day in the Archives, another day trying to take sneaky peeks at files, another day under Official Hensen's disturbing gaze.

I'd been searching for two weeks. Two weeks of trying to find something, of expecting Kore's plan to be put into effect. But what exactly was he planning? If he was using the drug he'd used on my brother, it didn't look like it was going to kill anyone. Was he hoping the disruption would be so widespread that he could just march into the government sector and take over? Was he expecting Hensen to help him? I imagined them standing side by side, slapping one another on the back as Governor Jerrill was arrested. I had a feeling it was more likely to end with a stabbing than mutual congratulations.

By the time I arrived at the Archives, Governor Jerrill and Hensen were already prowling around. I watched Hensen out of the corner of my eye. While he seemed to be legitimately searching for the plans, he didn't seem as concerned as Governor Jerrill. Was it because he didn't want them to be found, he had them already, or because he didn't want Kore stopped anyway?

'Good morning, Eden.'

'Good morning, Official Hensen, Madam Governor.' It was a good thing I'd had so much experience keeping my face neutral. With any luck, neither of them had a clue that I thought one of them surly and negligent and the other the greatest danger this city had ever seen. I simply went back to my work, noticing that my cart was full.

'We've been through those files,' the governor said. 'We have a list of some others we need to check.' She sent it to my link before turning back to Hensen and talking under her breath to him.

I looked around for my fellow workers. They'd taken to coming in late, especially since we were often kept there well past our hours due to the governor's demands. The only reason I turned up early each morning was because I too, was searching, although as subtly as possible. It was a good thing I'd always been dedicated to this job or the two of them might have gotten suspicious.

I wondered where Miss Gregor was. Sometimes she came instead of the governor, but Hensen always came, making my skin crawl whenever he walked past.

I looked at the files they'd been scouring. Only half were digital, the other half were paper records. I glanced over each one as I put them back. Had the treatment plant plans been included in one of the news publications? I could see an early edition of the *Sendirian City News*. It was dated about twenty-three years ago. I should have checked when the publication had started.

I looked at the dates and subjects listed for the digital files as I put each one back. They contained articles about the water grid and the electrical system, as well as sewerage, transport, practically every system our city had, but water was a theme running through most of them, so they must be aware of what Kore was planning. It was a pity no one in the Archives had catalogued what was in all the newspapers. I knew that Susan had been planning to do it but we'd never had the time.

'Are you enjoying your work here, Eden?'

I felt my heart leap into my throat. I'd been too engrossed to realise that Hensen had sneaked up behind me.

I turned to face him and I think he was trying to look contrite for making me jump. At least, I guessed that's what the manic evil grin was meant to look like.

He held up his hands. 'My apologies. I didn't mean to startle you.'

But I had the perfect explanation for it. 'I'm sorry, Official Hensen. I still get afraid of shadows. It reminds me of Izrod taking me away.'

'Of course,' he said, curling his lip. I smiled affectionately, as I thought he meant his tone to be warm and comforting, not cold and hateful.

'Is there anything I can find for you, sir?' I asked. 'A file you need?'

'No, no,' he said. 'Just making conversation.' He glanced back at Governor Jerrill. 'The governor's a bit out of sorts today.'

The governor was always out of sorts. I continued with my work, wishing he'd go away. I couldn't check anything with him standing there.

Just as I finished putting away the digital files, the governor came over with some more newspapers, still loosened from their book-like folders. 'Here, Eden,' she said, piling them all on top of my cart. 'These can go away as well. I also need the newspapers for years twenty-five through to thirty.' She glanced at Hensen. 'We haven't checked those yet.'

'Yes, I know. Let's keep looking.'

I inserted the different papers back in the correct folders then headed down the nearest passageway, slotting things in where they belonged. It was quiet in the depths of the Archives—away from the pervading evil of Official Hensen. I worked methodically, hoping to be left in peace.

No chance of that. It didn't take long for Governor Jerrill's patience to run out. 'Eden, please hurry up with those papers. We don't have all day.'

I grabbed a number of the folders containing the papers she'd requested and headed back with them, handing them over. 'I'll get the rest out while you look at these.'

'Thanks,' she spat, and Hensen sneered at me.

I continued my search, putting away what had been examined and pulling out the folders they'd requested. I sneaked looks at the papers they'd been through, as well as the ones I found for them. I glanced in the flickers of the light, trying to hide behind shelves so I could search more thoroughly, always keeping an eye on the governor and Hensen to make sure I was out of their line of sight.

Finally, I'd put away everything they'd already viewed. There didn't seem to be anything relevant.

The new folders were a different matter. I pulled them out and strolled along, seeking the dark corners so I could skim through them before I took them back. I could hear the two of them talking as they looked through what they had. It didn't sound like they were having any luck.

The elevator doors opened. Some of my fellow workers were finally arriving. That would make it even harder to check all the folders.

I grabbed another folder and quickly skimmed through the papers inside. I was about to slam it shut when something caught my eye.

There was a prominent photo in the corner of one page that looked like it had been taken when the water treatment plant had first opened if the caption was anything to go by.

Governor Fortescue with James Fittell, designer of the Osten Bridge Treatment Plant.

Oh, no! It couldn't be.

The famous Fittells. That's what Derek had said when I'd first come to the Archives. I thought he'd just been making a stupid joke, but I'd been wrong. Because there in front of me was a photo of James Fittell.

My father.

I hugged the folder to me and retreated further into the blackness. They couldn't see this. They especially couldn't know I was related to him. What if they connected us? Derek clearly remembered the name. But then, did people like Governor Jerrill and Official Hensen even know my last name? And surely if my father had designed the plant then they would already know him.

But *I* didn't know anything about this! I had no memory of Dad being anything other than a raging drunk, staggering from vendor to vendor for his next drink. Did Mother know? She couldn't have mentioned it?

My deadbeat dad would probably know how to get into that plant, if he could remember past last Thursday, anyway. So maybe it didn't matter if they saw it. I didn't even know where my father was. He might have completely disappeared. And even if he hadn't, could he find the information in his alcohol-soaked brain?

I couldn't take that chance. Leon and I had to get to him first. I didn't trust Official Hensen not to twist this into something terrible. While I didn't particularly care if he snarled in my father's face, I was afraid he might realise the best way to get my father to talk—offer him money.

We needed to keep this information out of Hensen's reach.

My corner of the Archives was still quiet. Could I rip this page out without anyone hearing? The other workers had been called to the head keeper's desk and Governor Jerrill was giving them instructions. It was now or never.

I slowly and carefully released the lever and pulled the paper out. Fortunately, the page with my father's photo on it was loose. I hoped they wouldn't notice it was missing; some of the older records were incomplete, so with any luck, they'd just think it was one of those. I quickly folded it up and shoved it down the front of my shirt, positioning it so no one could see it, then I put the rest of the paper back in the folder, reactivating the lever so it held everything in place.

Then, making sure my face was under control, I continued selecting the folders Governor Jerrill had requested, nodding to my fellow workers as they joined me. We moved quietly and serenely through the Archives, doing what we could to keep our stressed-out leader and her treacherous official satisfied.

The day dragged on forever. I managed to take a bathroom break at one stage and folded up the page, putting it into my pocket. It was better than having it rustling every time I moved and making bulges in the front of my shirt that seemed to blink *she's hiding something!* I continued my search throughout the day, checking folders when I could. After all, where there was one photo of my father there might be more.

Finally, the day ended and as soon as I was out of there, I clicked my link. I needed to talk to Leon as soon as possible. He'd been coming to my unit most days for the past couple of weeks, often taking me to the Underground to visit my family, but sometimes just to talk.

To my surprise, he was already there when I walked in the door. I suppose it was dark out, so he'd had cover. 'Wow, you sure move fast.'

'Nah, I was already on the way when I got your signal. What's up?'

I took the page out of my pocket and unfolded it in front of him. I wasn't sure he'd recognise the much younger and clearly sober person in the photograph. He opened his mouth to say something, looked at the caption, at me, then back at the photo, and groaned.

'Yeah, that was pretty much my reaction,' I said.

'Did you know anything about this?'

'Are you kidding?' Did he think I'd kept this quiet out of some absurd loyalty to the drunken lout he'd kicked out of our house? 'I don't remember my father ever having a job more prestigious than a labourer. I sure don't remember him having any skills. And working for the government sector? Every memory I have of us is in the poor sector. There's nothing else.'

'Do you think he'd remember anything about the plans? Could he help us?'

'Who knows? I mean, if you give him enough booze, he'll tell you anything, but whether he could actually recall useful information, that's anyone's guess.'

He looked up sharply. 'Either I'm getting to know you better or you're showing your emotions more.'

Rats. That was something I didn't want to do. 'Sorry.'

He held out a hand to me. 'That's all right. I don't want you to feel that you can't do that. It's just that you need to keep your face neutral. Not here, obviously, but keep it under control everywhere else.'

I slumped in one of my lounge chairs. I was tired of keeping control. Tired of this never-ending back-and-forth taking me back to my father just when I thought he was out of my life forever. 'I guess we need to find him.'

Leon sat down on the floor next to me. 'Yes. Any idea where he might have gone?'

That was easy to answer. 'Anywhere he could get a drink. He doesn't have anyone else to sell to Kore, except maybe himself, but he'd be so full of booze he probably wouldn't feel anything Kore did to him, which would be a shame, but hey, if I'm not there to see it, I guess it doesn't matter. And the chances aren't great that he'll be able to remember anything about his glory days, or whatever. I doubt he'd be able to tell us anything useful.'

He watched me carefully, then gave a half-hearted laugh. 'You're definitely getting more in touch with your feelings.'

I worried that I'd spent the day leaking fear and hatred for my father through my eyes. Would Official Hensen have picked up on it? Would he know what it meant if he had? But apart from my initial moment of shock, which had been shrouded in the shadows of the Archives, I was pretty sure I'd kept a reasonable amount of control.

So what was different now? Had it really been that hard to keep it in? Or was I so ready to share myself with Leon that his presence was like a release valve on the horrors of my past?

I looked at the man sitting next to me. Izrod. My friend. The one who'd saved my brother and me, my whole family. Was he the reason I was sitting here venting? Why did I feel comfortable enough around him to even do that? Because of the strength and nobility I'd seen in him from the moment I'd opened my eyes to the world Kore had cursed me to?

I wondered if he'd caught any of my thoughts on my face. A slight smirk appeared and I got the feeling that he'd picked up on something, which made me blush, and that didn't help.

'Even if he can't remember anything, we need to find him,' he said. 'He may know enough to get us inside. Do you know where he used to get his drinks?'

'The vendor carts outside our old unit block. He used to walk up and down, getting a drink from each one. When he could afford to, anyway. When he had no money he'd walk up and down, begging.'

He stood up and took my hand. 'Then that's where we start searching.'

CHAPTER EIGHTEEN

When we were finally out of the government sector, he suggested taking me to the Underground. 'I'll get your dad and bring him back there.'

'No way,' I said. 'What if you can't find him? You may need my help if he's not where he normally is.'

He folded his arms. 'So tell me where else you think he might be.'

I folded mine back. 'Take me with you so I don't have to.'

He scowled but I wasn't giving up. 'Look, I might remember a place after you go and then what do I do? I can't send you a message on the link.' His secret alert button made no difference when it came to actual messages. Anyone could see them if they knew how to hack into your file.

'Fine.' We started to move from shadow to shadow in a rhythm I was getting used to. I found myself correctly anticipating the steps he took, the best places to hide. A lot of it was in alleyways, as there were plenty between the tall unit complexes. Some of them were barely wide enough to fit him and so full of dust that it coated our shoes, but we shook it off silently and kept going.

We soon reached the marketplace in the poor sector. Many vendors only operated in the daytime, but they were usually replaced at night by some offering different kinds of wares. Three women leered at Leon and invited both of us to see what they could offer. There was a vendor with Skyhigh, something that I knew kids in the learning sector had taken. You could always tell by the way they swayed as they walked, their glazed eyes seeing nothing. A few had been kicked out for using it.

But drugs like that had never been my father's vice of choice. Soon we reached those vendors, the night ones, whose drinks were stronger than those in the daytime, made from cheaper spirits. Not as classy or tasty as the others, at least, according to my father, but less expensive.

I looked for any vendor I recognised, someone who might know where Dad was, but I wasn't in the habit of going out at this time of night, and certainly not in this area, so no faces stood out to me. Leon eventually started showing the photograph of my father to see if anyone had seen him, slipping some credits to them via his link in exchange for the information. But no one had. I couldn't tell if they were lying or if they didn't associate the young, fit, cultured version of my father in that picture with the wreck of manhood he'd become. They also didn't seem troubled by the fact that they were conversing with Izrod. Maybe they'd seen him around. Maybe they thought he fit in. Maybe it was just the money he offered.

Eventually, Leon turned to me. 'Let's check your old place.'

'The old unit block?'

'No, the shack.'

I scoffed. 'He wouldn't have gone back there. There's no credit for him to find.'

'We'll look anyway,' Leon said. 'It's worth a try.'

It didn't take long to get to the litter-riddled street. We didn't see many people. I jangled with nerves the further we got. Leon stepped closer to me, as though hoping his presence would steady me. Then I was more worried by the fact that he'd worked out I was nervous.

We arrived at our hovel and everything looked the same. I'd thought it might contain new tenants or simply be silent and empty, but the door was ajar when we got there. Leon pushed it open wider and we stepped inside.

I froze as I saw him sitting there, leaning against the wall. He looked up as we entered, his eyes red from drink. He squinted at us, then cringed against the wall as his gaze met Leon's. He glared at me but he seemed so powerless and weak in my new eyes that it was pitiful rather than frightening, although it still made me want to throw up.

'What are you doing here?' he said, his voice a low croak.

I looked at Leon. Was he going to lead here? But he stayed silent. Looked like it was my job. And it made sense. I knew my father better, more's the pity.

'Looking for you,' I said.

Dad struggled to his feet. I was still amazed that he'd stayed in an empty shack that clearly contained nothing of value. 'Well, I'm here,' he sneered. 'Where else would I be? The place I last saw my family.' He snuffled.

Leon glanced at me. Was he wondering if I would be affected by my father's sorrow and start to fold? But I wasn't Mother. I could see dirty footprints about the place. He'd definitely been looking for something. Probably prying up the floorboards to see if he could find anything hidden underneath, perhaps to trade, since the only other thing he had left to trade was himself.

'You mean that time he threw you out after your latest attempt to beat us until we gave you money?' I said.

He began to approach, making sure he stayed as far from Leon as possible. 'Of course I wanted to see you.' His lips trembled, the bottom one jutting out, and he seemed to be trying to put love into his eyes, but it wilted like an old flower. 'I love you and your brothers and your sister. And your mother. You know that.'

He looked like he was going to reach out and stroke my cheek. Leon took a step forward. That was enough to make my father retreat. He staggered back to the wall and slumped against it. 'Now that freak has taken my place. Taken over the love you had for me in your heart.'

'Love in my ...' How could he be so delusional? There was nothing in my heart for him except disgust. 'I can't remember ever feeling any love for you.'

'Eden,' Leon said. He nodded at the door. I got the idea—it wasn't wise to stay much longer.

I turned back to my father. 'Anyway, Dad, it's your lucky day. Because you've got something we need.'

He glanced from me to Leon in alarm. 'What? My blood? A kidney?'

Leon snorted. 'I don't think they'd be useful to anyone.'

He backed up as far as he could. 'You, you're going to hand me in to that K-K-Kore.' He stabbed a finger at me. 'You're going to let him take me there, to pay me back for what I did to you and Jed.'

It was so tempting to let him think that. It was tempting to do it, to throw him in Kore's path, let him use my father for whatever he wanted. But it was too dangerous now that he knew something Kore would be anxious to hear. 'No, Dad. It's information we want. If you cooperate, you might even get paid.'

***

We managed to cajole him back to the Underground with promises of payment and booze. It rankled me to think that I'd have to give him what he wanted, just as we always did, but we needed his help. I just hoped there was enough left in his foggy mind to actually be of use.

Leon made us wait in the foyer under Knifer's watchful gaze while he went in to talk to Sasha. By the time Leon ushered us in, she had her meeting room ready for us. Leon must have told her what motivated my father because there was a flagon of beer sitting on the table. Dad's eyes lit up as he saw it and he fell into a seat, his fingers wiggling as he reached out for it.

Sasha pulled the flagon out of reach. My father tried to snatch it, but Leon stood on one side of him and Knifer on the other. He flinched as they towered over him and shrank back in his seat. 'Okay, what do you want? I assume it's not money. It's not like my family supports me, after all.'

'It's difficult when you've already bled us dry,' I said.

Sasha unfolded the newspaper page Leon had given her and held it up for my father to see. 'That's you, isn't it? James Fittell.'

My father squinted at it, heat climbing up his neck and blazing in his eyes before it fizzled out. He sat back, slouching in his chair like a puppet whose strings had been cut. 'That was a long time ago. What's that got to do with anything anyway?'

That was a relief. He didn't have a clue, which meant that Kore hadn't been knocking on his door, and neither had Hensen.

Sasha read aloud from the news sheet. 'Engineer James Fittell was able to redesign the desalination plant so that the parts of it that had been destroyed in the Unbidden Conflict could be repaired. As head of water treatment in the government sector, he and his team have given Sendirian City access to clean water again, pumped directly into each unit block.' She looked up at him. 'Well done. But then, I guess that happened before all this.' She gestured between him and the drink.

Dad's face darkened. 'How about because of it?'

'Whatever the reason, we don't care. We're only concerned with how much you remember about your marvellous reconstruction.'

'Why?' His gaze flitted from Sasha to Leon to Knifer to me. 'Aren't you the Underground? I'm not stupid, you know. I know who's out there. Why are you interested in the water system? You planning to blow it up? No, I don't think you'd need to know how it functions to do that. Just smuggle a bomb onto the site. Poison it, then? Are you planning to kill everyone in Sendirian City?'

He laughed at his joke and kept laughing until he read our faces. He sat up straight and I thought he was going to make a run for it. 'Look, whatever this is about, I don't want any part in it.' But his eyes shot to the drink and I was glad that Kore hadn't gotten to him first.

'We're relieved to hear it,' Sasha said. 'That makes it likely that you'll see the benefit of helping us.'

'Helping you?' His eyes were blank. 'Poison it? No. Not poison it? Wait, are you telling me someone *is* trying to poison it? Seriously?'

'How easy would it be for them to do it?' asked Leon.

'Poison the entire city? Just about impossible. There's a whole system of water treatment and dosing that's designed to remove any impurities, such as irritating things like poison, before it even gets to the final stage.'

'What about doing it in the final stage?' Sasha asked.

'That's when it's in the water reservoir,' Dad said. 'It has plenty of security—at least, it used to—and then the water's channelled straight into underground pipes made of concrete and welded steel. They survived the conflict, so you can't just crack into one and pump your poison in. Not to mention that, if you wanted to use that point to kill everyone in town, you'd need a truckload of the toxin. It's a megalitre system, so you can't just put a drop or two in the reservoir and expect everyone to fall down dead.'

What did Kore intend? We were pretty sure his aim wasn't to kill anyone, just drive them insane for a day or two, presumably long enough for him to try and take control of the city, but if he needed a significant number of people affected, he'd need to pump it into the reservoir, wouldn't he? Was there another option?

Leon pushed himself away from the wall. 'What if he didn't

want to kill everyone? What if he wanted to target specific areas, maybe a few? What if he wanted to poison people closer to where the water was fed into their sectors? The water has to come out of those underground pipes at some stage.'

Surely that would make Kore's takeover strategy less effective. But given how aggressive Jed had become, and him only a thirteen-year-old boy, maybe Kore didn't need a whole city of crazies. Maybe pockets of insanity would do.

My father rubbed his eyes and looked at the drink again. 'Look, all this thinking is making my head pound. Do you mind if I …?' His fingers inched towards the drink.

I wrinkled my nose in disgust. Sasha, as pragmatic as ever, slid it towards him. He downed it in a couple of seconds.

'There. That's so much better.' But his eyes were still bleary so I didn't know what he meant by 'better'. Better than what, sobriety? 'Anyway, I guess you could aim for the testing points if you didn't want to kill everybody. That would be the best way.'

'What testing points?' said Knifer.

'Each sector has a testing point so that water can regularly be tested to make sure that it's still potable.'

'What?' I said.

His eyes dripped scorn. 'That means *drinkable*.'

I opened my mouth to berate him, but he ignored me, continuing his tale. 'It's a useful way to find the location of any problems with water quality. When I was working in the water department, they had instructions to test them every month or so, but I don't know if they still do that. Government employees would be responsible for that, although I don't think those testing points have any security, so it probably wouldn't be too hard to access one and poison it. Only the water to that sector would be impacted, though.'

'Do you know where the testing points are located?' Leon asked.

Dad coughed discreetly and peered into his empty mug. With a careful look at me, Leon reluctantly refilled it for him. 'Your answer better be worth it.'

There was no missing the menace in his tone, but Dad seemed oblivious. 'Oh, it will be. By the way, should I be asking you what your intentions are towards my daughter?'

Sasha and Knifer both looked away awkwardly and Leon looked like he was about to rip Dad's head off. Trust my father to comment on something that didn't concern him. 'Since when have you cared about that?' I asked.

'Since you're my daughter, that's when.'

I still wasn't sure what Leon and I were, but I felt a glib answer was best for Dad. 'I'm sure Leon could get you all the drinks you wanted if he felt like it, so he's probably ideal for me.'

'Not that I would,' Leon stated flatly.

'Which makes him less than perfect after all.' The second drink was making my father bold, but he was still lucid enough to notice the flash of Leon's eyes. 'Right. The testing points.'

'How would Kore go about getting the poison into them?'

'Well, he'd need to shut off the flow on the low side of the pipe first, that's where it comes out of the testing site. Once that's done, the water stops inside it. That's when you're supposed to take the sample. It would be as simple as using a syringe to put the poison in instead of taking a sample out. Start the flow up again and off it goes.'

I turned to Leon. 'Would Kore even know to do that? That's not as easy as just making a hole in the pipe.'

'I don't know. Maybe he has a contact on the inside? He has contacts in a lot of places. Someone who's susceptible to Alpha-D. Then they'd tell him everything.'

'The guy left in charge at government after me knew how to do it, but I doubt he'd let Kore stick him with any of his little formulas.

Be more inclined to kill him just for getting too close.' Dad's face filled with hatred. 'Then my own daughter goes back to work for government, after what they did to me, and refuses to let me benefit. I guess everything comes full circle.'

'Well, I didn't even know you worked for government so it had nothing to do with me getting a job there,' I said. 'Besides, if they fired you, I'd say it means they've got some sense, don't you?'

My father flung his beer against the wall and lunged for me. Leon jumped on him, pinning his arms behind his back. Dad whimpered and cried in between blasting me with curses and abuse. 'You're on their side. I knew you would be. I knew it! After all I did for you!'

Leon dragged him to the door but I grabbed him by the front of his shirt, almost yanking him out of Leon's grasp. 'What did you ever do? Except steal from us and terrify us and hit us. Take everything of value in the house and sell it just so you could get drunk. Break Mother's heart, a woman who loved you, although I'll never know what she saw in you. I would rather have never been born than have you as a father. You disgust me!'

My father stopped struggling in Leon's arms and blinked at me. 'Well … I don't know what …' His words drifted off as Leon dragged him out of the room.

I looked around at Sasha and Knifer. He gave me a nod of respect, she, a curious look.

'So you do have some spirit after all,' she said. 'Go back to your family. Check and see how they are. Leon will get whatever he can out of your father.'

I gave her a half-nod and turned to leave.

'And Eden?'

'Yes.' I struggled to be polite. I was too exhausted.

But the look on her face surprised me. It was one of calm acceptance. 'Welcome to the Underground.'

CHAPTER NINETEEN

Knifer led me to the small unit they'd given my family. It was really just an area screened off by a curtain and some sheets of cardboard. There were similar 'units' throughout the room where everyone seemed to live, as Knifer gave me a nod and headed off to one nearby, kissing the woman in the doorway.

Kathleen held me and Lenny toddled over to say hello. Mother gave me a warm hug and Jed did little more than nod. It was hard to see the pain etched deep on his face. His experience at Kore's seemed to have broken him. After years of putting up with Dad, I'd thought he would be able to shrug it off, but maybe it was just one step more than he could take. Or maybe there was some persistent effect from Kore's formula that kept him cowed and beaten. I dreaded to think what would happen if it got into even a fraction of our population.

'I just wanted to let you know that Dad's here,' I said. I saw fear bloom on their faces and hurried to reassure them. 'He's only here to help us with some logistics. He's with Leon.' The fear flitted away as quickly as it had come. They knew Leon would never let Dad near them.

I turned to Mother. 'You didn't tell me Dad used to work for government.'

'Did he? He never said so. He was working as a labourer when we met. I knew he'd been married before, but he never mentioned working for government. Do you know what he did there?'

I wasn't sure I wanted to go into specifics so muttered something vague and that seemed to satisfy her.

What had happened to make my father lose such a prestigious position? Why hadn't he told his wife? And did I really care?

I went in search of them, all the time berating myself. What the hell did I care about my father's sob story? Was it really just about something that could help us win? If there *was* something, then Leon could tell me about it. I didn't need to hear it from the mouth of the devil. But I continued looking anyway.

Eventually, I found them at a table in a corner of the community hall, Leon holding a drink out of Dad's reach while he hissed in desperation. He stopped and paled when he saw me.

'What do you want?' He looked down at the table. 'I thought I was the disgraceful father, not worth my daughter's attention.'

I wasn't going to sugar-coat it. 'You are. But I want to know why you never told Mother you worked for government. Don't you think she deserved to know?'

'Know how far I'd fallen, you mean?' he sneered. 'Your mother didn't need to know anything except that I made enough money to keep food on the table and in the mouths of an ever-growing brood of children.' He looked away again. 'Not that I ever wanted any.'

'Sorry to be such an inconvenience,' I shot back. 'Besides, you eventually seemed to give up on the idea of feeding us. There were so many more important things to spend money on. Well, one thing.'

My father's eyes were back on me and I got the feeling he was seeing me for the first time in years. 'You know, you remind me a lot of me.'

Thanks for the compliment.

'You went out and sought work. Wanted to better yourself. Wanted to do something that would take you somewhere.'

'Anywhere away from you was fine.'

He twisted his mouth. 'Okay, I get that I'm not exactly a stellar father, but you don't know what I went through.'

'I'm not sure I care.'

He stood up, snarling. So did Leon, making sure he didn't come too close to me. Dad glanced at him and some of his intensity faded. He sat down again. 'I started working at the water department in the government sector straight out of the learning sector. They were still rebuilding back then and they needed anyone who showed a bit of promise.' He puffed his chest out. 'I showed more than that, so it wasn't long before I was heading up their project to get water back into homes.

'There was so much work to be done. The plant was practically gutted inside, although the pipes underground were more or less intact. I had to redesign the entire facility. They gave me employees, equipment, everything I needed.

'But there was one man I worked with. He was responsible for organising the chemical treatment of the water. He had an amazing mind. Knew chemicals like nobody else. But I could see he was ambitious. He didn't want to just be involved in some low-level job. He had grander things in mind.

'We got the plant up and running and everything was functioning perfectly and he was the one who supervised the installation of the testing sites. But I had to sign off on them, making sure they worked right. I was sure they would. I'd checked that everything was built to the best standard, and the testing sites I saw were all perfect. But he said I didn't need to check them all. There were a lot and we had so much to do. I trusted him. More fool me.

'Then all I had to do was sign off on it.' He mockingly scrawled

195

in the air. 'That meant my name was on it. And do you know what he had them do?'

'What?'

'Use cheap material on the joins on some of the other points. Several of them leaked, flooding the surrounding streets and buildings, losing us litres of precious water, and who'd approved all the testing sites?' He pointed a thumb at his chest and slumped back down at that table.

'It was deliberate. I know it was. But it's all flooded and everyone's pointing the finger at me. And they'd been just about to offer me a job as the head of the water department at government. Guess who got it instead? Mr Chemical Genius himself.'

'Kore?' said Leon.

Dad gave him a derisive look. 'What, that low-level gangster? He wasn't even in Sendirian City back then.'

'The low-level gangster you sold two of your children to?' I said.

'Well, that should tell you a thing or two. I would never have sold you to *that* man.'

'It's nice to know you have some standards.' He'd sold us to someone who wasn't *quite* as bad as his worst enemy. What a concession.

'And all the way along, he's just kept advancing. If you see him at government, don't trust him. Mr Genius Dale Hensen. Huh, genius at nothing but climbing over everyone to get to the top.'

I felt like the floor had disappeared from beneath me. 'Do you mean Official Hensen?' My father knew Hensen? He had caused Dad's fall?

That got my father's attention. 'You've met him? Be careful. He looks friendly, but he'll turn on you in a flash.'

I knew how true that was. I saw villainy in every corner of Hensen's face every day.

Hensen knew Dad, knew him well enough to betray him. Did he know I was James Fittell's daughter? And what about him being some kind of chemical genius? Wasn't that Kore's ballgame? Maybe they were competitors, or maybe Hensen had given that up to progress up the chain of command in the government sector.

Leon left Dad to gulp down the drink he'd finally been allowed to have. 'Come on, I need to get you back home.'

With a nod to Knifer and a reminder to watch my father so he didn't cause trouble or try to leave, Leon led me out. He was silent as we slipped through the darkness back to my unit, but he came inside with me when we arrived at the air conditioning vent.

'What do you think about what your father said?' he asked.

I'd been mulling over it the whole way, my thoughts pulling me first in one direction, then another. 'I don't know what to make of it. He's not exactly the most reliable at remembering stuff, but it makes sense that he'd remember something bad someone did to *him*. And it's not like I trust Hensen. I can see how evil he is every time I look at him.'

He began to pace up and down. 'It's difficult to know what to do.'

I sat in the lounge chair and watched him as he marched. 'Do you think he's right about Kore? He doesn't seem to think he's a threat.'

'There's every reason to believe that Kore also knows his way around a laboratory.' He stretched out his hand. 'I have that evidence for myself. But not being anything more than a low-level gangster? What is Kore, then? And is he the real danger here?'

'Who at his organisation told Sasha about Kore poisoning the water?'

'There were a few people, but the most prominent she mentioned was Justin. He's also the only one I'd trust … sort of.'

'Would he lie to you?'

'I wouldn't have thought so. Alpha-D didn't work on him either. I saw that early on. And even you thought he was okay.'

'Well, that's good enough, I guess.' I hoped that meant something. What if this thing I could do was unreliable? And had Justin been that trustworthy? It was difficult to say. He'd looked strange to me but I couldn't put my finger on exactly why.

'And now we have to trust my father.' It was difficult to even spit the words out. 'Maybe what he said was garbage. Hell, all the alcohol's probably destroyed his memory anyway. Useless drunk.'

He raised his eyebrows.

Was I being a bit too expressive? 'Sorry.'

'I guess it's useful to vent sometimes,' he said. 'Try and get it out. It's healthy, so they say.'

'I wouldn't know.' Did I sound bitter? I felt it.

His eyes changed, filling with so much compassion. 'I know you don't. But don't feel that you ever have to hide who you really are from me.'

I tried to laugh but it fell flat. I was tired of the constant weight on my shoulders, the overwhelming burden of the life my father had given me. Why couldn't I escape it?

I ended up crawling out of the lounge chair and sitting on the floor. 'I've never really been good at sharing my feelings with others.'

He came and sat beside me. 'I can imagine. With a father like that, I bet there have been a lot of things you've had to hide.'

He was so close he was practically leaning against me, and he brushed the back of my hand with his own. It was so odd, my response to him. Part of me craved his touch, trusted him so much it hurt. The other part shied away from even this level of contact.

I worried that he'd take my hand or put his arm around me. I wasn't sure what I'd do if he did that. Snuggle into him or push him away? Or both?

My trust had been broken so many times, shattered into a kaleidoscope of misery. By my father, the man we needed now. And it wasn't just him either. It hadn't been unusual to hear the sound of fists connecting with bodies in the units around ours. But then, we lived in the poor sector, where relationships were often just a question of survival. I wondered if that was why my mother had married my father. I knew she loved him; she loved everybody. But to stay with him, to keep us there with him ...

Leon's voice broke the silence. 'My mother died when I was so small I don't even remember her. It was just Dad and me when I was growing up.'

I tried not to reveal how much I was listening to him. He'd told me that his mother had died, but nothing about his father. Had he been abusive too? Had life on the streets been Leon's safest option?

I think he saw those questions on my face. 'My father was nothing like yours. He was a kind man, decent and loving. He did his best for both of us after we lost my mother, but he was a labourer and not a great one at that, so work was hard to come by. We lived in the poor sector at Reacher's Pass, surviving day by day, trying to get enough food to keep going.

'Then he got sick, and you know what that's like when you live in the poor sector. We didn't have the money for fancy doctors and hospitals. We managed to get some medication for him, which we thought would help. He kept getting this bad throat, you see. He'd cough until blood came up. Then he got weaker and weaker. Eventually, they took him to the poor sector hospital. I was only eleven and I couldn't look after him anymore.'

The poor sector hospital—the doorway to death. That's what everyone called it, even in other sectors. Only under their breath, when they thought no one was listening. Not because anyone cared enough to try and make things better, but because it kept the truth at bay.

'I only saw him there once or twice before the end. He was so frail the final time, he said not to go back. There was no point. He could barely talk anyway. Two days later, a medical attendant came around with his personal effects. He'd already been cremated and he gave me his sympathies, but there I was, left with a photo of my mother and me and a measly credit line, nothing else.

'I couldn't stay in the unit. I had virtually no money and wasn't old enough to work. So I lived on the streets, stealing what I needed. That's when Kore found me and asked me to join him. I was never sure exactly what it was about an eleven-year-old that interested him. Maybe he thought I was so young it gave plenty of room for experimentation. Maybe he thought I was older.

'You know the rest. Kore turned me into this.' He spread out one of his large hands. 'Eight years later, and I'm no longer under his control. I wonder how he feels about that. He used to treat me like a son ... when he wasn't chopping pieces off me.'

He turned to me, answering my unspoken question. 'I want you to know that not all fathers are like yours. You hate him and I understand why. He's made you afraid of all men. But Eden, you don't need to be afraid of me.'

'I'm not.' Was that true?

Judging by his face, he didn't believe me, and his expression darkened. 'But then, it's not like I'm pure and spotless either. I kidnapped people off the street. I took them to Kore.' His shoulders slumped. 'Maybe I am a monster.'

I had barely spared a thought for the other people, like the moaner and the shrieker. Leon had taken them, just as he'd taken me. Had he had a choice? Kore had to believe that he was all in. But those families, the ones who'd lost their loved ones, I doubted they'd see it that way. It was all right for my family—Leon had saved us. In our eyes, he was a hero time and time again. But to others ... 'At least you didn't kill them.'

Guilt and anguish slid across his face. 'A couple of them I did.'

I felt cold at his words. He'd killed some of them, innocent people like me. They'd only been there because he'd plucked them out of the masses, deciding they were the best way to keep up his front. And even if he hadn't killed them himself, he'd known what would happen to them.

But some had escaped. Who had seen to that? 'How many got away?'

That seemed to bring him back a little. 'Only six.'

'And who got them out?' I wasn't sure why I was doing this. Maybe it was because of the overwhelming trust I still felt for him. Maybe because I knew with everything in me that he was good and noble and true. He might not always be that, but who could, especially in this world of ours?

He shook his head. 'It's not enough, you know. I mean, I was always selective. I tried not to choose innocents. I looked for people … well, to be honest, people like your dad. There are a lot of them out there, from all walks of life, men and women. I tried to make taking them away less of a nightmare for someone.'

'But there were others who weren't like that. Who were like you.' Anguish filled his eyes. 'I don't know why you don't see that. Why do I look so trustworthy to you?' He looked at his hands. 'Why don't you see the blood?'

He lowered his head. Was he crying? Oh, please no! I could wipe away Lenny's tears or even Jed's, but Leon's? And this was far beyond the grief of either of my brothers, even in those low moments when their despair couldn't be driven away by hugs and a mother's love. Leon's sobbing was a heart-wrenching cry he seemed determined to contain, although he was fighting a losing battle.

I crawled in front of him, almost into his lap. 'Well, if I can see it, it must mean something.' I tried to pull his hands away from his face and after a moment, he let me. 'You did what you did so Kore would trust you. He never would have otherwise. If you hadn't, he would have turned on you.

'And you know me. I'm not some little wide-eyed girl who sees in black and white. We all have shades of grey. You do. I do. Do you know how relieved I felt moving here, leaving my family behind? I may as well have left them in hell.'

'You couldn't do anything about that.'

'Maybe so. And maybe I could have done more.' I encouraged the light back to his face with a smile. 'So you see? We both have darkness.'

His eyes searched mine. 'And I think we're both determined to get past it. I can't ever go back to Kore's and I'm not sad about that. I need to make sure I walk in the light now. For myself ... and for you.'

His hand curled around mine and I let it. It was so warm and gentle, surprisingly soft for someone who used his hands to pull himself up on cables and scale walls. Our gaze held as he cradled my face in his hands and dropped a gentle kiss on my lips. I could feel my body trembling at the avalanche of sensations that caught me off-guard. I drew away, terrified of what I was feeling, but I caught sight of his face and saw love there, love for me, love that my new talent told me was genuine.

'Sorry,' he said, his eyes exploring mine. 'I don't know what came over me. I didn't mean to be pushy.'

'It's all right.' And I knew it was. I hadn't been expecting his kiss, but I hadn't hated it either. In fact, part of me wanted more. It seemed to have changed something in my mind, or maybe just cemented it. I just knew I'd be happy if he was always close to me, but I felt like I'd known that ever since I'd woken up in Kore's dungeon and seen his face.

Light came back to his eyes and he smiled. 'So what does this mean?' He gestured between the two of us.

He was asking me? 'I don't know. This isn't something I know anything about.' It felt strangely good to confess this to him. 'I mean, kids in the learning sector ... some of them liked each other.' I couldn't make myself say 'dated'. That seemed a ridiculous concept for a little thing like me and a freak like him, with all our baggage and bruises and scars, the ones on his hands, the ones that weren't as easy to see. 'A guy there once told me he'd only ever love a girl if she liked digital chess.' I gave him a shy smile. 'Do you think that's a normal requirement when you're going out with someone? I've never played it myself. Not really one for games.'

The last of the darkness fled from his face. 'Me neither. Kore wasn't one for games, except the fatal kind. But maybe we can learn those things together … if we manage to live through this.'

Leon didn't let me go and I didn't shrink away from his embrace. I put my cheek against his upper arm as he cradled me there.

'How do you think we find out more about what Kore's going to do?' I asked when he drew away.

He sighed. 'I'll talk to Sasha. I may need to go back and try and find out more from Justin or someone else at Kore's. That's the only lead we've got on what might be happening.'

'What if we're wrong? What if that's not the plan at all? He could have lied to you.'

'I know. But everything points to something happening and this is the only intel we've got.' He glanced at my room. 'I need to go. I'll come back tomorrow night and let you know what's going on. Be careful of Hensen. If he knows you're James Fittell's daughter …'

'He may not even know my last name. And even then, couldn't there be other Fittells around?'

'I've never met any,' he said. 'Don't rely on that.'

'I won't. And you be careful. All this sneaking back and forth to see me might get you caught.'

He was unconcerned as he climbed back into the air conditioning vent. 'Only if I get careless. And I don't get careless.'

***

203

It was back to the Archives the next day, but not before I noticed something new. New to me, anyway.

For the first time, I realised how many water pipes lined the walls of buildings in the government sector. I saw a testing point on my way to work and the dirt and grime on it told me it hadn't sprouted up overnight. A pipe led away from it, hugging the side of a building, before disappearing into the wall. I walked on, going through the checkpoints, noticing more pipes and some water main points. My father had talked about them too.

It was like waking up to Kore's formula all over again.

How many other things were around me that I didn't notice but that might be incredibly important? What stopped me from seeing them? If only Kore's formula had opened my eyes to every intrigue and machination in the government sector. That would have been useful.

Back in the Archives, I put away items, pulled some out to deliver to departments, and listened to my fellow workers grumble. There was still no head keeper and they were fighting over who should get the role. No one seemed interested in mourning Susan. I wondered if she had any family to grieve for her.

I ignored them, especially since I was still the most junior of the juniors, so there was no way they were going to suggest me. Instead, I prowled around the Archives, heading to the back of the room because I remembered what I'd seen there the first day.

It was right at the back where the passages were darker, the ceiling lower and the flooring less sturdy. I remembered those large throbbing air conditioning vents, along with Adriana's explanation of the fire equipment. Hose. Sprinkler. Axe. And the hose was next to a testing unit that looked so old there was no doubt my father must have signed off on its installation himself, all those years ago. I could tell by the thick layer of dust on it that it hadn't been touched in ages.

I hurried back to the relative brightness of the administration area.

It was unnerving, having one of those testing points in the Archives itself. What if Kore decided to target it? Would we all be in danger? I didn't think it was likely he would, but what did I know? What if it started leaking like Dad said the others had done? But surely it would have done that before now if it was going to blow.

Was it possible that Kore would target us here? Was that the reason Susan had died so suddenly? Did her death mean that the Archives was vulnerable?

***

I activated my link as soon as I finished work for the day. I hoped Leon would be in my unit when I got back there, but he wasn't, so I ate some dinner, did a few circuits of my tiny home, always checking on the air conditioning vent, then did laps of the living room.

Where was he?

Finally, I heard the sound of the vent being removed and raced into the bedroom just as he pulled himself out.

He took me in his arms. 'What's wrong? I'm sorry it took so long to get here. There are new security measures on the streets so I had to find a different way to get in.'

'I went into the Archives today. It has its own testing unit, sitting right at the back near the air conditioning ducts,' I said. 'Could Kore be planning to poison it, do you think?'

'I can't see that being his target. How would Kore even get in there? It's too well-guarded. There are heaps of other locations he could reach without that much trouble. He could drug the whole poor sector. Or the medical sector. Or security. Imagine how much chaos that would cause.

'We're having a planning meeting tonight. I've been in contact with Justin and he's delivering some intel. He knows what Kore's planning and wants to help us stop him. I wanted to take you, but I'm not sure we'll make it in time now, especially since we'll have to take a long way around.'

'Well, we'd better get going then, if we don't want to miss out.'

So it was back to the air conditioning vent until we reached the bottom of the building, where Leon went out first. He made me wait until he'd checked the street extensively, then at his nod, I scrambled out.

'Come on,' he whispered. 'We need to be quick.'

It was the slowest journey I'd ever had with him. We'd always had to keep to the shadows and sometimes even backtracked if we saw a security patrol, but that night they were everywhere, reaching into the darkness where we hid. The streets were also devoid of the usual night vendors. Even the homeless seemed to have vanished. It was like the whole city was on edge.

Eventually, we arrived at the Underground. I looked around the hall. There were forty or so people, most of whom I'd seen during one or more of my visits. Knifer was there, and the rest were like him—a hard-bitten motley crew of men and women, most flicking knives or small axes, hefting them, feeling their weight, practising with them. I could feel the breeze from one a few metres away as he twirled his axe, ending in a large swipe, presumably as he thrust it into someone's skull in his imagination. I hoped it wasn't mine.

Leon moved me a little further away from him, which didn't reassure me.

At the front of the hall, sitting at the head table, was Sasha. Beside her was Justin. He kept shifting, as though he was expecting an attack at any moment and wanted the chance to escape before it came.

Sasha looked up as we entered. 'Now we're all here, we can begin.' She indicated the twitching man next to her. 'Justin has brought us intelligence of Kore's plan. Eden, can you confirm Justin is trustworthy?'

All eyes swivelled to me and Justin jumped to his feet. 'You can't be serious. Kore was never satisfied with the results of that experiment.'

'That's because we hid the results from him,' Leon said.

'No, he used that formula a couple more times after that. He didn't even try to refine it further. Returned to his chaos plan.'

I could see Leon was thrown by that. 'Did he say why?'

Justin shifted in his seat. 'I don't exactly understand Kore's talk about all his experiments. You'd have to ask him.'

Which wasn't going to happen.

But Sasha wouldn't let it go. 'Eden, do you think Justin is trustworthy?'

'He looks … shifty.' I thought that was why I'd had trouble getting a read on him the first time we'd met.

'Shifty?' Leon asked.

'Like he's moving around, not just in his body, but in his mind.'

'That's because I know I'm risking my life just being here,' Justin spat. 'If Kore finds out …'

I wasn't so sure that was why, but Sasha inclined her head in acceptance. Maybe she figured they could overcome Kore regardless of any double-crossing. 'Justin has information about Kore's plan. He intends to cause chaos by injecting his formula into the water supply at several points throughout the city.'

'He's going to target the poor sector first,' said Justin, 'then the middle-level sector and the medical sector. That will cause maximum mayhem and stop anyone from being able to treat the people his formula affects. He will then continue to inject it into any sector he can reach after that, except the government sector and security sector. It's too hard to gain access to them. He hopes that will make the people suspicious of the government and rise up and overthrow them.'

'Does he know how to poison them?' I asked. And exactly how had he found that out?

Justin moved uncomfortably. 'He told me he did. Who was I to argue? I'm in charge of getting people into those areas, not doing the actual poisoning myself.'

'And why leave the security sector untouched?' I asked. 'What if they fight back?'

Justin shifted again. 'I don't know. Ask Kore. All I know is that's what he's planning.'

'At least, that's what he's told *you*,' said Leon. 'It's possible he's realised you're relaying information to us and is trying to throw us off.'

Or that Justin himself was trying to lead us astray.

Sasha let out a weary sigh. 'All the signs suggest that Kore is planning a major offensive early tomorrow morning. We need a plan of attack if we're to have any hope of stopping him.'

Leon clenched and unclenched his jaw. 'All right. Thank you, Justin. You can go.'

Justin glowered at Leon as he rose to his feet. He seemed about to protest, but Leon's gaze remained on him, ominous eyes that almost forced him from the room. Knifer followed him out, probably to make sure he left.

'He doesn't need to hear what we're doing to stop Kore. Although admittedly, what we can do is limited,' Leon said. 'I think we send three different teams out, each to the three major locations. But we'll need additional teams for other sites. We should also have one on Kore's lair in case he does something else entirely and we need to adjust our plans.

'I'll lead the team going to the medical sector, as that's definitely one we need to keep safe.' He looked at Knifer as he came back into the room. 'Ernie can lead the team to the poor sector and Craig the team to the middle sector.'

The meeting dissolved into everyone being broken up into additional groups while I wondered how someone like Knifer could have a name like Ernie.

Eventually, Leon turned to me. 'I'll take you home now. I need to be back in time to go out with my team.'

It took just as long to get home again as we tried to avoid the new security points. I was reluctant to go back; surely I could help. Couldn't I do more than prowl around the Archives looking for lost papers?

I didn't dare talk to Leon during our travels. I was afraid someone might overhear, but when he left me in my unit and immediately turned to leave, I stopped him.

'What if this whole thing's a trap?' I could tell he knew it was a possibility. I reached out and touched his arm, reassured by the heat of it.

'If it is, we'll know soon enough,' he said grimly. 'Try not to worry. We need to do this. And we're pretty inventive. If things turn out different from what we've planned, most of us can meet any challenge.'

'What about Hensen? He has access to the Archives. What if he decides to target it? If he and Kore are working together …'

'I guess that's possible,' he said. 'But even then, he'll just infect more people with Kore's formula and there's going to be enough of that going around as it is. Why would infecting a few government officials in administration be better than infecting security or medical sector officers? It doesn't seem a prime target to me.'

'All the same, I'll go in early tomorrow. Keep an eye on it.'

He placed his hand on my cheek. 'Not too early. You don't want to raise any eyebrows.'

I looked at him and realised just how much he meant to me. I couldn't stop the gnawing doubt from spreading through my body. It was like I wasn't going to see him again. The thought of him gone from my life left me bleak and cold.

I'd never thought this kind of thing would happen to me, that I could care like this for another human being, especially a man. I laid my hand over his on my face, wishing I could hold it there.

He pressed his lips to mine quickly. 'I've got to go. Stay safe.'

He put the vent back in place and slipped away, leaving me in silence and darkness, contemplating what was to come.

CHAPTER TWENTY

I couldn't sleep. I kept tossing and turning, straining my ears for any sound from outside, not that there was much—government unit buildings were fairly soundproof. Would I be able to hear the sounds of a rebellion if it had begun, crazed people from the poor sector attacking folks at random, flinging things at them with their briefly elevated strength, destroying everything in their way?

What about Leon and the others? Would they be safe? What about my family? I should have stayed at the Underground. Maybe I could protect them. But what could I do? I'd been completely useless when Kore's goons attacked us. I'd probably just get in the way.

I got up early, sick of tossing and turning with no sleep in sight. I had an early breakfast, then did some laps of the room, then had another breakfast, wondering how early was too early to arrive at the Archives. Maybe I could make an excuse, that I needed to check some files or something. Not to mention that it might be safer in there anyway, behind all those checkpoints.

In the end, I couldn't take the silence anymore. If anyone wondered why I was there two hours earlier than my usual starting time, I'd tell them the truth—that I couldn't sleep.

At the first checkpoint, they were half-asleep themselves and scowled at having to process me so early. One guard scanned my link, setting bleary eyes on me as I explained that I just couldn't sleep so thought I might as well work. Then he thumbed me past him, onto the next one.

The next two did more or less the same. They seemed to buy my explanation of a sleep-deprived worker looking for a distraction. Maybe they thought it had something to do with my kidnapping all those weeks ago. Maybe they didn't care.

Finally, I got through the checkpoint at the door of the Archives building. They were the most surprised at my early morning visit.

'Derek's not here to take you down in the elevator,' one said as she scanned my link.

'That's okay,' I said. 'I've done it before myself.' It wasn't hard. Press a button and down it goes.

After they let me pass, I padded my way quietly through the lobby. It was strange to see it devoid of the usual foot traffic. I stepped into the elevator and it began its groaning journey down to the Archives.

Once there, I grabbed my cart. It held the usual records people had sifted through late in the day that I hadn't had time to deal with or that had come in after I'd gone home. I trundled it along, shelving a digital record here, a paper record there.

I felt drawn to the back of the room, to the testing point. I needed to reassure myself that it was untouched. I looked for any sign the dust had been disturbed but it was just as filthy as the day before. No fingerprints, nothing unusual. I heaved a sigh of relief.

The grinding noise of the elevator caught my attention. It was still so early. I wouldn't have expected any keepers to be down here yet.

I waited quietly, creeping further into the shadows, my heart suddenly beating in my throat. What if it was Kore or one of his people? What if they'd decided to target the Archives after all? I ducked behind some shelves at the back of the room. If it was Kore's goons, could I make it to the elevator before they saw me?

The doors opened. I couldn't see them from where I was and I stayed crouched low. I was relieved when I only heard one set of footfalls. It would have been difficult to escape if there was more than one. And whoever it was, they didn't seem to be creeping or furtive. It was a bold, firm step—purpose-driven.

'You can come out, Eden. I know you're there.'

My body went rigid with terror. It was worse than if it had been one of Kore's men, or even Kore himself.

It was Hensen.

Had Kore sent him? Was he suspicious because I was there so early? It wasn't unreasonable that I was working. I might not usually get to work at the crack of dawn, but I usually beat everyone else.

His steps slowed. I heard his foot tap. 'I haven't got all day.'

I figured it was best to play innocent. I trundled my cart towards him. 'Oh, hello Official Hensen. What are you doing here so early?'

His eyes were cold and sharp, his mouth set in a line that could have been chiselled from concrete. 'I could ask you the same thing.'

'Me? I couldn't sleep. I thought I may as well be working.' I kept my expression normal and locked every feeling up within me. If he was there for some nefarious reason, maybe my presence would stop him or slow him down.

'You're so good at that, aren't you?' He laughed—a harsh, grating sound—then pulled something out of his pocket. It was a black thing that looked like it was made of metal, with a funnel protruding from the front. Was he going to use it to poison the testing point?

He held it up in front of my eyes. 'Do you know what this is? It's called a gun. You don't see them much anymore, mainly because we destroyed all the ones we couldn't commandeer. And these ones are especially attractive. No one can use this but me. Isn't that special? You know, it's amazing the perks that come with this job. I could never have gained access to something like this without it.'

My blood froze. They'd mentioned guns in the learning sector, always in stories of blood and war and death. I didn't know how one worked, but I knew it could kill me where I stood.

I aimed for looking curious, rather than petrified. 'Why did you bring it down here? Is it to be archived?'

'No, Eden.' His arm shot out, snapping at my wrist, twisting it behind my back. Or at least, he meant to. Dad had tried this manoeuvre on me many times and I slipped out of his grasp and bolted for the shelter of the shelves.

I'd made it no further than the end of the first row when something exploded above my head. I ducked to the ground, seeing sparks fly. I hadn't realised that a gun could be so loud. My ears were ringing.

'If you're planning to go back and tell anyone, you can't,' came Hensen's voice. 'I've disabled the elevator. No one can use it again unless I'm with them.'

I was crouched close to a string of shelves, searching for him. There he was, standing calmly, the gun still in his hand. He waved it at me. 'Don't think you can try and escape. I'm a good enough shot that I could take you out if I wanted to. So come back here.'

I looked at the shelf above me. There was a hole the size of a thumbprint in it and the metal was curled in as if someone had struck it with a riveter. And he expected me to just walk casually back and join him?

He pulled a black case out of his pocket. 'I knew you'd make an interesting subject. But never mind. I have something important to do. Actually, you're going to do it for me.'

He unzipped the container and pulled a syringe out of it. There was no doubt what it was for, but I had to play dumb. 'What's that?'

Annoyance flashed across his face. 'Don't play that game with me. I know your boyfriend and his cohorts think they're putting a stop to this. I was only too happy to lead them astray. I know you

214

know everything, so please, don't treat me like a fool.'

Boyfriend? He meant Leon! How did he know about us? 'So what are you doing here? With that?' I asked.

He rolled his eyes. 'Poisoning the government sector. Although I'm going to get you to do the actual poisoning.'

I grasped for something I could do to stop him. I was hardly strong enough to tackle him to the ground, especially since he was armed. I'd be dead before I reached him. And if Dad was right, he knew about having to stop the flow of water in the testing point first, so that wouldn't slow him down. And what if he managed to stick me with the formula?

No, there was only one thing I could do. I folded my arms in front of me, a classic defence gesture I'd used often with Dad, slumped my shoulders and pressed the secret button on my link three times. It had to be more than once or Leon wouldn't come until later. It should make him realise something was up. I prayed that he'd check it for my location and not go straight to my unit.

But how was he going to get in here? The same way he got upstairs? The huge conduits for the air conditioning at the back of the Archives were even bigger than the ones leading to my unit. I had to hope it would give him direct access.

In the meantime, I decided to keep Hensen talking. 'But why would you want to do that? Why help someone like Kore?' There was no point in continuing with the clueless act. Hopefully, he would humour me.

A look of distaste crossed his face. 'Help Kore? Help *him*? I thought you were smarter than that, but then, I thought he was smarter too, so maybe I'm not the best judge of character. I told him to ditch that freak you call your boyfriend, but for some reason, Kore couldn't. A misplaced sense of fondness for something he created, I guess. And then there was the idea that Alpha-D actually worked.' He laughed mirthlessly. 'It was the only formula he ever truly came up with himself. I was only too happy to let him think that it worked for a while, but it became a liability. Oh well, it won't matter for much longer.'

What did he mean? 'You're not helping Kore?'

'Hello? I'm not *helping* Kore. He's my employee. Or was. Now he's only good for one thing—a convenient distraction. Your friends from the Underground should be able to stop him with no problem since Justin told them exactly where he'll be, although he'll probably have time to use chaos before they get there. And then security will catch all of them together. I really wish I could be there to see it.'

This was worse than I could have imagined. I felt a surge of adrenaline shoot up my spine. Would Leon escape? Was he even now fighting for his life against some security worker? He was Izrod. They would have a take-no-prisoners approach with him. What about the others? Were they all dead?

Maybe it *was* up to me to stop Hensen. He thought I was stupid. Perhaps that was what had made him stop and talk. Or maybe he liked to gloat. Had he been missing an audience?

I could play that role. 'Isn't Kore responsible for that vial in your hands?'

He gave me a contemptuous look. 'Kore, responsible for *this*? You've got to be kidding me. Oh sure, he can chop up body parts and do some amputations and reattachments, even some basic chemical muscle strengthening, but create something like this?'

He held it up to the light, looking into its depths like it held the secrets of the universe. 'This is *my* creation. Kore was simply a convenient way to test it.'

My mouth went dry but I kept my face in order. I couldn't lose it now. I tried clueless again. 'But *he* created it, didn't he?'

He leaned down and looked into my eyes. I had been watching him move closer to me all the time while I stood my ground. 'Oh Eden, he didn't create this any more than he created the formula he used on you. I know it worked, by the way. I know you can see things you couldn't before. I know the world looks so different to you now, as though you're seeing it afresh, with the eyes of a child.

'I was so sure it would be successful that when Kore told me it had failed I didn't believe him. That's when the cracks really started showing in our arrangement, not that they weren't there before.'

'You're wrong,' I said, keeping my expression surprised. 'It didn't do anything to me.'

'Eden, please. I told you not to bother lying. How do you think I know, anyway? Because I used it on myself. Kore has no idea, of course. I gave him some watered-down batches he could use for a couple more experiments to prove that it didn't work, so it's just going to be our little secret.'

I kept my face confused as I felt my heart beating its way out of my chest.

'So you can stop trying to hide your feelings from me,' he said. 'I can see who you really are. I know you're just a scared, pathetic little wide-eyed idiot who'd do *anything* if Daddy just *loved* her!'

I felt anger replacing my fear, but shock layering over everything else. Could he really see that? *I* wasn't even sure that was how I felt! But if he'd taken the formula too …

What did I do?

'Now, all this talking has been pleasant, but we really must get on.' His hand tightened around my arm and he started dragging me to the back of the room. 'At first, I thought I should leave you unharmed but I knew you'd be a problem. Then I realised it doesn't matter if I leave a few bruises on you. I will have been valiant in my efforts to try and stop you.'

'I'm not doing anything you say.'

'Yes, you are. You're going to take this syringe full of chaos and you're going to stick it into the testing point. Of course you know how to do it; you found out from your father. It'll be great to implicate him

217

in this—yet another twist of the knife. That never gets old.

'It will be discovered that not only have you been working with Kore and the Underground, who are, of course, in league with each other, but you're high up in the command chain. That's why you were able to put that drug in Susan's drink, which led to her unfortunate heart attack. Kore gave it to you for exactly that purpose.'

'What?' I struggled to keep the air in my lungs. 'I'm seventeen. I'm just out of the learning sector. No one's going to believe that.'

'They will when they discover all the messages on your link. It's not hard to backdate or fake them if you have people in the tech sector in your pay. There'll be ample evidence when they investigate. Yes, the sad little girl, so traumatised by what the big bad government sector did to her poor old dad, she decided to take revenge on them. You getting together with Izrod made it so much easier. Do you know how many photos I've got of the two of you together? It's been so entertaining to see you helping me out so much.'

I dug my heels in and tried to twist away from him again. 'I won't do it. I won't!'

He turned on me. 'Oh yes you will, or I'll drag your mother into it. And your brothers and sister. I'll have them all committed. I'll have your mother put in jail and your siblings put in foster homes. I'm sure those lovely people will give them such a good life. Most of them are just like your father. So you'll do as I say or I'll make sure they suffer.'

'You can't do that! You can't!' I continued to struggle against him, trying my best to get away, but he held me in a grip stronger than I would have thought possible. Enhanced strength? Anything was possible.

'I can when I'm governor, especially since Governor Jerrill's nasty accident last night. I've framed you for that as well. Did I forget to mention that?'

I couldn't do this. But how could I not? I knew he was planning to kill me—he'd said as much—but I couldn't let my family suffer because of this. Would he really leave them alone? I didn't trust him, not for a second. I was sure that whether I was dead or alive, he would ruin my family, probably out of some bizarre final retribution on Dad.

He could damn well try and force me, but he would fail. I'd had bruises before—too many to count. I would make him leave so many on me that no one would believe that he'd just tried to stop me. Hell, he'd have to shoot me before I did anything. I wondered how long I could keep going with a bullet in me. Could I last long enough to be riddled with them? There was no way anyone would believe that he'd needed to go so far to stop a tiny little thing like me.

I heard a faint noise coming from the back of the Archives, just a slither of sound. Was it Leon? I knew how quiet he was and I couldn't imagine him having made that noise unless he wanted to be heard. Why would he announce his presence to Hensen?

Hensen scowled. 'I suppose it's that idiot boyfriend of yours. Well, I've got contingency plans in place for this too.' He put the syringe back in his pocket and pulled me closer, putting the gun to my head.

We reached the back of the Archives—Hensen's destination. He looked around carefully, checking the shadows. He went along the length of the air conditioning conduit—I assumed he knew how Leon travelled—until he reached its vent. He peered around and raised his voice. 'Your boyfriend is here, I think. Hey there, freak! Unless you want her dead, I'd be very careful what your next move is.'

The blast of water came so fast that I had no time to brace myself. It made us both stumble, the gun flying out of Hensen's hands. Only then did I see Leon with the fire hose, spraying Hensen with another burst.

'Run!' he said. I darted behind some nearby shelves while he continued to spray gushing water at the floundering official. But there was no way I was going any further until I was sure Leon was safe.

He dropped the hose, grabbed the axe off the wall and brought it down on the joins connected to the testing point, grunting as he hacked it. The metal shrieked as it came apart; an ugly grating sound that echoed throughout the Archives. There was a gurgle and a spurt, then a fountain of water poured out.

But Hensen had found his gun. Leon dived to the side, getting soaked as water continued to pour from the joins, while the flow from the hose lessened to a trickle. Hensen fired at him, the sound echoing through the room. I crouched with my hands over my ears as Leon barrelled into me, sweeping me behind him.

'Stay down,' he said in a low voice.

'I can hear you,' sang Hensen. 'Enhanced hearing too. Another little formula of mine.'

I glanced at Leon, then down at our feet. Water was flooding throughout the Archives. Given how big this room was, I had to hope that the level wouldn't get high enough to drown us.

But as we crept down the aisle in the direction of the elevator, Leon raised the axe and smashed it into one of the fire sprinklers on the ceiling. He struck it until it started to come off, gushing more water out. It must have triggered the others because water began raining down, icy droplets drenching us. I could feel cold seeping into my clothes and wiped my eyes to keep the drizzle out, but it kept coming, pouring down from all over.

Then, typical of our city, the lights went out, but this time they didn't come back on and the Archives was plunged into darkness.

Leon brought his mouth to my ear. 'We need to get out of here. Do you know the way?'

'Yes.'

'I'll keep you on your feet and watch out for Hensen.' He put a hand on my shoulder. 'Lead on.'

I scrambled to assemble a map of the Archives in my mind. The hardest part was trying to work out where we were at the moment. Once I'd done that, I could find the way easily.

We'd been at the back, near the ancient records. I peered into the blackness but couldn't see anything and the water swirled at my feet. I put a hand out to find the nearest set of shelves. What did it feel like? It was the older metal kind—the ones that had been buckling after so many years. Yes, I could feel the dip in one. That meant we were amongst the records from before the Unbidden Conflict.

I ran my hand along the shelves. One was positioned higher in the next bay. That was where the ancient geographical records for the world beyond our city were stored. My fingers traced the spines of some of the ancient books and I reached past them, hunting for the next shelf.

A shot rang out and Leon crouched over me. I felt something speed over my head and hit the shelves above us. Could Hensen see in the dark? Had he enhanced his sight as well as his hearing? I put that thought out of my mind as I came to a junction in the shelves.

I knew this place. It was the awkward part that was so narrow the carts always got stuck. There was a slight rise in the floor. I could feel it under my foot. This was where the ceiling became higher as well. I dragged Leon on and we kept going.

But the water was rising. It must have filled the whole chamber because it was lapping above my ankles. How high would it get? What if we couldn't get out? Hensen had said he'd disabled the elevator. Would it work anyway, now that the power was out? There was still the ladder leading up to the next level. Could we find it in the dark? Would we be able to open the trapdoor?

I reached out again. This was where one shelf ended, a horizontal line cutting through it. My hands reached out for it. Ecology. Flora and fauna. I grabbed it and hung on, pulling Leon around, until I reached the end of the horizontal line of shelves. On the other side was more recent history, but still paper records.

I stretched over to the next line of shelves. Infrastructure. The building of Sendirian City. Its re-establishment. Now we were at the digital records. I could feel their storage bays under my fingers. Hand over hand I went on, Leon still clutching my shoulder. We were nearly there.

I gasped with relief when I collided with Susan's desk. Then it was just manoeuvring around the other desks and through the chairs. I felt my way along each, reaching out in the dark to find the elevator doors.

The lights flickered on briefly, then off again, but it was enough for me to see the way. The elevator doors were shut. I reached them, pressing the door button over and over again, but they didn't budge. Leon put the axe between them and tried to pry them apart, but it didn't work.

There was a zing above our heads and we both had to duck as Hensen shot at us again. But I was pretty sure he was only guessing. How could we get out?

The emergency release. I fell to my knees and rummaged around for the little door. I prayed that the water hadn't affected it. My fingers quickly found it and I pried the door open and snagged the release.

'Try the doors now!' I said.

Leon put his hands on their edges and dragged them apart enough that we could get in sideways. The water raced in with us, tugging at my ankles, its cold making me shiver. The crack of the gun echoed through the Archives, a spark flashing as the bullet hit the elevator doors and rebounded with a clang. Hensen couldn't be too far away. It was only the dark that would save us now.

'The door in the ceiling!'

Leon reached up and felt around just as we heard the zing of another shot. He ducked quickly, then leapt up, shoulder to the trapdoor, crashing into it with all his strength. The hinges shrieked and it sprang open. He grabbed me, lifting me with one hand. I latched onto the edges of the door and dragged myself through.

He came after me, having to bring one shoulder through at a time, too big for anything else. I heard the sound of more shots, much closer this time. Hensen must have reached the elevator.

Leon slammed the trapdoor shut and wedged the handle of the axe underneath it. We heard more shots peppering the roof of the elevator with a clamour that made me cover my ears. I winced and ducked, but the elevator contained them.

A feeble emergency light blinked in the elevator shaft and I could see the door to the floor high above me. The ladder was just a step or two away. I began pulling myself up, Leon following me. I kept glancing back, listening for any sound of Hensen breaking through the trapdoor, but there was nothing.

Finally, we reached the floor above. I grabbed the catch on this door but my fingers were bruised from the other one and weren't strong enough to release it. Leon stepped up the ladder, his feet on the rung below mine and his hands on the rung above my hands, and managed to move the catch himself.

So it took Izrod to get an employee safely out of the Archives via the emergency exit. I would be putting in a complaint to management.

He lifted me up and out onto the lobby floor, hauling himself up after me. We lay panting there, squinting in the light.

'Are you all right?' he asked hoarsely.

'I think so.'

Our eyes met and he reached for me, pulling me close. 'We're safe now. We made it.'

I heard the sound of footsteps and felt the panic bubble up. Was it Hensen? Before I could turn, there was a truncheon in Leon's face. 'Don't move!'

Door security stood over him, snarling, their truncheons swinging as they beat him. He held up his hands and I leapt to my feet, grabbing one's arm to stop him.

But two more of them appeared beside me and dragged me off. I fought, arms flailing, elbows digging into any ribs I could find, kicking out as hard as I could. Experience with Dad had taught me the best places to aim and I kept up my assault.

Then two more appeared, then three, then four. They crowded around Leon. I could hear his grunts as he tried to fend them off and then he gave up, lying on the floor, covering his head.

Two guards grabbed my arms and pinned them beside me as Leon was buried under a mountain of security officers.

'No! Don't hurt him. Don't hurt him! Leon!' I tried to twist away, but the guards wrestled me to the ground, putting handcuffs on me. Then they pulled me to my feet and I lunged forward, desperate to break through the mob surrounding him.

Elena Gregor came into view, arms folded, face serious. 'Take her to the prison bay.'

Terror held me by the throat. Who'd put Miss Gregor in charge? Was she working with Hensen? That would mean death for Leon and me, and my family would be next, destined for whatever misery Hensen had planned for them. I couldn't save them. We were done for.

And these guards, even if they weren't in Hensen's pay, they'd finally found the hideous monster they'd been searching for all these months. How many of these officers who were snarling and bashing him had lost family and friends, people who'd been snatched by him, taken away, never to be seen again? They would show him no mercy.

I pleaded anyway. 'You can't hurt him,' I said as they hauled me away. 'He's not a freak. His name's Leon and he's been helping combat Kore and Hensen. Hensen orchestrated all of this. Leon's not a threat. He's not a threat! Leon!'

CHAPTER TWENTY-ONE

They'd told us about the security bay in the learning sector, especially when we'd been punished. 'This is nothing like you'd get in a security cell!' I'd never really cared; no punishment they gave me compared to the hell I had to live at home.

It was much the same here. If the foreboding scowls on the two guards were anything to go by, they expected me to be trembling in terror. But even though they shoved me a bit, it didn't affect me. My father would have done that if he was feeling kind.

I was marched into a building with straight walls and grey everywhere, up their elevator (which was much quieter than the Archives' one) and along a drab corridor until we arrived at a cell. It was simply a room with one door and basic amenities inside.

I was pushed in and looked at the bland interior. There was a cot and a wash area. No windows except a small one in the thick door they'd closed behind me. It wasn't that uncomfortable. I probably would have settled down for a nice quiet sleep if it hadn't been for Leon.

I had no idea what they'd done to him after they'd taken me away, and neither my empty threats nor my pleading had made the guards pay attention to me. It didn't matter how many times I said that we were innocent, that it was Hensen, that he could still be down there poisoning the government sector, it hadn't changed the pace of their walk or their silence.

And I knew, deep down, there was no reason they should believe me. Hensen had made it clear that he'd framed me for Susan's death, for the governor's too, although I couldn't believe she was dead as well. And I'd been kidnapped and miraculously reappeared still in charge of my senses, unlike everyone else. I'd also been caught locked in the arms of Izrod himself. They had every reason to think we were the bad guys.

What if Hensen was in charge now? What if Miss Gregor was working with him, or for him? If this had been their plan all along, everything was lost.

I lay on the cot. The mattress was made of shiny material that stuck to me. There was a plastic sheet on top of it that crackled every time I moved. I hadn't expected luxurious accommodation, and it didn't make any difference that every time I rolled over the sheet came with me. I doubted I could have slept anyway.

I got up again and paced. Then I sat down but my leg jiggled so much that I started to pace again, all the time aware of the video camera on the wall. Was it working all the time or did it shut down when the lights flickered?

After a while, they shoved some water and food through the little window in the door, then slammed it shut again before I could say anything. I avoided the water—what if Hensen had managed to get chaos into it? But then, if he had, all the guards would probably be running around screaming, hitting each other with their truncheons. I still didn't want to risk it, but I figured I might as well eat to pass the time.

I hoped being imprisoned like this wasn't going to become a habit for me. I could think of things I'd rather be doing than being trapped in a tiny box like this. This was the second time someone had shoved food through a gap in a cell door for me. At least the bread and stew they'd given me this time had some flavour, even real chunks of meat, not bland, runny gruel like I'd had at Kore's.

I was munching on the bread when the door opened. It was Marshall Avery. I examined his face for any sign that he thought me a traitor, that he was corrupt, that he was affected by chaos, but his expression seemed as calm as usual. 'Eden? Please come with me.'

I opened my mouth to pepper him with questions about Leon, but I didn't want to annoy him, so I shut it again.

What if I was being taken to Official Hensen so he could make a show of how I'd betrayed him? And how Izrod had tried to kill him. I could imagine his smug face as they marched me away. There would probably be someone from the media sector snapping photos. I could see the captions now—*Izrod's lover causes chaos—caught in the act of poisoning government employees.*

Marshall Avery led me down a featureless corridor into an equally featureless room. There was a chair, then a desk, then a chair. Metal and grey, like everything else around me. Then he left. I couldn't think of what else to do, so I went around the desk and sat in the chair facing the door. There was no way I was putting my back to it.

I was wondering how long I was going to have to wait when the door opened and Miss Gregor came in. Two security guards came with her, one standing on each side of her, as she sat in the chair opposite me. She had a folder of papers in her hand, with some digital files as well. She plugged them into her portable computer and started checking them.

She glanced up at me, her face severe and businesslike. 'When did you start consorting with Izrod, Eden?'

Why did she have to start like that? 'His name is Leon.'

'I know,' she said, turning a page in her file. 'Leon Rogers, to be precise. Son of Graham Rogers, labourer, and Mamie Overson, both deceased. But you didn't answer my question.'

This was my chance to tell her what had really happened. But how could I be sure she wasn't there on behalf of Official Hensen? How did I know she wouldn't take what I said and twist it this way and that? Every word I said could condemn me.

But I could think of nothing else to do but tell the truth. 'He saved me when I was at Kore's.'

'Wasn't he responsible for you being there in the first place?'

'Yes, he was, but he was working undercover. He wanted me to …' how much of this should I tell her? '… undergo Kore's latest procedure.'

'Why you?'

That was the question I'd asked myself many times. Why me? I was good at hiding things, I could cope with pressure and I knew how to keep my cool … outwardly, at least.

But I couldn't stop myself from blurting, 'Because he believed in me.'

Believed in my ability to keep quiet. Believed that I would help him, without even really knowing me. It was amazing how much he'd trusted me.

She looked up. 'Believed in you?'

'That I would keep quiet about what I could do and would help him.' That was the easiest way to explain it.

'And what did Kore do to you?'

'He injected me with something that allowed me to see who people really are.'

Her eyes examined me. 'Did it work?'

I still wasn't sure. 'I saw things differently afterwards, so I guess so.'

'Describe it.'

How could I describe something so surreal? The best way was the example I was anxious to push home. 'I immediately realised Leon was trustworthy and wouldn't hurt me.'

'You're sure that wasn't intended?'

I'd been through this enough times in my head. 'Then why didn't Kore look like he was trustworthy? Why no one else in Kore's gang? Why just Leon?'

She digested that and then asked something I wasn't expecting. 'And what do you see when you look at me?'

'Someone capable and confident.' Although I was starting to think everyone saw her that way now.

'And what did you see when you looked at Official Hensen?'

This was dangerous territory. I still had no idea where Hensen was. But what could I say but the truth? However, I was going to be careful how I said it. 'I didn't trust him.'

She seemed satisfied with that answer. I wasn't sure why.

She turned back to her computer. 'Just making notes,' she said. 'They'll go with the official recording of this interview.'

I should have realised they'd be recording it, perhaps via the camera on the wall.

'What were you and Izrod ...' She looked at me. 'What were you and Leon doing in the Archives?'

'I work there.'

She rolled her eyes. 'All right, let me be more specific. Why did you go down there so early? Did you know that Official Hensen would be there? Did you go there to meet him?'

'No. I had no interest in meeting Hensen anywhere.' *Please, please let me be doing the right thing.* 'I knew that Kore was planning to attack water testing points in the city with a formula that would have made everyone crazy. Leon and some others were trying to stop him. I couldn't sleep, so I thought I'd go down into the Archives. Official Hensen came down there too. He told me he'd framed me for the head keeper's death and Governor Jerrill's as well. I didn't even know she was dead. Is she?' It seemed so hard to grasp that he'd caused so much heartbreak.

Miss Gregor kept on with her questioning. 'How did Leon end up there?'

I didn't want to tell her this, but how else could I explain? 'I let him know I was in trouble.'

'How?'

I shifted in my seat. She must have noticed and to my surprise, waved that question away. 'We'll come back to that. So Leon found his way into the Archives. I believe he used the air conditioning vents. Is that correct?'

I didn't want to say this either, but there didn't seem much help for it. 'Yes.'

'So you called him because you wanted him to stop Official Hensen. Is that correct?'

'Yes.'

She typed some more notes and the silence dragged on. Eventually, I couldn't stand it any longer. 'Miss Gregor?' I said tentatively.

The guard on her right leant over. 'That's Acting Governor Gregor to you.'

So *she* was in charge now. Why not Hensen? Had she defeated him in a takeover?

'There's no official determination on Governor Jerrill's cause of death yet, but there's no doubt in my mind what it will be.'

'I didn't do it!' I said. 'You've got to believe me. I had no idea she was dead until Hensen said.' If only he hadn't told me. I'm sure the shock of that news would have pierced even my reserve.

She looked up. 'Official Hensen was found with a syringe on him. We're still to determine exactly what it is, but our experts seem certain it matches what we found on Kore's people.'

'It was his, not mine. I swear.'

'His fingerprints were on it, not yours. And you weren't found with any gloves on you, nor were any found in the Archives, not that we can search it extensively at the moment. Then, of course, there's the gun that was under Hensen's sole control. I'm sure he was planning to tell us he took it down there to try and stop you.'

It sounded like … 'Does that mean you believe me?'

'Kore and his people are under arrest. But the things we found at his headquarters were … very revealing.'

I bet they were. Vials of formulas, cells full of victims, laboratories for treating his human experiments. 'And Official Hensen?'

'Official Hensen is dead.'

I went numb. We'd killed him. Leon had trapped him in the Archives and he'd drowned. While I felt relief at the thought that I'd never have to look into those menacing eyes again, it told me what we were facing. While they might believe that we hadn't killed Susan or Governor Jerrill, we had been responsible for the death of an official.

'Yes,' Miss Gregor continued. 'We found him in the Archives, a gunshot wound to his head. The shot that killed him ricocheted off the elevator ceiling.'

Wait, what? So his death couldn't be put at our door unless she needed convenient scapegoats. Or was she saying that just to get a reaction from me?

She made some more notes on her computer. 'This interview is at an end.' She turned to one of the security guards. 'Please take Miss Fittell back to her cell.'

I felt a dead weight in my stomach. She didn't care. A desperate part of me wanted to beg for her to listen but why would that work? Even if she wasn't in league with Hensen, who was I to her? Just a junior employee in the lowest department in government. She would make her decision and I'd have to live with it. I didn't want to waste my breath screaming protestations of innocence so she could ignore them.

I went back to my cell quietly and it wasn't long before another meal was presented to me. I ate it silently, wishing I knew what was happening out there, particularly where Leon was. What were they doing to him? Even if Miss Gregor believed he'd been trying to stop Kore and Hensen, there were still a multitude of other reasons they'd want him. He had, after all, been terrorising the city for months. They would never let him walk away from this.

***

I stayed there another night and another day. At least, it seemed like it was that long, and they turned the lights off for what I assumed was 'night'.

I was slowly demolishing my dinner when the door opened and Marshall Avery walked in. 'Eden, follow me.'

He led me back down the corridor towards the elevator. We took a short trip, before exiting into another room of the security sector building. It had several desks, each with an officer sitting at them and someone in front of them. I thought I recognised a couple of people from the Underground.

I could see the security sector lobby through a door at the end of the room. Was I being released? Best not to get my hopes up. There could be a catch.

He led me over to a desk where a senior officer sat ticking things off on her computer. She looked at Avery. 'This is Eden Fittell?'

'It is.'

'Miss Fittell, your mother is here to collect you. But first …' She held out her hand, and when I didn't move, Avery put my wrist in her hand. She removed my modified link and gave me another one.

'You're free to go.' She pointed to the door at the rear. 'Just through there. She's waiting for you.'

I didn't move. 'What about Leon?'

She didn't look up. 'I'm not at liberty to tell you anything about that.'

I fought off despair at the clanging finality of her words. I looked in every corner of the room, hoping to see him being processed somewhere. Just to catch a glimpse of him. But a guard was holding the door open for me. *Better hurry up*, his look said.

I marched through the door into a throng of people. The security sector's lobby was humming with officers racing everywhere. Had something else happened or were they just mopping up after the catastrophe?

'Eden!'

I turned to see Mother hurrying over to me. I wasn't one for motherly hugs, but I decided it was worth it. Then I quickly pulled away. 'What's been happening? Do you know where Leon is?'

She glanced at the people around us. 'Not here. Let's get going.'

We made our way to the doors and through the checkpoints before she said anything. 'We've gone back to our home. The security sector came to the Underground yesterday and arrested almost everyone, although they let the families go.'

'Do you know what happened? I mean with Kore?'

'Not really. After the teams went to stop Kore's people from carrying out their attack, the security sector arrived at the Underground. No one from the teams came back, or at least, they hadn't by the time we left, so I assume they were taken into custody. Did you see anyone?'

'Possibly a couple. Do you know where Leon is?'

'No. There've been reports that Izrod has been captured, but nothing's been officially confirmed by the government sector.'

So he was probably still in there. Surely what I'd said to Miss Gregor meant something. Or hadn't she believed me? If not, why had I been released?

I didn't bother talking on the way back to the shack. I wondered if I would be allowed to get my things from my unit. I guessed I didn't have a job anymore, but no one had said anything about that. No one had told me to report anywhere or that they wanted any more to do with me. I was, after all, an unimportant link in the chain.

When we reached the house, Jed was there looking after Kathleen and Lenny. Mother declared that she was off to buy some food for them. Where had she got the money? Maybe she was going to beg.

She'd barely walked out when I stood up. 'I'm going to the Underground.'

Jed didn't even blink. 'I knew it wouldn't take you long.'

Whatever. I had no answers and I needed them. I had to find out whether Leon was alive and unhurt. Was he being charged? Was he going to jail? Surely they could see that he wasn't the villain here. Was I really the only one who could see his goodness, his honesty, his trustworthiness, his loyalty?

But how many people did he kidnap, Eden? People with families. People who worked in the government sector. People who could have gone on to have families of their own, living and loving, enjoying life. He cut that short, taking them away from the people they loved forever.

Yes, but what choice had he had? And he'd tried—I knew he'd tried so hard—to do the right thing. Even in the deepest dark, he'd sought the light.

I was careful the whole way there. There were still security patrols on the streets and I occasionally heard the whine of a security vehicle siren. I stayed out of the way, head down, hoping no one would think I looked guilty enough to stop.

It had occurred to me, given what my mother had said about the members of the Underground being arrested, that it would be deserted. Imagine my surprise when I saw Sasha there. But then, if anyone had been going to get out of this unscathed, it was her.

She tilted up her nose at the sight of me. 'What do you want?'

'Where's Leon?' I demanded. I'd better get an answer to this question soon.

She looked me up and down. 'You don't know?'

What did that mean? Was he dead? Executed? Imprisoned somewhere?

But she didn't seem disturbed, only irritated. 'I assumed that's why you're here.'

She beckoned to me to follow, leading me through to the main area, which was being packed up by people I'd never seen before. 'Who are they?'

'Government sector workers. They've come for all our records, resources, anything not tied down. Also, they've taken the plans for my food distribution program for the poor. Apparently, the government sector's going to take responsibility for it now. They're planning to revamp the whole poor quarter, fix up the units, make it nice for everyone. Finally give proper homes to the people who've been victims of fires or other government mismanagement.' She sniffed. 'I'll believe it when I see it.'

'But what about Leon?' If I had to ask one more time …

She pointed to a corner and there he stood, lugging out some furniture for a government worker. There were bruises on his massive arms, bluish lines probably left by the truncheons when he'd been beaten. Not that they were stopping him from hauling an old table that would normally take two people to carry.

He saw me and opened his arms. I fell into them, trying not to show just how much I was shaking as relief washed over me. He was here. He was safe. How long had he been at the Underground? He'd probably been released before me!

I felt a sudden swell of anger and had to stop myself from swatting at him, worried I'd hit the worst of the bruises. 'Why the hell didn't you let me know you were all right?'

'I didn't know where you were. And I didn't get a location from your link.'

Oh, that's right. 'The security sector confiscated it.'

'Of course they did.' He cradled my face between his hands, checking me over. 'You're all right? They didn't hurt you?'

'I was more worried about you.'

He sighed. 'Let me move this for Jeff. Then I'll explain.'

I wasn't about to be left behind so marched determinedly along beside him.

'We're just getting all this stuff loaded up,' he said. We went out to the alley behind the Underground's headquarters where large vehicles were chugging as they waited to receive loads of goods, transporting them … where?

My mouth fell open as I saw Marshall Avery. I put my arm protectively in front of Leon as he lowered the table he was carrying to the ground.

Marshall Avery held up his hands. 'It's all right, Eden. I'm not here to hurt anyone. I'm just organising this convoy.'

It was all I could bear. 'What's going on? Someone please tell me!'

Avery stepped out of Leon's way, looking warily at him as Leon hefted up the table and put it in the back of one of the vehicles. 'That's the lot,' Leon said.

Avery eyed him suspiciously. 'It's amazing what a bit of intel can do, isn't it?' Now that the vehicle was full, the marshall sealed it up and thumped it. I heard a driver rev the engine.

'Leon, please. What's happening? Where's everyone going? Will they be all right? Why are you here and not in jail?'

He looked amused. 'Would you prefer that?'

'Of course not! But I didn't think they'd let you go.'

He laughed. 'I know. But as Marshall Avery said, it's amazing what a bit of intel can do. Or in this case, a lot.'

He took my hand and we started walking along the street.

'My team barely made it to the medical sector before some of Kore's gang showed up. We took them on and made sure no one got near the testing point. Several of them had syringes, so Kore had clearly expected opposition. If half his team went down, he anticipated that someone would make it through.

'Then security came out of nowhere. At first, I thought they might have already been infected with chaos, but they were way too in control for that. We scattered, and that's when I got your signal. I knew you had to be in trouble; you wouldn't have contacted me otherwise.'

'You got away?'

He let out a chuckle. 'Security may have been ready for us, but they weren't ready for *me*. Truncheons don't usually make much of an impression. They tickle more than anything.'

Given the bruises on his arms, I wasn't so sure about that, but I didn't want to interrupt.

'I charged my way through them, which allowed some of my team to get away as well, but I couldn't stay, not with you in danger. Apparently, it was the same with all the teams—security turned up and arrested everyone.

'When they took me away from you at the Archives, there were questions galore and I was a little concerned that I was going to be put in the deepest, darkest cell and left there, but then Miss Gregor came to see me. You were right about her—she's definitely more than she ever let on. I got the impression she's had Hensen under surveillance for some time.

'Of course, that didn't mean I was going to get off scot-free, but it didn't take her long to realise I had something of value, something she was desperate for.'

'Which was?'

He nodded at the disappearing convoy. 'Like Avery said—intel.

I'd been with Kore for years. He didn't tell me everything, but I knew his business ties and that he'd gotten a lot of funds and equipment from certain dealers. I dropped a few names in passing and it seems I've just revealed a stack of government abuses dating back to before I was even born, for here and Reacher's Pass, even Twin City. I was able to give Gregor dates and locations and that helped her piece things together from the files they found at Kore's place.

'Naturally, I wasn't going to give her something for nothing. I said I'd give her whatever I knew in exchange for clemency, for me and for you.'

So his knowledge, all the things he'd endured with Kore, had paid off like this? I felt my body relax, even as my mind struggled to believe it.

He'd saved us. Even saved the whole city. What if his intel meant that things could be fixed up? The power grid, the poor sector ... 'I guess I owe you again.' And not just me, but everyone.

'You don't owe me anything.' He led me back towards the Underground. 'Of course, if it makes you feel obliged to keep seeing me, a lowly government consultant, while you're a high-up junior keeper, then I might be okay with you feeling that way.'

'Am I a junior keeper?' I said sarcastically. 'After we destroyed the Archives?'

He looked surprised. 'Sure you are. Gregor didn't tell you that you still had a job? Someone's screwed up. I'll have words with them.'

'You're a consultant? What does that mean?'

'At the moment it means I help sort things out as we process everything from Kore's lair, and here. I don't know if I'll be involved in helping the homeless and the poor, but apparently, they're going to do that too.'

'Yes, Sasha mentioned that.'

His face was just as sceptical. 'She's not convinced it's going to work. Or be long-term. Or be anything more than a PR stunt. I don't care, as long as they do something.

'So,' he said, turning to me. 'I'd better get you home.'

'Which home?'

'Your unit! Did you really think they'd kick you out? Someone's dropped the ball. Come on, let's go.'

He led me back towards the government sector, which was the most bizarre thing I'd ever done with him. We didn't dart from shadow to shadow. We didn't shelter behind garbage bins. We didn't hold our breath while security marched past. We wandered down each street in the light, when it wasn't flickering, him nodding to any security sector officers we passed. They regarded him cautiously, but they didn't touch him.

When we reached the first checkpoint, the guards looked at him, askance. 'We can't let you in,' one said, barring his way.

He folded his arms. 'And why not?'

The guard faltered under Leon's gaze. 'Because ... because you're not an official government sector worker.' His voice shook.

Leon's gaze was like steel for a moment, then he smiled. 'That's fine. Checkpoints are no barrier to me anyway.' He pulled me closer and kissed me. 'You go home the normal way. Maybe I'll see you later?'

I wasn't ready to leave his side. 'Maybe I can come your way instead?'

That made him laugh outright. 'Sure. Let's show these guys how it's done.'

He gathered me in his arms and vaulted over their heads, darting between two buildings. The guards yelled and I thought I heard them coming after us, but they weren't quick enough to catch Leon. In a flash, he had the grate off an air conditioning duct and we scrambled inside.

When we made it to my unit, I was glad to see the place again, relieved that everything—not that I had much 'everything'—was in its place.

He lingered in the air conditioning shaft, looking at me uncertainly.

'Are you going to come in?' I extended my hand to him.

He smiled. 'Sure.'

He followed me as I wandered into the living area, feeling light with relief. The danger was over. No more Hensen. No more Kore. No more evil. Hopefully. As Leon and Sasha had said, we'd have to see if it stuck, but for the moment, we were free.

I went to the refrigerator and opened it. What did I have for my hungry guest? 'What do you want?'

'Oh, nothing like *that*,' he said, his hand resting on my hip.

His tone was both playful and heated. I turned towards him and he lifted my chin, placing a kiss on my lips. I wrapped my arms around him and stood on the tip of my toes, trying to reach him as his lips continued to press onto mine, gently at first, but then with more purpose.

He swung me up into his arms and took me over to the couch, laying me on it. He leaned over me and kissed me.

It didn't take long before we became lost in each other. I held him close to me, feeling the warmth of his body as his large frame enveloped mine. His lips wandered over my eyelids, down my cheek to my neck, back to my lips, as my hands clung to his broad shoulders, trailing down his arms, revelling in their heat.

I enjoyed the feeling of his body pressed against mine and how protected I felt, as if all the nightmares of my past were being burned away, leaving … what? A new me? I felt elated, as though I was floating, joy filling every corner of my mind. Who would have thought it would be like this for me? For us?

Then I heard the front door chime. Guess who?

I opened the door to the two security guards trying to look tough. But I could see their knees knocking. The first officer pointed at Leon. 'He doesn't have permission to be here.'

Leon rolled his eyes. 'All right. I'll go and get permission first.' He kissed me in the doorway and held me for a moment. 'Go and get some sleep. I'll see you tomorrow. And the day after. And the day after. Besides, I'd like to see your mother and officially ask if I can date you.'

That was ridiculous. 'Like she's going to say no.'

'Probably not, but I'll ask anyway.'

'Leon?' I said just before he shut the door.

'Yes?'

'Don't ask my father.'

He cocked his head. 'Why would I do that?'

CHAPTER TWENTY-TWO

I was a little nervous to return to work, despite what Leon had said about me still being employed. After all, we'd done a pretty good job of trashing my workplace. Was any part of the Archives left? When I'd last seen it, it had been ankle-deep in water, with more gushing in. How were they even going to get the water out?

When I arrived the lobby was bustling, people from the maintenance sector fussing around the elevator shaft. Did I have to take the ladder down? Would they even let me pass?

There was a huge tube on the floor throbbing so loudly I wanted to block my ears. It bobbed and weaved in a wobbly dance.

The workers looked up as I approached and the woman who I assumed was their leader squinted at me. 'Yes?'

'My name's Eden Fittell. I'm a junior keeper. Is it possible to get into the Archives at the moment?'

She nodded at the ladder inside the shaft. 'If you want to use that you can go down. There are already people down there. It's the only way in or out at the moment. Watch out for the drainage pipe.' She gestured at the snakelike tube.

I stepped past her, one of the maintenance men giving me a hand to reach the ladder. But the climb down was relatively easy.

A stench wafted up to me, a bit like dirty washing multiplied by the power of ten. I tried not to gag.

Acting Governor Gregor was down there with Derek, Adriana and Reggie milling around, looking like they were doing something, only they weren't.

And I could see why. The water had dislodged many of the shelves, which had never been that stable anyway. Although a few of the wall ones were still standing, most of the others had collapsed. The floor was a mess of pulped paper. Most of the digital records had fared better; their shelving system seemed to have protected them a little more, but the ones in the lowest drawers had been damaged.

'Eden,' said Acting Governor Gregor, 'I'm glad you're here. I was just talking to your fellow keepers about what we can save.'

Adriana spoke up immediately. 'Not the paper records, Governor. Not even these digital ones.' She kicked at some of the digital sticks at her feet. 'And the shelves will need to be replaced before we can do anything.'

'They don't need to be replaced,' Reggie said. 'We just need the maintenance team to come down and fix them to the wall.'

Adriana marched over to a set of shelves with a scowl. 'Oh, you think this is salvageable, do you?' She lifted a shelf, which had buckled.

'Yeah, but that one was buckled before this and we still used it. A lot of them weren't perfect but they still did the job.'

Derek picked up the digital files and peered at them. 'These might work if they could be dried out. Can we ask the tech team what they think?'

As they continued to banter back and forth, I moved further into the Archives to where some of the swollen paper records lay strewn across the floor. I opened the book-like cover and looked at the paper inside. Could the pages be pried apart? I slipped my finger under one, only to see it rip away.

I put down that one and picked up another. It didn't seem as wet. I tried to pry the pages apart and found that I was able to do it.

'I think this one can be saved,' I yelled back to the others, continuing to pick my way through, looking for other folders with pages that seemed at least reasonably okay. I found some more and tried to pull each page apart. Sometimes it worked, sometimes it didn't.

I took the good ones back to the admin area and put them on one of the tables. 'If we dry them out here we could save some.'

Governor Gregor came over to look while Adriana scoffed at me. 'This stuff isn't any use. You can hardly read it.'

I held up a page for the governor. 'I can read that,' she said. 'Good work, Eden.'

Reggie folded his arms and Derek groaned. 'We can't wade through all that and pick out the pieces that are okay. That will take days.'

I returned to the shelves, looking for more salvageable pages. The governor turned to the others. 'Come on, get to work. Salvage what you can. Pile what can't be saved in a corner.'

I looked to the left of the elevator shaft where a few warped shelves had been put. 'We can put anything we can't save there.'

Adriana went to Susan's desk. 'Fine. Go and start. I'll see if I can get this computer up and running.' She pulled up a chair and tapped on the computer's side, trying to wake it.

Governor Gregor put her hands on the desk. 'What do you think you're doing?'

Adriana looked up in surprise. 'We've got to get a system going so we can catalogue what we can save.'

'True, but I fail to see why you get to sit here and do that while the others do the dirty work.'

She stood up uncertainly. 'Governor, we need a head keeper. It was hard enough managing without Susan under normal circumstances. We can't possibly do this without leadership. If I can start this computer going, I can catalogue what the others bring back, put it all in order.'

Governor Gregor nodded. 'I agree. That needs to be done. I'll get the tech crew to come down and see if they can salvage the computers or replace them. The Archives system will be on the server, so that can be used.'

Adriana looked smug but that expression was wiped away as the governor turned to me. 'Eden, can you see about contacting the tech team? Start organising places to put the various pages in some sort of order so they can be catalogued appropriately.'

'Certainly,' I said, carrying another pile of papers back to the desk. 'There are seven desks here.' Even though two had wonky legs. We could prop them up with something. 'We can allocate seven different areas from the Archives, one to each desk, and put anything salvageable on each desk. I'll print off some labels so we know what goes where.' If I could find a way to print them.

'Good work.' Governor Gregor said. 'I knew you'd have a system you could put in place straight away. And you got stuck in immediately, getting the job done instead of standing around and expecting someone else to do it.'

'The head keeper should be the organiser,' Adriana grumbled.

'Exactly,' said the governor, 'which is why Eden is now head keeper.' She barely paused as the others gasped. 'I'll make it official as soon as possible and I expect you to all defer to her.'

Protests rose from all around, complaining about how I was at the bottom of the pack, the newbie, the nobody. She waved them away. 'I've made my decision. I've been watching everyone here long enough to know who's the best for this job.'

'Someone consorting with Izrod,' Derek spat.

'Consorting with our undercover agent,' the governor said

without missing a beat.

What? I examined her face. There was definitely subterfuge there, but she looked perfectly matter-of-fact as she continued, 'Yes, the man known as "Izrod" has been our undercover operative for some time. That news is scheduled to be released by the information sector today.' She turned and gave me a wink.

So that was her plan. Not only would Leon be accepted, but it would look like he had been in league with the government the whole time. I was fine with that if it meant he could come and go as he pleased, although I wondered how people who'd lost loved ones would feel about it, knowing Izrod had kidnapped them. Maybe they would spin that as well, saying it had never been him in the first place, only Kore, the bad guy, who was now under lock and key in the security sector.

'Now get to work. I need to talk to your new head keeper.'

She took my arm and led me further into the Archives, dodging piles of mushy paper and the tube that was still pumping away. She saw me glance at it.

'It's draining the water away,' she said. 'It was the only way we could get it out. We had to get an expert in to shut off the water first, then drain what was left. It's nearly done.'

I looked at the isolated puddles around us. 'That's something. But if I'm head keeper, can I make a recommendation?'

She seemed amused. 'Sure.'

'We need another way to get out of the Archives. We almost didn't make it because it was pitch black, and then we had trouble getting the elevator doors open. And if there's a fire or something, we may not have a lot of time.' I knew that from experience. 'We can't be expected to climb into the elevator shaft and go up a ladder to escape.'

She pondered that. 'Good point. I know in pre-conflict days, buildings all had dedicated fire stairs. I'm not sure we could get one built down here, but we could put a ladder outside the elevator shaft and run it up through the floor to the next level via a trapdoor or something. I'll get the maintenance sector to look into it.'

That would have to do. It had been bad enough being trapped down here with water. I couldn't imagine what it would be like with fire and only an axe and a hose for protection.

'We'll still need access to some water, though,' I thought out loud. 'We need a fire hose.'

She led me to the back of the Archives. 'It's under construction now. In fact, that's what I wanted to talk to you about.'

The smell was almost overpowering as we continued to the back of the room, where I could see some maintenance personnel sweeping pieces of metal away from what was left of the pipes Leon had hacked through. But I couldn't focus my attention on them as I noticed the man giving them instructions.

My father. I almost choked on my breath. I looked at her, incensed, but then realised that she probably didn't know.

But she did. 'I understand. He's here under strict conditions. We have a good sobriety program and he's expected to get himself straightened out if he wants to keep working here. Otherwise, he's out. But we needed his expertise.'

Dad saw me and came towards me uncertainly. I shut down my face.

The governor looked between the two of us. 'I don't expect you to get along, but you need to play nice.' She walked back to the admin area.

Dad looked contrite. He'd combed his hair, which was normal, but his eyes looked as bloodshot as usual. I wondered if the governor had checked if he'd had a drink already. But then, if he went without drink straight away, they'd probably have to put him in a padded cell, and they needed him at least functioning. As functioning as he got, anyway.

'So I got a job,' he said. 'Wasn't that something you wanted?'

I said nothing. But while that used to bug him, this time he seemed to expect it. 'I'm back in the government sector. They reckon they're going to get me clean—'

'Yeah, right.'

He didn't disagree. 'Whatever. They need me, and that's what's important.' I could tell by his lofty look that this sudden need for his assistance had gone straight to his head. I bet he'd want a celebratory drink or two … or three. Or four or five.

'I'm not looking for forgiveness,' he said, 'but now that I'm employed, your mother—'

'Stay away from her.'

He pouted. 'I think your boyfriend would probably rip my head off if I didn't. But she loves me. You know that. So maybe he'll have to let me sooner or later. I mean, maybe Gregor's right. Maybe they can get me clean.'

I don't think he believed that, or even wanted it, and I didn't believe it at all, although something in me longed for it desperately. Maybe Hensen had been right. Maybe I did still love him. But did I love him more than I hated him? Could I ever forgive him?

I turned away. 'Don't bet on it.'

He went back to his work. I went back to mine.

CHAPTER TWENTY-THREE

I checked that everything was in order on my desk and that all the other keepers' desks were also straight and neat.

I looked down the aisles of shelving that ran the full length of the restored Archives. The smell still lingered, even after more than a month, but the bright shiny new shelving sparkled. Some of the shelves were empty, at least of paper records; we'd been able to salvage only about half of the damaged ones. But almost all the digital records had been restored.

I glanced at the newly installed ladder that rose beside the elevator shaft to an opening in the ceiling. I'd insisted that it be open—I didn't want us to have to fiddle with any trapdoors if we were fleeing for our lives.

I nearly jumped as the elevator doors opened. It no longer groaned and ground its way down. Now there was only a barely detectable woosh.

I cast my eyes around the admin area again. Adriana, Reggie, Derek and the other keepers all stood beside their desks. Adriana still hadn't ditched the resentful expression as she cast envious eyes my way. The others at least looked reasonably decent considering what an important occasion it was.

Governor Gregor came out of the elevator with her new assistant, Melanie Blake, a brunette who was so tall it looked like her spine had been stretched. I remembered the conversation we'd had when she'd first considered hiring Miss Blake.

'How ambitious does she look, Eden? Is she going to stab me in the back?'

'No more than anyone else here.'

Ever since she'd found out what I could do, she used it whenever she could.

Leon followed the two of them out of the elevator. He was dressed in a suit. He pulled at the tie and rolled his shoulders under the shirt. It had been hard to find one the right size for him. He smiled at me.

Governor Gregor passed Adriana, Reggie, Derek and the other keepers before arriving at my desk. 'Well, Eden. What a fantastic job you've done. Everything looks excellent down here. Don't you agree, Miss Blake?'

'Oh yes, definitely, Governor,' said Miss Blake in her submissive way. Only half of her deference was genuine.

'And what do you think? You over there, our newest consultant?'

Leon smirked. His fancy title meant that he told the governor how things were in the city and where she damn well better fix them up. He was direct, but she liked that, and although he didn't get everything he wanted, he got some of it.

He looked around the room. 'It's superb, of course, but I'd expect nothing less of Eden.'

Adriana shot me a glare but darted her eyes away as Leon looked in her direction, while Governor Gregor laughed. 'Yes, well, it's not like you're biased at all, are you?'

Leon met her gaze. 'I always tell it exactly as it is, Governor.'

'Don't I know it?' She began to journey down the aisles and I fell in step beside her, Miss Blake following her boss, Leon behind me.

Governor Gregor looked up at the empty shelves. 'It's a pity we couldn't salvage more.'

'At least we were able to image capture some of the ruined pages.' The tech guys had taken photos of the destroyed pages on the top of each sludgy pile and had been able to enhance the images so most of the wording was legible. It meant that we still had more pre-conflict records than we would have otherwise.

'Yes.' She cast her eyes on the floor, looking for dirt in the corner. She would find none.

After I'd led her around and shown her all the sectors, she returned to the elevator. 'I'm glad to see this place looking so much better now. But we've got a full schedule for the day.' She indicated that Miss Blake should follow her. 'Duty calls.'

Leon stayed behind and she didn't seem surprised. I could see the other keepers watching him carefully, but there was no way they were going to mutter against his astonishing new status where he could hear them.

He took both my hands. 'We still on for dinner tonight? No business meetings to keep you here late?'

'Sure.' It still seemed odd to hear him talk about mundane, everyday things like having a meal together. 'Dinner' sounded so … normal and boring. I hoped normal and boring would last a long time.

'And what have you got on today?' I asked.

'I'm going to see Sasha to check on what's needed in her sector.'

Sasha had been made head of the reconstruction of the poor sector. She'd thanked Leon for that, even though she knew I was the one who'd suggested it.

'Then I'm going to check all the sectors, make sure security's doing their job properly.' He glanced sideways at me. 'Although I could use your help there.'

'Why?'

'You could tell me if anyone's hiding anything. You know, you should leave the Archives and come and work with me.'

'No thanks. Normal and boring is much better.'

He took me in his arms. 'You don't think you'll get tired of this normal stuff? Normal can be overrated.'

'I think it'll be a while before I want any more excitement.' It was enough that I had to keep up with Lenny, who had just had his third birthday. He'd disappeared from Mother's new unit twice. The first time we'd been frantic, thinking Dad had taken him, but it turned out Lenny had just been checking out the building's plumbing system. Maybe he could take over Dad's job one day. Maybe he'd need to if Dad couldn't stay sober for more than five minutes.

'Besides,' I continued, 'I like it down here.'

I cast my eyes around the Archives again, looking at the gleaming shelves. I wondered how long it would take to fill them. Could we find replacement paper records anywhere? The hunt was on for them. Would we fill them with digital cartridges? Maybe. Whatever the case, and whatever form the information took, I wanted to be at the helm, keeping things secure, making sure the records were there whenever they were needed.

And with any luck, this thing Kore had put in my head would help me see more than anyone expected.

'Yes,' he said. 'I have to admit that you've got the right skills to be head keeper. But …'

'But?'

'But we might need a break from normal life sometimes. What do you think?'

I pressed my lips to his. 'Give me long enough, and maybe I'll be ready for us to take on the world beyond Sendirian City.'

WANT MORE STORIES BY
LYNNE STRINGER?

VERINDON: The Heir, The Crown, The Reign

Sarah Fenhardt is living an ordinary life in high school, trying to hide her crush on Dan Bradfield, who is dating her best friend, Jillian. But when tragedy strikes, her life is turned upside down. Sarah is desperate to uncover the truth, but it takes her to another galaxy and changes everything she believes about who she is.

The Verindon Trilogy combines the romance of *Twilight* and the excitement of *Star Wars* with an added element of *The Princess Diaries*.

The Verindon Alliance

As Princess Vashta of the Vendel finishes her combat training, she hopes to lead their forces into battle against her race's deadly enemy, the Verindal. But when Brandonin, the heir to the Verindal throne, comes to see her father, it's clear he desires peace, not war. When a new enemy arises, each race blames the other, although Vashta seeks Brandonin's help to fight this menace. But what can they do when Vendel and Verindal refuse to work together? Can they defeat this deadly threat or will it mean the end of life on Verindon?

The Verindon Conspiracy

Misilina has finished her training at the Academy on Verindon and hopes to prove that she's as good an agent as her father, Keridan. However, her first assignment is guarding Lord Jolan—her childhood tormentor and the son of Overlord Ardon—who is making a planetary visit to Darsair with his bride-to-be, Mandine, to help the Darsairian government improve conditions for the mine workers. But when the miners stage an uprising and attempt to kill Jolan, can Misilina and her fellow agents keep Jolan and Mandine alive?